PRAISE FOR THE
Odelia Grey Mysteries

10: A Body to Spare

"[A] witty series with its quirky,
well-drawn characters."—*Booklist*

"Offbeat…the suspenseful climax offers some
unexpected turns for everyone."—*Publishers Weekly*

9: Hell on Wheels

"Action-filled…Jaffarian neatly pulls all the plot lines
together for a satisfying outcome."—*Publishers Weekly*

8: Secondhand Stiff

"Witty and well-plotted."—*Publishers Weekly*

"Ina's goods may be secondhand, but Jaffarian's
are first-class."—*Kirkus Reviews*

"Odelia and her colorful family and colleagues
are as quirky and appealing as those found in
Sharon Fiffer's Jane Wheel series."—*Booklist*

"[A] clever, winning tale with lots of laughs
along the way."—*Suspense Magazine*

7: Hide and Snoop

"Despite Jaffarian's flirtations with vampires and ghosts, her original series is still her best. Odelia takes no nonsense from anyone and stops at nothing to give the bad guys what they deserve."—*Kirkus Reviews*

"Jaffarian is a skilled writer who is able to make extreme situations seem plausible and minor characters multidimensional. This character-rich series will appeal especially to readers of G. A. McKevett."—*Booklist Online*

"[An] enormously entertaining seventh cozy…tight plotting, first-class humor, and vivid descriptions."—*Publishers Weekly*

"It's nice to read a book in which the heroine is not obsessed over body image. Odelia…is happy, healthy, in love—and utterly charming."—Kathleen Henrikkus for *The New York Journal of Books*

6: Twice as Dead

"Plenty of humor, the charms of the feisty main character, and a great supporting cast add to the amusement."—*Booklist*

"Jaffarian outdoes herself this time with an exceedingly clever plot."—*Mystery Scene*

5: Corpse on the Cob

"Ultimately, *Corpse on the Cob* offers readers much food for thought."—*Mystery Scene*

"The personal story makes this among the most satisfying novels in the series."—*Booklist*

"Jaffarian's delightful fifth cozy to feature supersized sleuth Odelia Grey…Jaffarian keeps getting better and better at blending humor, suspense, and romance."—*Publishers Weekly*

"Like its predecessors, this title is a delight."—*Library Journal*

"A trip to the East Coast blows a refreshing fall breeze through Odelia's fifth. So does the switch of focus from workplace woes to family drama."—*Kirkus Reviews*

4: Booby Trap

"Leavened with lively humor, the action builds to a wickedly satisfying windup."—*Publishers Weekly*

"Concentrating on the puzzle and her trademark smart dialogue, Jaffarian does some surgery of her own, leaving a lean plotline for plump Odelia."—*Kirkus Reviews*

"A fun, quick read with a usually sassy detective, *Booby Trap* will keep readers of the series happy until the next installment."—*The Mystery Reader*

3: Thugs and Kisses

"The best title yet in a priceless series…a real treat for chick-lit and mystery fans who like feisty women."—*Library Journal* (starred review)

"Odelia is a character that could easily be a good friend. She's down to earth and likeable. While she doesn't fit into Hollywood's size 0 body criteria, she's a good plus-size fit for the real people and mystery readers of the world."—*Deadly Pleasures*

"Odelia Grey is delightfully large and in charge in Jaffarian's third entertaining romp."—*Publishers Weekly*

"The best one yet…an intriguing, well-plotted mystery that will entertain and inspire."—*The Strand*

"Snappy dialogue."—*Kirkus Reviews*

"Written with a light touch but a keen eye for detail, this satisfying entry in the Odelia Grey series also has room for a little romance."—*Booklist*

2: The Curse of the Holy Pail

"Jaffarian's writing is sharp and sassy—like her protagonist— and she knows how to keep the suspense high."—*Mystery Scene*

"Odelia Grey is a keeper."—*Library Journal*

"Jaffarian offers the perfectly flawed alternative for readers sick and tired of picture-perfect characters."—*Booklist*

"Plus-size paralegal Odelia Grey gets more than she bargained for when she accepts an unusual gift from a favorite client… Jaffarian plays the formula with finesse, keeping love problems firmly in the background while giving her heroine room to use her ample wit and grit."—*Kirkus Reviews*

"I have enjoyed both books in the series. Odelia is a resourceful woman, and I didn't chafe at her amateur sleuthing. The book has an inspired cookie recipe."—*Deadly Pleasures*

1: Too Big to Miss

"I'd like to spend more time with Sue Ann Jaffarian's Odelia, a plus-size fat-liberationist with a handsome wheelchair-bound lover. Odelia…does not hesitate to give justice a small, well-plotted forward shove at every opportunity."—*The New York Times*

"With a cast of diverse characters, an intriguing plot, and a credible heroine, this is an enjoyable read."—*Mystery Scene*

"[Odelia] is an intriguing character, a true counter against stereotype, who demonstrates that life can be good, even in a world where thin is always in."—*Booklist*

"Balancing her professional skills as a paralegal with her self-doubt as a sleuth, Odelia is one of the most believable amateur detectives in recent fiction. Beautifully plotted and carefully crafted, this is a marvelous start to an exciting new series. Strongly recommended."—*Library Journal*

"Plus-size reading pleasure—try this one on!"
—Lee Child, *New York Times* bestselling author

RHYTHM & CLUES

Photography by Ayman Samman

ABOUT THE AUTHOR

Like the character Odelia Grey, Sue Ann Jaffarian is a middle-aged, plus-size paralegal. In addition to the Odelia Grey mystery series, she is the author of the paranormal Ghost of Granny Apples mystery series and the Madison Rose Vampire mystery series. Sue Ann is also nationally sought after as a motivational and humorous speaker. She lives and works in Los Angeles, California.

Visit Sue Ann on the Internet at

WWW.SUEANNJAFFARIAN.COM

and

WWW.SUEANNJAFFARIAN.BLOGSPOT.COM

SUE ANN
JAFFARIAN

AN ODELIA GREY MYSTERY

RHYTHM & CLUES

MIDNIGHT INK
WOODBURY, MINNESOTA

FIRST EDITION
First Printing, 2016

Cover illustration by Ellen Lawson

Midnight Ink, an imprint of Llewellyn Worldwide Ltd.

This is a work of fiction. Names, characters, places, and incidents are either the product of the author's imagination or are used fictitiously, and any resemblance to actual persons living or dead, business establishments, events, or locales is entirely coincidental.

Library of Congress Cataloging-in-Publication Data
Names: Jaffarian, Sue Ann, author.
Title: Rhythm & clues : an Odelia Grey mystery / Sue Ann Jaffarian.
Other titles: Rhythm and clues
Description: First edition. | Woodbury, Minnesota : Midnight Ink, [2016] |
    Series: Odelia Grey mysteries ; #11
Identifiers: LCCN 2016026847 (print) | LCCN 2016032124 (ebook) | ISBN
    9780738718859 (softcover) | ISBN 9780738732008 ()
Subjects: LCSH: Grey, Odelia (Fictitious character)—Fiction. | Women
    detectives—California—Fiction. | Overweight women—Fiction. | Legal
    assistants—Fiction. | Missing persons—Investigation—Fiction. | GSAFD:
    Mystery fiction.
Classification: LCC PS3610.A359 R49 2016 (print) | LCC PS3610.A359 (ebook) |
    DDC 813/.6—dc23
LC record available at https://lccn.loc.gov/2016026847

Midnight Ink
Llewellyn Worldwide Ltd.
2143 Wooddale Drive
Woodbury, MN 55125-2989

www.midnightinkbooks.com

Printed in the United States of America

ONE

THERE IS NEVER ANY booze in your coffee when you need it—not that I'm a big booze hound. My husband and I enjoy beer with our barbeque, the occasional wine with our dinner, and the every-so-often Irish coffee or cocktail. My mother and my half brother Clark are both recovering alcoholics, but thankfully that insidious disease seems to have skipped me. Not that I'm not plagued with my own obsessions, but I seem to have dodged the bullet on the big three addictions: alcohol, drugs, and gambling. Still, right about now would be a good time to pull out a flask and pour a good measure of something strong and mind altering into the beverage in front of me.

I was sitting in a Starbucks in Long Beach across the table from a very annoyed Shelita Thomas. My mother was the cause of her irritation. The stone in her shoe. The pain in *my* backside.

"Your mother is a bad influence," Shelita said to me, symbolically snapping my mother's scrawny neck with each emphasized word. Shelita is African American and, like me, in her mid to late fifties. Unlike me, she was tall and bony. She clutched her coffee between her hands and pursed her full lips in disapproval until they resembled an overripe plum. "I don't want her spending time with my father."

Gawd, Mom, I groaned silently, *what have you done now?*

Shelita's father is Art Franklin, a lovely man who lives in the same retirement community as my mother, Grace Littlejohn. Art and Mom are good friends, and Art has been a guest in our home on several occasions, often serving as Mom's plus one at parties. I'd met Shelita a few times during special events at Seaside Retirement Community. She'd always been friendly, and we'd even exchanged phone numbers just in case an emergency came up with either of our elderly parents. When Shelita called me last night and suggested we meet for coffee this morning, the last thing I expected was to be dressed down like a lax parent of an out-of-control preschooler. But then Shelita is an elementary school principal, so I guess her response and behavior were natural.

"What are you talking about, Shelita?" I asked, anticipating that she'd have a ready list of Mom's supposed crimes. I really was in the dark about her concerns.

She took a drink of her coffee. It was the end of August, and even though a recent brutal heat wave had ended, it was still in the mid-80s every day. The last thing I wanted was hot coffee, so I had opted instead for an iced latte. With each word of complaint Shelita voiced, I pined for the missing booze in my beverage. The next time Shelita calls a meeting, I'm going to suggest a bar or I'm bringing a flask. Considering my mother, it's a wonder I don't drink more often.

"I received a call from the management office at Seaside yesterday," she told me. "Seems your mother and my father are pestering them about some resident they believe is missing. And I just know Grace is behind it, goading my father into doing something he ordinarily wouldn't do."

I pulled my cell phone out of my purse and checked it in front of her. There were no messages, and there hadn't been any calls from the retirement community. "Why would they call you and not me?" I asked.

"I went to college with Mona D'Angelo," Shelita explained. "You know, the woman who manages the front office at Seaside? She always gives me a heads-up when she feels something is amiss and thinks I should know about it."

In other words, Mona D'Angelo is a spy and a snitch, but I kept that to myself. "So what is Mona's concern?" I knew if it was about my mother, it could be anything. She was obstinate and pig-headed and followed her own drummer. She was definitely not a sweet old lady who knitted and blushed at swear words.

"Like I said, the two of them, Grace and Dad, have been hounding the front office about one of the retirees who they believe is missing."

"It sounds like they are merely concerned about their friend," I said, coming to Mom's defense. "Did Mona look into it?"

"Of course," Shelita answered with a definite nod. "You never know with older folks. He could have slipped in the tub or something. Mona and one of the security guards used a pass key and checked out the man's place and found nothing. It looks like this man simply left town. I understand he has a little dog, and the dog is gone too. So is his car."

3

"So what's the problem?" I asked, using a napkin to dab latte foam from my lips. "It seems to me that Mom and Art were just being good neighbors."

"The problem is, they won't leave it alone." Shelita frowned, knitting her brows together until they resembled a long black scarf hugging her eyes. Shelita had dark brown almond-shaped eyes like her father's. She also had a cluster of small freckles on each cheek and several across the bridge of her nose that strung them all together like a tin-can telephone. "Mona said the office did that check a week ago, and Grace and Dad are still insisting that something is wrong. They even called the police and reported the man missing."

I had my latte straw nearly to my lips again when my hand skidded the cup to a stop. "They called the police to file a missing person's report?"

"Yes, they did," Shelita confirmed. "The police came out, took a look around, and pronounced no sign of foul play or anything else."

"The Long Beach Police?" I asked as my stomach did a nervous jiggle. We knew one of the homicide detectives with the Long Beach Police well. Andrea Fehring was a by-the-book detective who didn't take lightly to civilians messing with police matters. She was especially sour on the whole idea when it involved anyone in my family since we've crossed paths on several occasions. Andrea wore two hats in my life: one as a sometimes-friend and the other as a cop who'd love to see Greg and me move to another part of the country and take Mom with us.

"Yes, of course," Shelita answered, impatience creeping into her words. "Seaside is in Long Beach."

The police check must have been done by routine patrol cops and wasn't on Andrea's radar because if she did get wind of Mom's obsession with this missing geezer, she'd be the one calling me, not tattletale Mona or anxious Shelita.

"Odelia, weren't you the one who found that corpse in the trunk of your car earlier this year?" From Shelita's tone, it sounded like she was asking if I was the scamp who'd put paste on a schoolmate's peanut butter and jelly sandwich.

I closed my eyes and took a deep breath. "Yes, I am."

"Maybe your mother's imagination has been stirred up by that?" she suggested. "Which is fine. I just don't want my father involved."

Apparently, Shelita didn't know about all the other bodies I'd found or the scrapes I'd been in, some with Mom. The proper principal also probably hadn't heard about my playground nickname of Corpse Magnet, given to me by Seth Washington, one of my dearest friends. If she had, I'm sure she would have worked it into the conversation by now.

"Look, Shelita," I said, trying to sound reasonable and not on the defense. "I really think Mom and Art are just concerned about their neighbor, and their imaginations ran away with them." I was making sure I made Art an equal partner in the mischief. Mom wasn't about to take this rap alone. "They are retired and have little else to do with their time. They also like each other and are grown adults with all their faculties. I can't tell my mother she can't play with Art any longer, any more than you can tell your father that my mother is off-limits." I took another deep breath. "My mother's a piece of work. You'll get no argument there from me. But Art hardly seems like an obedient puppy just following her around."

I could tell Shelita didn't like my response one bit. She drank down the rest of her coffee with one gulp, dabbed a napkin gently over her red-purple lipstick, and rose to go. "I'm still going to suggest to my father that he find someone else with whom to spend his time." She slung her tidy purse over one shoulder.

"Knock yourself out, Shelita," I told her, "but don't be surprised if you meet with stubborn refusal from your father. You work with kids. You should know that telling someone with any amount of determination *not* to do something is a sure way for them to dig in their heels, no matter their age."

Then I added silently to myself: *and that goes double for my mother.*

As I watched Shelita leave, I called Mom and told her I wanted to drop by.

TWO

My mother looked about to pop her dentures from excitement as I made my way from the curb in front of her townhouse to her door. She had been sitting on her patio waiting for me with Art Franklin. I hadn't told Mom that I'd met with Art's daughter, only that I wanted to talk to her. As I got close, Mom hopped up to greet me over the low block wall that separated her patio from the rest of the front yard.

Seaside isn't a rest home. It's one of those over-fifty-five developments consisting of several acres of attached townhomes pleasantly placed throughout a honeycomb of paved walks, well-maintained greenbelts, and pristine streets. It has a large swimming pool, a recreation room, and a gym, along with regularly scheduled activities. The residents putt around on golf carts behind a security wall with a twenty-four-hour guard at the gate. The only thing Seaside didn't have was a golf course, which kept it from being considered luxury digs.

Mom's development is located in Long Beach, right on the border with Seal Beach, the town where we live. There is a huge retirement community in Seal Beach, with a golf course, several pools, and more amenities, but my mother passed on it because it was too large for her liking. Clark lives in one of the swankier specimens of such a geriatric village in Arizona, just outside of Phoenix. Mom likes visiting Clark at his place but prefers to live where she can meet and know most of her neighbors. Personally, I think she likes having less people to keep track of when she's being nosy.

Mom is quick to point out to me that even though my husband, Greg Stevens, isn't old enough to meet the minimum age requirement, I am, so we should consider buying a place at Seaside. And I am just as quick to point out that we have a seventy pound golden retriever, a big no-no at a place with a pet policy restricting animals to twenty pounds in weight. Wainwright isn't even allowed to come with us when we visit Mom, making it necessary for Mom to come to our place when she wants to visit her granddoggy. They also have a one-pet-per-household restriction—another strike against us, thankfully, since we also have a cat.

It's too bad Seaside doesn't have a weight restriction for its residents and guests, then maybe Mom would get off my back. My name is Odelia Patience Gray, and I weigh in at around two hundred twenty pounds on a five-foot-one-inch frame. Surely I would be over any weight limit in their resident policy if they had one, and then I wouldn't be spending my Tuesday afternoon listening to my mother's harebrained ideas. Of course, that would mean she'd just get in her car and drive to our house, which means I couldn't make an excuse to leave after a suitable time like I can when I visit Seaside. Both had their drawbacks and their charms.

"Hi, Mom," I said in greeting over the wall. "Hi, Art." Art lifted a glass of something in greeting.

"The door's open," Mom told me. "Come on in."

After entering her townhouse, I dropped my tote bag on the coffee table and exited again through the patio door to join Mom and Art, careful to shut the slider behind me to keep in the air conditioning. Bending down, I quickly kissed Mom on the forehead. Art flashed me a beautiful smile, bright white against his semisweet chocolate skin. He still had all his own teeth, which he was happy to brag about without much prompting.

Art Franklin is a very well-preserved man, widowed and in his early seventies. He'd retired from the post office after serving it for over forty years. He was good-natured and smart. When Mom first moved into Seaside, Art seemed very interested romantically in her, but over time she seemed to have dampened his ardor and he scaled back to just being her good friend, at least for appearance's sake. Since coming to California Mom has had a couple of suitors, much to our surprise since she's often cranky. Art was our favorite. Greg and I even joked about adopting Art and sending Mom packing to his family on holidays. I'm sure Shelita would just love that.

"Are you not interested in dating Art Franklin because he's black?" I had asked Mom once while we were out to lunch alone.

For a long time Mom had stared at me like I'd just told her I'd been kidnapped by aliens and had suffered a probing. Finally, she'd said, "Do you really think I'm that type of person, Odelia?"

"No," I'd answered honestly, "but he's so nice and has all his own teeth, not to mention a great sense of humor—a trait that helps in getting along with you, I might add. I'm just wondering why you don't seem interested in such a nice stable man."

"He's too young for me," she'd said and slurped a spoonful of soup.

"He's just a few years younger than you," I pointed out.

"I like him just fine as a good friend, Odelia. We have a lot of laughs together. Now mind your own business." She took another mouthful of soup.

"Why? You never mind yours." I took a bite of my sandwich and chewed as more thoughts came to mind. "Is he terminally ill? Is he hiding a criminal record?"

"MYOB," she'd snapped, clearly agitated at my questioning. She looked up from the depths of her bowl. "I'm old, Odelia. I've been married twice and have no desire to have another husband. Art and I are good as we are. We have fun, then he goes home to his place. I like it like that."

My eyebrows raised higher than twin Golden Arches. "Are you and Art sleeping together?" This was not an original thought. Greg had once asked me if I thought Mom and Art were doing it.

Mom put her spoon down with a hard thud, hard enough to make the salt and pepper shakers on the table snap to attention. "Yes, Odelia," she hissed across the table. "Art Franklin and I are having hot monkey sex at night on the shuffleboard court."

Seeing that it was Grace Littlejohn saying those words, I wasn't sure if it was true or not.

"Once we even got caught by the nighttime security guard," she added. "He joined us for a threesome."

Okay, now I knew she was being facetious—disturbing and facetious. It was difficult enough getting the picture of Mom and Art doing it out of my head, but Mom in a threesome was surely going to send me into therapy.

That whole conversation came to mind now as I watched Mom and Art sitting contentedly side by side on padded plastic patio chairs while sipping iced tea. On a table between them was a plate of my mother's yummy banana bread. Thanks to her AC, Mom baked year-round. I sat down, took a slice of the bread, and bit off a large chunk.

"There are no nuts in it," I complained around a half-full mouth.

"Art's allergic to nuts," Mom said. "I also made a batch with nuts. It's inside. You can take a loaf home to Greg." I took note that she didn't include me in the gift of banana bread. Mom adores my husband.

I continued chewing and shook my head. "Greg's out of town for the next week to ten days. It's his annual trip to visit the Phoenix and Colorado shops. I put him on a plane early this morning. He's going to stay with Clark while he's in Phoenix."

Mom touched the side of her head with an index finger. "I'd forgotten that his trip was coming up."

"Greg does that every year?" Art asked.

I nodded as I swallowed my second bite of nut-free banana bread. "Yes. He and his partner Boomer meet in Phoenix to check out that store and meet with its manager for a few days. Then they'll fly up to Colorado to have their annual meeting and go over the books at Boomer's branch." I grabbed a napkin from a small pile on the table. "Greg also wants to visit some friends from college who have recently settled in Denver."

"Are they still thinking of starting another store?" Mom asked, knowing that it was something Greg and Boomer wanted to do but had held off doing because of the economy.

"They revisit that possibility every year," I told her. "Greg is thinking if they do, it might be in Seattle. He's learned of a shop up there for sale, so instead of starting from scratch, they could buy it and turn it into one of their shops."

"Isn't your friend Dev Frye up in Seattle now?" Art asked.

An elderly couple, both with hair as white as snow, strolled by. As they passed, they waved to us. Mom and Art waved back. Mom leaned toward me and whispered, "That's George and Eleanor Brown. Enlarged prostate and incontinence issues."

"Yes, he is," I answered, ignoring Mom's commentary on her neighbors. "He's the one who told Greg about the shop for sale."

"Maybe he could get Dev to run it," Mom suggested. "It would give him something to do in retirement."

I laughed, not imagining Dev for a second sitting on a porch cataloging his neighbor's health issues. "Greg said the same thing."

Six months earlier our good friend Dev Frye had retired from the Newport Beach Police Department and moved to Seattle to be with his girlfriend Beverly. He'd been a homicide detective for a long time and a good one. We all miss him a great deal. We heard from him via email about once a month. He reported that things in Seattle were fine, but Greg and I both thought he sounded bored.

Mom put her glass on the table and got up from her chair. "Let me fetch you some iced tea," she said to me.

"I can get it," I protested.

"Nonsense," Mom said. "I need to get up and move my old joints anyway, or would you rather come inside where it's cool?"

"No," I answered, "outside is fine. There's a nice breeze now that the heat's given us a break."

She looked at Art. "You need a refill?"

Art looked down at his glass. "No, thanks, Grace. I'm good."

"When I come back," Mom said to me, "Art and I can tell you about these suspicions we have about a neighbor."

"Is that what you've been bothering the management office about?" I asked, my last bite of banana bread halfway to my mouth.

Mom shook a bony finger at me. "I'll bet that Mona D'Angelo called you. She's such a snitch." Before I could respond, Mom disappeared into her cool condo. I turned to Art with unasked questions plastered across my face.

"I'll let Grace tell you the details," Art began, "but have you ever heard of Boaz Shankleman?"

I ran the name through my memory bank, then slowly said, "I don't think so. Does he live here at Seaside?"

Art nodded, then took another sip of his tea. "Yes, he does. How about Bo Shank? Does that name ring a bell?"

This time a sharp ding went off in my head. "Bo Shank? Do you mean the lead singer for the old band Acid Storm?" I gave my head a gentle shake. "He lives here?"

"Yep," Art answered, "but he goes by his real name now: Boaz Shankleman."

"I loved that band when I was in college," I said with excitement. "They had a couple of hit albums, then disappeared. I believe the band broke up."

Mom returned with my iced tea. I took it from her and took a long thirsty drink.

"I'm so glad you called today, Odelia," Mom said after settling back into her chair. "I was going to call you anyway. We need you to help us. We think something's happened to Bo. He's gone missing for a couple of weeks, and no one will do anything about it."

"Maybe he's off visiting his kids," I suggested.

Art shook his head. "Doesn't have any. At least that's what he told us."

"In fact," Mom added, "Bo claims he doesn't have any family. He told us he was married once in his forties for a couple of years, but that's it."

"He can still take a vacation, can't he?" I asked before taking another sip of tea.

"He can and he has," Mom answered, "but he always tells us when he does. He usually has Art take care of his plants when he leaves town."

"And Ringo once in a while," Art chimed in. "If he doesn't take him with him, which he usually does."

"Ringo?" I asked, still in shock that one of my favorite singers from the '70s was living in the same place as my mother.

"That's his taco terrier," Mom clarified, still leaving me in the dark.

"A taco terrier?" I asked, sounding like a repetitious dunce.

Mom let out a big loud sigh. "As nutty as you are about animals, Odelia, I would have thought you'd know what that is."

"Educate me," I said, getting annoyed with her attitude. I turned to Art, the much nicer of my two current companions.

"A taco terrier," he explained, "is a hybrid—half Chihuahua and half toy terrier. It has a sturdier body than a full-bred Chihuahua, but it's still pretty small."

"It has the big ears of a Chihuahua, too, but it's not as yippy," Mom said. "At least Ringo's not obnoxious."

"Okay," I said, getting the conversation back to the original topic. "Recapping, you haven't seen Bo in a while."

"It's been a couple of weeks," Mom said.

"You haven't seen Bo in a couple of weeks," I clarified, "and he didn't tell anyone he was leaving town."

"Right," Art said, "and he's not answering his phone or returning voicemails. Grace and I have both left several messages. We also have his email address, and he's not answering that either."

"Considering that Bo lives alone," I said after thinking about it a few seconds, "I can see why you're both concerned, but if the dog and car are gone, then Bo probably went on some extended trip and forgot to tell you. Maybe it was a last-minute thing." I took another sip of tea. "Art, if you took care of his plants and dog once in a while, did he give you a key?"

"I always returned it when he came back," he said. "He never offered to have me hold on to it. And this time he didn't even ask me to look in on the plants."

"By the way," Mom interjected, "Art and I have exchanged keys. I keep it in the junk drawer along with your extra key."

"That's nice to know," I nodded, trying to keep my earlier ideas out of my head. I took another drink of tea. "I understand you asked the management office to look into it."

"So Mona did call you," Mom said, peeved. "She treats us all like a bunch of special-needs kids." She twitched her nose. "It's annoying." I didn't say how I already knew about this. I'd rather she think Mona D'Angelo was a snitch than Shelita was coming to me, wanting to break up this friendship. "Yes, we notified the management office. They went over there and knocked quite loudly, and then the security guard opened Bo's place. Art and I went with him."

"Not a thing was out of place—and no Boaz or Ringo," Art reported. "The plants needed watering, but that was about it. The guard let me water them while we were in there."

I put my tea on the table and got up to stretch. It was nearly noon and I was starting to feel very warm sitting outside, even if we were under the shade of the patio roof. "I still think you're going to find out that Bo went on a long trip or vacation and simply forgot to tell anyone. It might have been last minute." I waited, wondering if Mom was going to tell me about contacting the police. When she didn't, I decided not to bring it up. I'd learned long ago with Mom to let sleeping dogs lie—taco terriers or not.

Picking up my tea glass, I opened the slider to go into the house to get my bag. "I have lunch plans with Zee," I told them, "so I have to shove off."

Mom followed me in and Art followed her like ducklings crossing the street in a row. "Aren't you going to snoop around a bit?" Mom asked. "That's what we want you to do."

I picked up my bag and pulled out my car keys. "I'm sure Bo put an emergency number on his Seaside application. Do you know if the management office called it?"

Art and Mom looked at each other, then shrugged in unison.

"Tell you what," I told them. "How about I swing by the front office before I leave and inquire if they did that or not?"

"Sounds good," Art said with his killer natural smile. "I think they're tired of hearing from us anyway."

I turned to my mother. "Will that make you feel better, Mom?"

She crossed her arms in front of her, clearly not happy with my meager offering. "Well, it's a start," she groused, "but I think he's met with foul play, Odelia, both him and the dog. And the sooner we start looking into it, the faster we can solve it."

"Why do you say that, Mom? Was Bo a shady character or into drugs or stuff like that?"

"He's a great guy," answered Art.

Mom nodded in agreement. "Yes, one of the best around here, funny and smart." She uncrossed her arms and rubbed her abdomen. "I've just got a gut feeling about this, Odelia, like I ate something bad. Do you know what I mean?"

I knew very well what my mother meant. Gut feelings were a family trait.

THREE

"So what did the front office say?" asked Zee after I told her about Mom and Art's concern and my coffee with Shelita.

I picked up a piece of my turkey club sandwich, ready to take a bite. "They said they did call his emergency contact, and that person—his band manager, I think they told me—said he had no idea where Bo is at the moment and hadn't heard from him either." I took a bite and chewed. "But Mona in the front office also told me that he said it didn't strike him as odd at all that Bo took off on a long or unplanned trip without telling anyone. He claimed Bo did it often."

"But Grace and Art thought it odd?" Zee asked.

"Yep. According to them, he would have someone at least check on his plants while he was away."

Across from me, Zee was working on rebuilding her burger. No matter what she orders, Zee has to take it apart, then reassemble it exactly the way she wants. Only soup is safe from this habit of hers. I simply pick up what's in front of me and dive into it like I'm bobbing for apples.

"On the way here, I called Mom and told her what Mona said, but she's still not happy."

Zee stopped fiddling with her food and looked at me. We were sitting outside at a favorite café, and she was wearing sunglasses. The darkness of the lenses and frame nearly matched her dark skin, making her head look like a large, round chocolate truffle. "So what's your next move?" she asked.

I shrugged. "Nothing more I can do."

"Don't give me that." She fixed me with her ninja mom stare. Zee was now an empty nester, so I was getting it more and more since her kids weren't around, like she had that look stored up inside and if she didn't let it loose on someone, she'd burst at the seams. She picked up a sweet potato fry and aimed it at me like an extra finger. "I know you and I know Grace. Neither of you can keep your nose out of anything."

"How is Hannah feeling?" I said, changing the subject to Zee's very pregnant daughter, who lived on the East Coast. The pending birth of her first grandchild was Zee's favorite topic.

"She's fine and big as a house," Zee said with a wide smile that rivaled Art's. "And about to pop!" To confirm her claim, she pulled out her phone and showed me a recent photo of Hannah. My unofficial goddaughter did, indeed, look about to explode.

"I'm surprised you're still here in California." I licked mayonnaise off a finger.

"Seth and I are leaving tonight, as a matter of fact." Zee bit half of her fry and chewed it. "We were going next week, but Hannah said she thinks the baby is coming early, so we're hopping a red-eye tonight."

"Give Hannah a big hug for me, and I have a gift for her in my car." We each took another bite of our food.

"So, what are you going to do about this Boaz guy?" Zee asked again, after taking a drink of lemonade.

"What can I do, Zee?" I asked, trying another maneuver by answering a question with a question.

Zee wiped her hands on a napkin before speaking. "Odelia, I've never seen you at a loss before on what to do in such circumstances. Do you need a dead body before the Sherlock Holmes part of your brain kicks in?"

Ouch!

But she had a point. There was no body and my big behind wasn't in a jam, nor was anyone I loved in danger. This was a simple snoop job, with the only downside being that I might end up annoying the hell out of someone. My mother and Art had already paved that highway ahead of me.

"Yeah, you're right. I guess I could snoop around and see if I can find out something. And doing that would make Mom happy. The folks at Seaside didn't give me the name of Bo's manager, but that shouldn't be too hard to find out. He'd either be the one from before, which means he's probably mentioned on Acid Storm's Wikipedia page, or he's someone who books their current gigs."

Zee looked at me with surprise. "But I thought Acid Storm broke up decades ago."

I nodded as I chewed and swallowed the bite of sandwich in my mouth. "They did, but I think I remember reading somewhere that some of the members of the band still make occasional guest appearances. Of all the guys in the band, Bo Shank would be the biggest draw, even now. Either way, I'm sure I can track down his manager online."

I took another bite of my club sandwich and washed it down with a healthy gulp of iced tea. What I could also do was check Marigold, but I didn't mention that to Zee because I had never told her about the ultra-secret Internet search engine I'd stumbled upon via Barbara, a contract researcher that my boss, Mike Steele, and I had used in the past. When she retired and moved into a rest home, Barbara had given me her passwords to several of her subscription search engines, and I had paid her for the time left on them.

When I'm not stumbling over dead bodies, I'm a corporate paralegal at a law firm called Templin and Tobin, or T&T for short. The T&T main office is in Los Angeles, in Century City, but I work in their Orange County branch. Several attorneys and staff migrated to T&T from our previous law firm, including Steele, who manages the OC office. Marigold has proven itself quite useful in my paralegal work. Now when Steele needs useful information on a party to a business transaction, especially if he's smelling something a bit off, he gives me the job instead of contracting it out. I haven't exactly told Steele about Marigold, just that Barbara gave me a lot of her research information when she retired.

Marigold isn't exactly in the deep dark web, where nefarious activities of all kinds take place, but it's not crawling on the surface waving a red flag announcing its existence. You have to be referred to it by another user to even know it's there. It can pull information on anyone or any company, much of which is public but not easily attainable and certainly not conveniently located in one spot. And some of it may not be public but gathered from servers that the folks who operate Marigold have accessed, legally or illegally.

Marigold was invaluable to me after that body was found in the trunk of my car in February, and it might be useful now in finding a lead on the whereabouts of Boaz Shankleman. As soon as I got home after lunch, I would run his name through Marigold's digital brain and see what cropped up.

After lunch Zee and I went to a local baby store and ordered a gift for Hannah's baby from Greg and me. We were getting her a stroller, and I wanted Zee with me to make sure I ordered the right one. My mother had had one of the ladies at Seaside knit a darling blanket, booties, and cap set for Hannah, and I passed that gift along to Zee to carry with her on the trip since they could be packed easily.

"I didn't know Grace did such beautiful handwork," Zee said as she stroked the blanket. "These are gorgeous. Hannah is going to love them." I didn't wrap the items because I wanted Zee to see them. They were pretty spectacular and done in the softest yarn and palest green imaginable.

"She doesn't," I said as I stood next to my car in the parking lot of the baby store. Next to it was Zee's car. "My mother gets these from a lady at Seaside named Teri Thomson. Whenever Mom needs a handmade gift like this, she's Mom's first stop. Teri's work is amazing. Mom is a great baker; that's her talent. Speaking of which," I said as I dipped my head back into my car and pulled out a loaf swathed in plastic wrap. "Here's a loaf of Mom's banana bread for you and Seth."

"She's baking in this heat?" Zee asked as she happily took the treat.

"Yep. She loves to bake. She doesn't eat much of it, but she sure can crank it out." I chuckled. "Clark says she started baking when she stopped drinking. It's her therapy when she's anxious about stuff."

"I hate to hear that Grace is troubled," Zee said with genuine concern, "but I sure do love the results. Seth will eat this entire loaf tonight before we go if I don't watch him. Maybe I'll stick it in the freezer until we get home from Hannah's. He says I don't bake enough now that the kids are gone." She rolled her large expressive eyes and patted her round belly. "Like either of us needs it."

"Me included," I added. "It's like Mom's our dealer and her bread and cookies are crack. I'm putting my loaf directly into the freezer too, to save it for Greg."

Zee laughed. I love her laugh. It's as rich as dark chocolate and as merry as an elf's. "Right," she said, winking at me. "I'm betting it's half gone by noon tomorrow." Zee knew me too well. We've known each other for over twenty years. Hannah was just a toddler when I met Zee and Seth, and their son, Jacob, hadn't been born yet.

"Well, dear," she said, "give me a hug because I won't see you until I get back from my trip." We hugged tightly. After, she added, "And don't you go getting into any trouble while I'm gone, and especially while Greg's out of town."

"What trouble? I'm just going to look up some stuff on the computer and make a few phone calls to keep my mother happy. Pretty boring stuff. Not to mention, you encouraged me over lunch to do it."

"That's the plan, Stan," she said with another signature laugh. "If you help Grace with this, maybe you'll be too busy to get into any real trouble."

FOUR

When I got home, the first thing I did was put the banana bread directly into the freezer. Huh. A lot that smartypants Zee knows. I can be trusted with baked goods. I even did it before I greeted Wainwright and Muffin, although I had to maneuver a gauntlet of wagging tails and meows to do it.

Poor Wainwright. He usually goes everywhere with Greg. With Greg traveling for the next week or so, the dog was going to be singing the blues. I'd have to make sure we took two walks a day instead of just our usual morning walk down to the beach. Muffin, on the other hand, didn't care who was home as long as there was at least one warm lap in which to snuggle.

After taking care of animal greetings, I pulled out my laptop, grabbed a yellow pad and pen, and went out on the patio to work. I wanted to first initiate a Marigold search for Boaz Shankleman. That might quickly lead me to some people I could contact to ask about Bo, and that would put my mother and Art at ease. It helps on Marigold if you can provide as much information as possible to weed out duplicate names. Although I doubted there were many Boaz Shanklemans running around, I was able to pull Bo's date of birth from Wikipedia and insert that along with his name and alias of Bo Shank into the Marigold search engine. Marigold results were not instantaneous. It could take anywhere from thirty minutes to two hours, depending on how much there was to pull and how busy the server was at the time. In the meantime, I pulled up images of Bo on Google and checked them out.

He'd been a tall, sexy drink of water in his band's heyday, with a lean body and wavy dark hair that he wore down to about his chin most of the time. Over the years, Bo's hair had run the gamut of lengths from shoulder-length to almost a buzz cut. I'd lusted after the singer during his wavy mane period. Recent photos of him showed a man in his late sixties, still lean, still sporting a shock of wavy hair, but now it was steel gray. His taste in facial hair had been just as varied, from full and long to short, but never clean shaven. Even now he wore a Vandyke beard, much like my husband's but gray. Greg's beard was showing scant bits of gray, like patches of snow at the end of winter. Sometimes he likes it, sometimes he doesn't and threatens to shave it off, proving that men are just as vain about going gray as women. Bo's face looked like a rough road with deep tire tracks around his eyes and mouth, but even when he was younger Bo Shank hadn't been a pretty boy. He was still good looking though, even for an old guy, and in photos he still exuded a casual sexiness that was hard to ignore.

I opened the various current photos of Bo that showed him with people. On the webpages on which they appeared, some had captions noting who was with him. I saved the photos to my desktop that I thought might be important and jotted down the names of the people with him in each. There were a few of Bo holding a small dog. I opened the first one, but there was no caption. The second one yielded information. The caption for the photo read *Bo Shank with His Taco Terrier Ringo*. I enlarged the photo and studied the animal. Bo was sitting, holding the dog on his lap, a hand cupped against the front of the dog's chest, while he talked with an unidentified man to his right. Neither man paid any attention to the photographer, but Ringo did. He stared at the camera with open intelligence and confidence that told the world he was quite comfortable in his celebrity status.

I checked out a few more photos of Bo with Ringo. One showed the animal standing on a table on his small hind legs, his front paws on Bo's chest. The man and dog were snout to snout, sharing smooches. Clearly the animal loved his owner, and Bo loved him back. The dog's body was small but sturdy, especially through his chest, and his legs were stumpy. His coat was mostly white, with splotches of medium brown, as if he'd rolled around in soft milk chocolate, then shook most of it off. His eyes were large and dark and very expressive, while his ears were quite comical. They were too large for his head, like they'd been borrowed for the day from a larger dog. Ringo looked like an animal with a sweet and stable disposition, and he was evidently comfortable around people—my kind of animal.

My curiosity about Ringo satisfied, I continued going through more recent photos of Bo and noted the names and faces of the people with him when they were listed. I'd gone through almost two dozen when I hit pay dirt.

It was a photo of Bo with a man about his age but round and soft and bald, like a boiled egg wearing business casual. The photo was taken about six months earlier and the caption noted *Legendary Bo Shank with His Manager Titan West.*

Titan? It made me wonder if it was his real name or some nickname hung on him by snarky kids in school. The last thing this man looked like was a Titan. A Morris, maybe, or even a George or a Howard.

I googled Titan West and found a simple but very professional website for Titan Entertainment. From the information on the site, Titan West headed an agency that represented tribute bands and old-time musicians still pumping cash out of the baby boomers who had followed them way back when. Among the bands he represented was Acid Storm, but it wasn't listed as a tribute band. Confused because I knew the band had broken up decades ago, I clicked on the link that brought me to the group's bio, which included a close-up photo of the band. Bo Shank was in front, arms crossed in front of him, one eye half closed in a surly look that suggested he didn't give a damn if you hired them or not. The photo looked familiar. Switching to Amazon, I looked up Acid Storm's albums, which were still available in used condition through outside vendors.

Sure enough, gracing the front of one of Acid Storm's first album covers was a very similar photo, with Bo giving the same challenging stare; the other two band members on either side of him but slightly in the background were wearing the same serious scowls. The difference, besides the newer photo not being an album cover, was that Bo was older and one of the band members standing with him was much younger. He wasn't a kid, maybe in his mid-thirties, but young enough that when Acid Storm was riding high in the charts, he probably wasn't alive or at most had been in diapers.

The other band member was about the same age as Bo and looked familiar. I toggled back and forth between the two photos until I was reasonably sure that the third guy was also an original member of the band.

Bo Shank had been the lead singer of Acid Storm and the most well-known of the original trio, but he was certainly not the only member who grabbed attention. The lead guitarist, an English guy by the name of Kurt Spencer-Hall, was notorious for wild nights and partying with teenage girls, often underage. I dug deep into my memory for the name of the other band member. I could have looked it up but wanted to see how well my gray matter had stood up over the years. As I recall, the drummer's name was David Oxman, the other original member in the current band. I looked it up online and was pleased to see that I was right. It was Kurt Spencer-Hall who had been replaced by the young guy.

I toggled over to the Marigold site and input searches for Titan West, Kurt Spencer-Hall, and David Oxman. My search results for Bo had not shown up yet, so I went back to the bio page for the new Acid Storm group and checked on the identity of the young guy. His name was Simon Tuttle. I ran a Marigold search on him as well.

I returned to the Titan Entertainment website and the page for Acid Storm's upcoming events. If Acid Storm was in the middle of a string of shows, that could explain Bo's disappearance and whereabouts. Then I remembered that Seaside had said his manager had no idea where Shankleman was. Seems he would if they had a show scheduled. But I checked anyway.

The events page listed shows up until the beginning of last month, but nothing was going on right now. In fact, there was nothing listed for the rest of the year, and it was only August. I found that odd. Nostalgia bands were a big hit at fairs and other summer and fall outdoor events. I looked at the page again. There was no mention of the band being closed to bookings.

I did a Google search to see if there was any mention of Bo Shankleman or bookings for Acid Storm not on the Titan Entertainment page. There was nothing. Everything was pointing to Boaz and Ringo hitting the road for a little off-the-book road trip.

I took note of the number for Titan Entertainment and punched in the numbers on my cell phone. According to its website, it was located in Santa Ana. One quick call just might take care of this mystery. After the fourth ring, right before I expected it to go to voicemail, the call was answered.

"Titan here," a man's voice barked.

"Is this Titan Entertainment or Titan West?" I asked, toggling back to the photo of Titan West with Bo Shank. The voice didn't match the photo.

"One and the same," the man said. "State your business."

It didn't seem like a very professional way to answer a business phone, but I wasn't about to give him a tutorial on phone etiquette. "Mr. West," I began.

"Titan," he said, cutting me off. "It's just Titan."

"Okay, Titan." I took a deep breath. "My mother lives at Seaside Retirement Community, where Boaz Shankleman also resides."

He cut me off again, this time with, "So? What's that got to do with me?"

"Mr. Shankleman hasn't been seen in a couple of weeks, and my mother is worried."

"Why? He banging her?"

I clamped my mouth closed at the vulgar question, lest I say something equally bad. "No," I quickly answered, "but he is a friend and neighbor, and she and some of the other residents are concerned."

"Yeah, so I heard." He cleared his throat. "Some woman from the front office there called me a few days ago looking for Boaz. As I told her, I don't know where he is and don't care."

"Aren't you his emergency contact and his manager?"

"Yeah, I guess. At least the first part, which I need to change. As for the manager end, he fired me a few months back."

"So that's why there are no bookings for the group on your website. I thought it seemed strange that the listings stopped. Did you and the band have a falling out?"

He laughed. "Just artistic differences."

"Do you know who's representing the band now?"

"Not for sure, but I have my suspicions. And she can have them. Acid Storm burned out decades ago, and it's still a bunch of burnouts. Cydney Fox ruined the band back then, and she's going to ruin what's left of it. Mark my words." He hung up.

Cydney Fox. The name sounded familiar, but I couldn't immediately place it.

I was about to do a Google search for Cydney Fox when my cell phone rang. It was Greg. I eagerly picked it up. "Hi, honey," I said into the phone. "How are you doing?"

"Just fine, sweetheart. I had a few minutes before Clark and I left for an early dinner and thought I'd check in with you."

Dinner?

I glanced at the time on my laptop. It was past five o'clock. Holy moly! I'd been researching for over two hours. "Wow," I said to

Greg, "I had no idea it was that late. I've been working on the computer since I got home from lunch and shopping with Zee."

"You doing something for the office?" he asked.

Okay, here's where it could get sticky. I wasn't about to lie to my husband, but if he knew I was nosing around about people, he might get upset. Usually when I did that, it meant someone was dead and I was up to my neck in trouble. Before I could make up my mind about what to say, the dead air on the phone made him jump to the worst-case scenario.

"Oh my God, Odelia!" Greg shouted. "I haven't even been gone twenty-four hours and you've managed to find a dead body?"

"No. No. No," I hurriedly assured him. "There's no body. I swear."

I heard voices, then a second later I heard my brother's voice as Greg switched his phone to speaker. "Dammit, Odelia, now what are you into?" Clark barked into the phone.

Clark was a retired cop who now headed up security for a company headquartered in Phoenix. The ultimate owner of the company is Willie Proctor, a friend of ours who is also a felon on the run. On paper, though, it's just a normal company with a normal . board of directors.

"I'm just helping Mom," I snapped. "She and Art are worried about one of their neighbors. He's been gone for a few weeks, along with his car and his dog, and they're concerned. I'm sure he'll turn up after having taken a little road trip. He's an entertainer, so he's probably in Vegas or someplace like that."

"What's he do?" asked my always suspicious brother.

"Do you remember the band called Acid Storm?"

"Sure," both Greg and Clark answered.

My husband was ten years younger than me, so he would have been a very young teen at the time. "You listened to Acid Storm, Greg?" I asked with doubt.

"My brother had their albums," he answered. "After my accident, I pulled them out and played them all the time, to the point where my mother threatened to throw them out. It was angry music, and I was an angry kid."

Greg had become a paraplegic after a fall from a bridge at the age of fourteen. In spite of it, he'd managed to finish high school and college, build a great business, and develop an incredible and genuine positive outlook on life, but I knew it hadn't happened overnight and without overcoming great obstacles and setbacks.

"Well," I continued, "here's a newsflash: Bo Shank, the lead singer, lives at Seaside."

"Get out of here!" Greg exclaimed.

"It's true," I confirmed, "but he goes by his real name of Boaz Shankleman."

"Hey," said Clark, "I've met that guy during a couple of my stays with Mom. I had no idea who he was, though. He was just introduced to me as Boaz."

"So it's Bo Shank who's missing?" asked Greg.

"Yep," I answered, "along with his dog, Ringo. I've been looking into him online and just got off the phone with his former manager. He doesn't know where he is, but it seems Acid Storm might have new representation since the band still performs nostalgia gigs. I'm betting he's on one of those trips and just forgot to tell anyone at Seaside."

"Sounds reasonable," said Clark, "although I thought that band broke up years ago. Wasn't there some scandal?"

"I think you're right, Clark," I answered. "Only Bo and David Oxman are still performing. The third member of the band, Kurt Spencer-Hall, was replaced by some young guy when they got back together." I paused. "So you see, no dead bodies."

"It's still early," Clark scoffed.

FIVE

I HUNG UP FROM Frick and Frack after Greg and Wainwright had a slobbery moment via the phone, after which I brought all my stuff inside and thought about dinner. Nothing caught my interest as I stood in front of the open refrigerator door hoping something would magically appear. It was nearly barren, but I didn't feel like grocery shopping either. Spying Wainwright's leash hanging on its peg by the back slider, I had an idea.

I grabbed my tote bag and stuck my laptop into it, then grabbed the leash. I didn't need to call to Wainwright. As soon as the animal saw his leash off its peg, he bounded over, tail wagging and ready to go. In doggie years he's an old guy, but jiggle his leash and he behaves like a puppy. I barely had the leash attached before he was pulling me toward the front door. We could have been going out the back to the car, but the smart dog had read my mind.

Our home is only a few blocks from the ocean and the Seal Beach pier. Wainwright trotted along happily as we made our way down the street toward the ocean. He'd get his walk and I could grab dinner at a small café across from the beach. It had a patio facing the street, and I could keep Wainwright with me on the patio while I ate. When I got down there it was still a bit early for the usual dinner crowd, so Wainwright and I easily found a spot where we could both people watch. A few neighbors waved hello as they passed, and one stopped long enough to give Wainwright an affectionate pat.

"Hey, Odelia," Brad Hornby said as he handed me a menu. "Where's Greg?"

Brad was one of the owners. He handled the front of the house while his father, John, a former stockbroker, did most of the cooking. When they were busy, John's wife, who also made some of the baked goods, helped wait tables. The Hornbys had bought the café several years earlier when John had burned out on the business world and went to cooking school. They'd renamed it the Hornblower Café and transformed the place from a casual coffee shop into a great little eatery popular with locals and tourists alike. Greg and I loved having breakfast here on weekends. They weren't open every night for dinner, but tonight was my lucky night.

"He's on a business trip," I told Brad as I looked over the specials tacked to the front of the usual menu. "It's just Wainwright and me tonight."

"The seafood salad is super," Brad told me, pointing it out on the list of specials. "It's a variety of fresh grilled seafood with a lot of great local veggies and the house vinaigrette."

"Sold," I told him, "and give me a glass of your house chardonnay with it."

After Brad left with my order, I took out my laptop and opened it. I could continue my research while having dinner. I noted in my email that some of the Marigold searches had come in, but not all of them.

My dinner came. The salad was delicious, especially with the chilled wine. Brad also brought Wainwright a bowl of water and a bit of cold roast beef. While I ate, I opened one of the Marigold reports and read. I started with the one on Boaz Shankleman. He was sixty-seven years old, born in Syracuse, New York, to Sarah and Benjamin Shankleman, both deceased. He had two older siblings, a brother who died in 2001 and a sister two years older named Harriet Mayer who was still living in Syracuse. *Odd*, I thought. Mom and Art had both said Boaz told them he had no family. If Bo didn't show up, I would look up the address and phone number for his sister and give her a call. He might have gone to visit her. She might even be ill and he went to be with her. There were so many possibilities as to why this man wasn't in his home at the moment, and most of them didn't involve foul play.

The report noted that Bo had been married only once, to a woman named Courtney Phelps back in the nineties, but it had lasted less than two years and they had no children. Contacting his ex-wife would be a long shot, so I left it for last, in case I ran out of options.

It was interesting to read about the life of a celebrity from my younger days. I hadn't been the sort of fan to follow celebrity gossip or news, so all I really knew were the basics: the band's music and eventual breakup. As Clark had said, it had been big news back then, occurring about two-thirds through a world tour and causing the cancellation of the rest of the bookings. Acid Storm had been sued by concert promoters and venues left and right. I slowly shook my head back and forth, now remembering the brouhaha that had been splashed across tabloids and magazines more than thirty years ago. The tour, the band, and even the corporation set up to handle their business affairs had been torn apart and bankrupted—all over a woman.

What was her name? I stopped reading and stared out across the road to the ocean on the other side, digging through my brain like a seagull diving for scraps. Considering how many people were out walking, biking, and skateboarding, you'd think it was a weekend night instead of a Tuesday. I glanced down at Wainwright, who was asleep next to my chair, his head resting on his crossed paws. He was no help.

What was her name?

I could just look it up, confident that it was a big-enough story to pop up with the right keywords, but I wanted to remember it on my own like I had with the other band member. It was huge news at the time. Just because I didn't exercise my body that much didn't mean I was going to let my brain get as soft and flabby as my ass.

"Hey," the college-age girl seated at the table next to me said to her companion, a boy about the same age, "did you see the trailer for that new show on Fox? It looks pretty cool."

Her question flickered in my memory like a spark trying to catch on dry tinder. Fox. Cydney Fox!

"That's it!" I said aloud, then glanced over at the young couple, who were now staring at me. I jabbed at my laptop screen. "Sorry, just some exciting news in an email." They shrugged and went back to their meals.

Titan's bitter words replayed in my head: *Cydney Fox ruined the band back then, and she's going to ruin what's left of it. Mark my words.*

Memories of what had happened decades ago bubbled to the surface of my gray matter like gas in the goo at the La Brea Tar Pits. A young woman named Cydney Fox, who'd been seriously involved with David Oxman, was also having an affair with the notorious womanizer Kurt Spencer-Hall. When Oxman found out, he left the tour, the band, and Miss Fox. But it went beyond that. Soon after, several young groupies came forward claiming Spencer-Hall had drugged them to get into their panties. It was all very sordid and splashed about for months in the tabloids before dying a natural death—and that was before the Internet. If it happened now, it would be spread across the world in 140-character sound bites underscored with snarky comments directly from the public. Before finishing my meal, I requested a Marigold search for Cydney Fox.

Wainwright and I walked a long double loop back home. We both needed the exercise, especially me since I had also opted for a slice of Hornblower's spectacular double fudge chocolate cake after dinner with a cup of decaf coffee. Usually Greg and I split the piece of cake, but tonight I gorged myself on the gooey richness. My reward, I guess, for making sure the banana bread made it untouched into the freezer.

The animals and I had a quiet night. I retired to bed early and read until I was too tired to see the words—at least until the phones, both our land line and my cell, which was on the nightstand, started playing a pesky game of tag.

SIX

First one rang, then the other, then the ringing went back to the first phone and the round robin started again. I thrashed about on the bed like an unruly drunk trying to clear sleep from my brain. The other side of the bed was empty. It took me a groggy minute to remember that Greg was out of town. I finally grabbed my cell, worried that something had happened to him, but the call had been missed again.

I glanced at the display. I didn't recognize the number that had called, but it was local. I sighed with relief. Greg was in Arizona on a business trip. I'd talked to him earlier in the evening. The phone display also told me that it was about one thirty in the morning. Maybe it was a wrong number. I hit callback, but the number that had called me was busy.

Before I could put the phone back down, the ringer on the land line in the kitchen started up. We have an extension in the bedroom with the ringer set to off, but it's on Greg's side of the bed. Most people call our individual cell phones when they're trying to reach us. Still entangled in the sheets, I now tried to wade my way across our wide California King bed. It was like trying to swim while an octopus gave you a hug. Both Muffin and Wainwright were on the floor, side by side, alert and worried that I was losing my mind. By the time I reached the landline phone on Greg's nightstand, the ringing from the kitchen had stopped. Then my cell phone started up again. Whoever was trying to reach me was insistent, even if I didn't recognize the number. Fortunately, I still had my cell phone clutched in my hand. I flopped onto my back on Greg's side of the bed and answered it with all the sleepy and frustrated charm I could muster. "This had better be good."

"Odelia, it's Mom."

My eyes shot open, and my head instantly cleared. I glanced again at the phone's display. This was not Mom's landline or cell number. I went on instant alert. "Mom? What's going on? Are you calling from the hospital or something?"

"Um, more like something." Her voice was low and a bit shaky.

Now I wasn't just on alert but cautious and worried. "What's going on?" I repeated. "Where are you?"

"Um," Mom began again, then paused.

"Mom," I said, my voice full of warning, "cut to the chase."

"Do you think you could call either Seth or Steele for me? I'd call them myself but the cops took my phone."

Seth or Steele? Cops? Seth Washington and Mike Steele are both lawyers. Why would Mom need a lawyer at this time of night? As my brain connected the dots, I let loose with a very naughty swear word I seldom used.

"Odelia," my mother snapped. "Getting vulgar isn't helping."

I took a deep breath and looked again at the time. It was now exactly 1:30 a.m. "Seth and Zee left tonight to see their daughter. I'll see if I can reach Steele. Where exactly are you?" Considering who she was asking for and the comment about the phone, I had a sinking feeling about Mom's whereabouts, but I had to ask.

"At the Long Beach Police Department," Mom answered.

I let out another expletive when I heard the answer I knew might come, then started untangling myself from the sheets. My feet hit the hardwood floor in the bedroom at the precise time I asked, "What did they arrest you for?"

"It's not for me," Mom explained. "And no one has been arrested. At least not yet. But we still need Steele."

"Is it Art?" I asked. I put the phone on speaker and propped it on the dresser while I started pulling on the clothes I'd taken off and discarded on a chair just hours before. If it was Art, why weren't they calling Shelita Thomas? Or maybe Art was on another phone doing just that. I groaned as I imagined what Shelita was going to say to me and Mom. Now she'd probably insist Art move out of the retirement community to get away from my mother.

"No, it's not Art," Mom answered, her voice getting tight with frustration and worry. "It's Lorraine. They brought Lorraine and me here, and it doesn't look good. She's the one who really needs a lawyer."

Lorraine? I combed my memory for someone named Lorraine at the Seaside Retirement Community and came up empty. I slipped my bare feet into my cheery striped espadrilles and grabbed the phone. "Have I met Lorraine?"

"Lorraine!" Mom insisted. "Your niece Lorraine."

41

I dropped the phone. It hit the hardwood with a loud clunk. Wainwright scooted over to see if it was an edible item that had slipped from my fingers. I pushed him away from the phone and picked it up, saying a quick silent prayer of thanks that I'd bought the heavy-duty case for it that Greg had suggested instead of the cutesy flimsy one I'd originally wanted.

"What's Lorraine doing in California?" I asked Mom. "More to the point, what is she doing at the police station?"

On the other end of the line Mom hemmed and hawed, then finally said, "Seems you're not the only corpse magnet in the family."

My butt hit the edge of the bed as my legs gave out. I came to a stop sitting on the floor, my back against the mattress. My fingers dug into the hard case of my phone until they went white.

"What happened, Mom?"

"Just get here with Steele. I can tell you both at the same time." The line went dead.

I remained sitting on the floor in a stupor. Mom had just suggested that being a corpse magnet was a family trait, like eye color or a long nose.

I closed my eyes, thinking—no, hoping—it was all a bad dream and I was still entangled in bedsheets. Wainwright gave me a big slobbery kiss up the side of my face. That was real and caused me to open my eyes. I was still sitting on the floor, dressed and clutching my cell phone.

It wasn't a dream.

It felt like the beginning of a nightmare.

I called Mike Steele. He wasn't pleased to be woken up but immediately kicked into action when I told him my niece Lorraine was being held in Long Beach in connection with a murder. He said he'd meet me there.

Some days I wish I'd never found my long-lost mother. Fortunately, I didn't feel that way often, but today had started with that thought and it wasn't changing as I finished dressing so I could head to the Long Beach Police Department in the middle of the night.

Mom had disappeared when I was in high school. One day she was there, an aloof yet functioning drunk. A different day I came home from school and she wasn't there—neither was a note nor explanation of any kind. She and her clothing were gone. She'd left behind our meager furniture, a few scattered dust bunnies, and me. For decades I didn't know if she was alive or dead until a few years ago when I located her in Massachusetts, along with my two half brothers. After a rocky start, Mom and I had reconciled, and she now lives in Southern California near me. One of my half brothers died, and the other, Clark Littlejohn, and I have become quite close. I also inherited two nieces, Lorraine and Marie, along with Marie's husband and daughter. I'd gone from virtually no family to a bucketful overnight. Trust me, it's a mixed blessing.

For the entire drive to the police station, I ran over the events of the previous day, playing them back from the moment I met Shelita for coffee until dinner. Not once did I recall Mom or Clark mentioning that Lorraine was coming for a visit. Nor do I remember ever receiving a text or an email about it.

As I pulled into the parking lot at the police station, I wondered if I should call Clark and let him know what was going on. The thing is, *I* didn't know what was going on, at least not yet. Better to find out the entire story before I cause my brother to have a stroke. And who knows, Mom could have called him already. Better she be the one to make his head explode.

SEVEN

EVEN AT TWO IN the morning, the Long Beach Police Department was buzzing with activity. When I didn't see Mom anywhere, I stepped up to the front desk and waited until the balding, middle-aged uniformed cop behind it got off the phone. When he did, he looked up at me, his small brown eyes scanning and measuring me, absorbing information I didn't know I was giving off. "How can I help you, ma'am?"

"I believe my mother and niece are here," I told him, keeping my voice low and away from the others waiting. "Grace Littlejohn and Lorraine Littlejohn. My mother called me."

After consulting something on his desk, he said, "Take a seat. Someone will be out to get you."

"Their attorney is meeting me here in a few minutes," I added. *Their attorney!* My insides quivered at the thought. "His name is Michael Steele. Can you send him back when he comes?"

"Take a seat," he said again, his voice a monotone. "We're really busy tonight. When he gets here, let me know. You can go back together."

This was not what I wanted to hear. I wanted to talk to Mom now, but before I could protest, the officer had called the person behind me to the window.

Michael Steele isn't a criminal attorney, but he could make the appropriate calls to such people in the event one was needed. I took a seat next to a fidgeting bleached blond and prayed that call would never need to be made. Steele isn't just an attorney; he's also my boss. He can be annoying as hell, but he's also as loyal and helpful to Greg and me as our dog, Wainwright. He also seems to adore my mother, or maybe it's more that he finds her to be cheap entertainment. Either way, as soon as I told him that Grace and Lorraine were being detained by the Long Beach Police and that a corpse might be involved, he'd jumped into action. Steele lives in Laguna Beach, about thirty-five miles south of Long Beach. Without traffic, it takes about forty-five minutes to get from there to Long Beach. With traffic, you'd better pack a lunch to make the trip. It comforted me to know that at this time of night—or, rather, morning—there would be little to no traffic, and that Steele drives a Porsche and has a lead foot.

Earlier this year Mike Steele had married a woman named Michelle Jeselnik, who is a pediatrician with a thriving medical practice in partnership with her father in Perris, California. She also owns a home there. Since the wedding, they divided their time between Steele's ultra-modern condo on the beach and her home in Perris, taking turns with the killer commute. Recently Steele told me that Michelle and her father were looking to expand by buying a pediatric practice in Orange County, with the idea that Michelle would work from there. They'd been given a lead on a retiring pediatrician looking to sell his practice located near CHOC, the Children's Hospital of Orange County. It seemed a perfect solution, and negotiations were about to begin. I counted myself lucky that tonight was a night that Steele was in residence at Laguna Beach.

I glanced at a big industrial clock on the wall. It had been close to a half hour since I'd called Steele. I fidgeted in my seat, anxious to talk to Mom. While I waited, people came and went, and the place finally started emptying out. The background noise consisted of ringing phones and low conversations, but it was nothing like the noise that filled the place when I'd been there during the day.

My mind buzzed like a disturbed hornets' nest. All I knew was that Lorraine Littlejohn was in town, and that being a corpse magnet might be genetic—in our case, definitely passed down through Mom's genes. What in the hell was Lorraine doing in town without anyone saying anything about it? Did she decide to surprise her grandmother with a visit? Or was she in trouble and showed up on Mom's door knowing that Mom would do anything to help one of her grandchildren? Again I thought about calling Clark and Greg, but there really was no need to call before I knew what was going on. I tried to tame my anxiety by playing a few games of Words With Friends on my phone. I always had a few games going, but because of the hour, I took my turn and no one on the other side took theirs. Well, that burned up a whole two minutes. I tried reading, but I was too antsy and my eyes were gritty from exhaustion.

Finally, I simply hugged my tote bag to me, closed my eyes, and tried to think of more pleasant things, like Greg and the warmth of our bed, Muffin's purring, and Wainwright's slobbery kisses.

"Grey," I heard a voice in a tunnel say. I ignored it. "Grey," it said again, accompanied by a shake of my shoulder.

I jumped, my eyes flying open to see Steele standing next to me impeccably groomed, wearing a suit and tie, and carrying his brief-case. For a second I thought I was in the office and had dozed off at my desk. But as soon as I shook off my catnap stupor, I realized I was still at the police station and had tipped over against the empty seat next to me. I shot a look at the big clock and was surprised to see that it was about three a.m. I had nodded off for almost thirty minutes.

"Sleeping on the job?" Steele asked, but his face held no humor.

"They said to wait here until you arrived," I told him, yawning and rubbing the sleep out of my eyes. Steele was clean shaven, but one whiff told me he had skipped a shower. Not that Steele smelled of body odor, but I know from years of working with him that he's a morning shower person and always arrives at the office smelling of this special soap he uses. I stood up. "You look pretty spectacular for someone who just rolled out of bed."

This got me a small smile. "Just don't look too closely. I had to shave while driving 75 miles per hour."

"You drive a stick shift," I pointed out.

"Exactly." He took my arm and guided me to the front desk. We were the only ones in the waiting area now, but it still took the offi-cer a few moments to acknowledge us.

"Michael Steele," Steele announced once he had the officer's attention, "here to see Lorraine and Grace Littlejohn. I'm their attorney, and this is Odelia Grey, Mrs. Littlejohn's daughter."

The officer looked us over for what seemed to be way too long, then picked up the phone and made a call, announcing us to someone on the other end. "Someone will be right out," he told us as he hung up. "Take a seat."

Steele and I remained standing while we waited. About two minutes later a side door opened and none other than Detective Andrea Fehring beckoned us through it. She looked tired, but—like Steele—professionally pulled together in her usual dark pantsuit and light colored blouse. Today her blouse was pale pink.

"Don't look so surprised, Odelia," Fehring said to me after we were inside the inner workings of the station. "I have your name and your mother's on an informal call list. Anything comes up with you two or with Greg, my colleagues do me a favor and call. Think of me as your guardian angel."

"Is that why they made me wait?" I asked, peeved. "So you could be called? I've been here almost an hour cooling my heels instead of with Mom."

Fehring raised an eyebrow at my tone, then said, "I understand your niece, at the insistence of Grace, clammed up as soon as the police detained her and said she'd only talk to her lawyer." Fehring shot a look at Steele. "No Seth Washington this time? Or is it your turn to babysit, Steele?"

"Seth and Zee are on their way to see their daughter, Hannah," I answered before Steele could say anything. "Hannah's going to have her baby any minute."

A slight smile crossed Fehring's lips. She was a mother herself and knew and liked the Washingtons. "Please tell them congratulations for me."

"I hate to break up this little coffee klatch, ladies," Steele said with his usual impatience with pleasantries, "but what's going on? All Grace told Odelia was that she and Lorraine were here, and that being a corpse magnet seems to run in the family. Are they under arrest for murder?"

Andrea shook her head. "No, they are being detained for breaking and entering."

My heart stopped. "You arrested them? Both of them?" Mom had definitely said they weren't arrested.

"Odelia," Fehring answered, her voice weary, "Lorraine was discovered inside a house that was not hers. She crawled through a window to get there. FYI, that's a crime. Grace was an accessory. Neither have been formally charged yet, but they could be. Plus, Lorraine Littlejohn did find a dead body, and until we find the killer, she's a suspect." Again the cocked eyebrow. "She's Clark's daughter, correct?"

"Yes," I answered, "his eldest, but none of us even knew she was in town. But what window and whose house?" But my gut told me the answer before I heard it.

"From what little the officers on the scene could get out of them before Grace played the lawyer card, they were checking on one of Grace's neighbors. Lorraine found the body."

My gut, as usual, had been right. Sometimes I wish it would be wrong.

My head exploded with possibilities and the urge to throttle my mother. It looked like Lorraine had shown up for a visit and Mom had put her to work snooping around. "So they found Boaz Shankleman dead?"

Andrea turned her attention to me, but now it was her laser attention, honed from years of being a homicide detective. "What do you know about Mr. Shankleman?" she asked.

I turned to Steele for support but saw he was waiting for an answer too. "Mom and her friend Art told me today, or I guess that would now be yesterday, that they were worried about a neighbor named Boaz Shankleman. He's also known as Bo Shank, from the '80s rock band Acid Storm. He lives at Seaside and has been gone for a few weeks. They've been trying to find out if he's okay." I paused, then remembered something. "But Seaside did a welfare check on him not too long ago at the insistence of Mom and Art, and he wasn't home. Did he finally come home and have a heart attack or something?"

"The victim wasn't Mr. Shankleman," Fehring told us as we walked down a hallway. "It was a woman named Cydney Fox."

I nearly stumbled. "Cydney Fox?"

Fehring stopped short and looked at me. "Do you know her?"

"Not personally, but I know who she is, or was. Years ago she broke up Acid Storm with a messy sex scandal. I can't imagine what Lorraine has to do with her." I followed this up by telling Fehring and Steele about my call to Titan West.

"So she broke up the group years ago and now was hired to manage them?" Steele asked. "That sounds pretty odd."

"Kurt Spencer-Hall, the person she cheated on David Oxman with, is no longer in the band. In fact, I think he died of an overdose many years ago." I wasn't about to tell them that I'd read that on the Marigold report just before going to bed, so I tried to make it sound like a casual bit of minutia any fan might know.

Fehring had been jotting notes on a small pad she'd taken from her blazer pocket. "The victim was found in Shankleman's home at Seaside," she told us when she was through writing. "Lorraine stumbled upon it after climbing through the window, probably at Grace's encouragement, knowing Grace. They called the police when they found the body. When the officers brought Lorraine in for breaking and entering and questioning about the murder, Grace told her to shut up until she had a lawyer. So that's all we know so far." Fehring put her hands on her hips. The stance showed the gun holstered at her right hip and the shiny badge fastened to her belt. "Sounds about right for your family, doesn't it, Odelia?"

I lowered my head into my hands and shook it back and forth in frustration.

"Can we see them?" Steele asked.

"Sure," Fehring said. "We have them in separate rooms. I'd suggest you tackle Lorraine first. She's scared and more likely to spill the truth without embellishment than Grace." A crooked grin broke across Fehring's face. "I'm also pretty sure this was Lorraine's first dead body. She's puked a few times." She looked at me, the grin gone. "Hopefully, it will be her last and she won't go into the family business."

As Fehring started down the hall to where they had Mom and Lorraine, I stopped her. "You don't think Lorraine killed Cydney Fox, do you? I can't even imagine her knowing her or even about her."

"The victim has been dead at least twenty-four hours, according to the coroner's initial assessment," Fehring told us. "Killed by several vicious blows to the skull."

I thought of poor Lorraine stumbling upon that scene and shuddered, wondering how much blood there had been and how bad the carnage was.

"Do you know where Lorraine's been for the past two days?" Fehring asked. "Was she here in California visiting Grace?"

"I have no idea," I answered truthfully. "I didn't even know she was in town until Mom called me from here. I do know that Lorraine wasn't at Mom's when I visited her yesterday morning, and Mom said nothing about Lorraine coming for a visit. Lorraine lives in Chicago with her fiancé."

"If you can get a solid alibi for her, all the better," Fehring told us, "but there's still the B&E issue, although I'll see what I can do to get that tossed out if she can provide an alibi for the time of the murder."

"Lorraine must have flown in from Chicago," Steele noted, "so her plane ticket should give her an alibi if the timing's right."

Fehring nodded affirmatively. "We'll check the airline records too to make sure she was on that plane. Have her give you the carrier and flight time, and we'll check it out right away." She looked down the hallway in the direction we were headed, then back at us. "Frankly, it looks like Grace and Lorraine had a bad case of nosiness and acted on it," Fehring continued. "Again, Odelia, par for the course in your family."

"Kind of like Cagney and Lacey," suggested Steele.

Fehring snorted. "More like Lucy and Ethel."

"What about Art Franklin, Mom's friend?" I asked. "Was he involved in these nighttime shenanigans? He was worried about Shankleman too."

"No one by that name has come up yet," Fehring answered. "Lorraine and Grace appeared to be alone when the responding officers got to Seaside."

I breathed a sigh of relief, not that this was going to keep Shelita at bay, but at least I wouldn't be dealing with her so soon after our last meeting.

I placed a hand on Fehring's arm. "Thank you, Andrea. I feel bad that you were called in the middle of the night, but I'm very happy and grateful that you're looking out for Mom and Lorraine."

She gave me a tight-lipped smile. "I've always wondered why Dev Frye was so intent on looking after you and Greg. I guess I'm beginning to see the disturbing appeal. You guys are like one of those reality shows where it's a really horrid idea and the characters are totally insane but likeable."

Next to me, Steele stifled a laugh. "I always think of them as a car accident on the side of the freeway. You hope there are no serious injuries, but you can't help but find it entertaining in a macabre way."

Fehring turned and set her laser stare to high beam on Steele's face. "What makes you think I see you as an innocent bystander, counselor?"

EIGHT

FEHRING HAD BEEN RIGHT: Lorraine did look scared to death. She was pasty white with deep, dark circles cupping her eyes like hands holding them up. Her long brown hair was tied back with a clip. She had just turned thirty but looked like a terrified child. She was wearing workout clothing too big for her slight frame.

"They took her clothing to check for trace evidence," Fehring explained, noting my surprise at Lorraine's attire. "I supplied some clothes out of my locker." I mouthed thanks in her direction.

Lorraine jumped up and threw herself into my arms. "Odelia! I'm so glad you're here." She began sobbing. I tightened my arms around her and gave her a comforting squeeze.

"It's going to be okay, Lorraine. We're here to help." I let her go. "This is Detective Fehring. She's a friend and also knows your father."

"To be clear, I'm not on the case, Odelia," Fehring said to me. "I'm only here because I know you and want to help where I can.

Detectives Khalil Mack and Michael Gonzales were called to the scene and will handle the actual investigation. They're good men."

I nodded my understanding and turned back to Lorraine. "And this is Michael Steele, an attorney. But he's also a good friend of the family and my boss. He's going to guide you through all this." Steele held out his right hand. Lorraine, in her stupor, studied it as if it would bite before shaking hands with him. "Lorraine, Steele is going to talk to you now, without the police. You need to tell him everything, okay? But first, please tell Detective Fehring here when you flew into town. Was it yesterday afternoon?" She nodded. "Then," I continued, "it's very important that you tell us now exactly when and on what airline."

Lorraine looked to Steele for permission. When he nodded, she gave out the flight information. I sighed with relief to hear the flight time made it impossible for Lorraine to be anywhere near Cydney Fox at the time of her death, even with a wide time frame. Fehring wrote the information down.

"What about Grandma?" Lorraine asked.

"Grandma's going to be questioned too," I assured her, "but Steele is going to talk to you first. You have to be very honest with him, okay?"

"After you and I talk," Steele told her gently, "the police will come in and question you, but with me here."

"Okay, Mr. Steele," she sniffed in a small voice.

Steele turned to me. "Grey, why don't you go sit with Grace while I take care of this?"

I nodded, and Fehring showed me out and down the hallway to another small room containing a table, a couple of chairs, and my mother. Unlike Lorraine, Mom didn't seem afraid at all.

"Is Steele here?" she asked as soon as she saw me.

"Yes, he's with Lorraine now."

"Good," Mom said with relief. "I wouldn't want her to get stuck with a bogus murder rap on my account."

"Speaking of which," I started as I took the chair next to Mom, "murder aside, Lorraine may be charged with breaking and entering. You might be too. Did you even think of that before you encouraged her to go through that window?"

Mom looked at me through her thick glasses, her mouth pursed. "Don't be ridiculous, Odelia, she's not some common burglar. She was checking something out for me. I'm sure they just brought us in for questioning." She rubbed her wrists, first one, then the other. She'd also been rubbing them when I first came in.

"Did they handcuff you?" I asked. If I'm lying I'm dying, but I could have sworn Mom's eyes lit up at the question.

"Yes, both of us, and they read us our rights, just like on TV."

"Now there's something to be proud of," I snapped.

"Yes, definitely something I can take off my bucket list," Mom snarled back.

Her glib attitude was making me nuts. "No wonder you called, wanting a lawyer." I stabbed the tabletop with an index finger several times, hard enough to break my nail. "Did you ever once consider the consequences of your actions? Did you?" My voice was rising with each word.

"There's no need to shout, Odelia," Mom scolded. "Lorraine's fine. They'll question us, and we'll be home before you know it. I doubt they'll hold us since neither of us have a prior record for burglary or anything else. It's just that last night I thought I saw a light on in Boaz's place. I rang the bell, but no one answered. I called the nighttime guard, but he ignored me." Mom stopped to sip from a cup. It looked like coffee.

Something about her comment bothered me. "Last night as in Monday night or last night as in a few hours ago?"

She gave it some thought, then said, "Last night as in Monday night."

"You didn't tell me about the light when you first told me about Shankleman."

Mom looked truly puzzled by the omission, then shrugged. The gesture gave me confidence that she wasn't lying. "I guess I forgot. But tonight I remembered it while talking with Lorraine, so she and I decided to check it out on our own. In and out: that was the mission, nothing else."

Mom took a turn at jabbing the tabletop, but her nail held. "If not for us, who knows how long that poor woman's body would have gone undiscovered?"

I took several deep breaths before I tried again to point out the dangers of Mom's behavior. "True, but what if Shankleman was home, thought it was a home invasion, and shot Lorraine?"

"He wouldn't have a gun," Mom said, dismissing the idea as just so much fiddle-faddle.

"How do you know?" I countered, my voice loud with frustration. "These days it seems everyone's got a gun. I'll bet even a few of the little old ladies at Seaside are packing." I paused, trying to get control over my anger. "At the very least, he might have hit her with a baseball bat. Even Greg and I have one of those. Not to mention, whoever was in there Monday night could have been the murderer and still there. He might have attacked Lorraine." I stopped to take another breath to calm my nerves and check my voice. I could see my words were finally getting through to Mom. She lowered her head over her coffee cup.

"Legal charges aside, Mom," I continued, "you put Lorraine, your granddaughter, in a very dangerous spot by encouraging her to do your snooping. And she'll probably be traumatized for life by finding that body. *And* she'll probably now have a criminal record for breaking and entering."

Mom reached into the pocket of the sweater she was wearing and pulled out one of her linen hankies. Taking off her glasses, she dabbed at her eyes, which were running like a leaky faucet.

Oh geez, I made my mother cry. I felt like a heel but knew I was in the right to be angry and to point out her stupidity.

"What was Lorraine doing here anyway? Were you expecting her to visit and forgot to tell me that too?" I struggled to get my voice packaged into a calm, tidy tone, but it was like trying to sit on an overstuffed suitcase.

Mom shook her head and continued mopping up the water-works. When she was done, she put her glasses back on and looked at me from across the table. "She just showed up today in a cab," she told me. "It was early evening. She said she'd just flown in and was on a two-week vacation from her job." The timing fit with what Lorraine had told us about her flight time.

Mom stopped to drink more coffee. Her spotted hands were shaking now that the full realization of what could have happened had sunk into her brain. "She told me that she and what's-his-face broke up."

"You mean Elliott, her fiancé?"

"I think he's an ex-fiancé now," Mom noted. "I didn't get the whole story, and Lorraine didn't want to talk about it. She just asked if she could stay with me for a bit to think things through. We went out for dinner, and that's when I told her about Boaz. I thought it might take her mind off of what's-his-face."

"And just when did the topic of Lorraine hauling her ass through Shankleman's window come up?"

"Later, after we got home."

"So you just casually mentioned to Lorraine that it would be a favor for her Grandma, and she jumped to do it for you?" My voice had quieted but taken on a very snarky tone. I was really trying to hit a balance between simple concern and outrage, but I wasn't succeeding.

"I didn't ask her to do it, Odelia." Mom looked directly at me. "It just sort of happened. One minute we were in my living room and I was saying how I'd like to get a gander at what was going on at Boaz's place. That's when I remembered seeing the light in there the night before. I'd met some friends, who live at that big retirement place by your house, for cards. When I got back to Seaside, I swung my car by Boaz's place on a whim, on the chance he might have returned. That's when I thought I saw a light. I told all this to Lorraine while we were watching the late news. The next minute, she was asking for directions to his place and was out the door with a flashlight."

"Just like that?" I asked.

"Well, alcohol might have been involved."

"Are you drinking again, Mom?" I asked with alarm. Mom had been sober for decades.

"No, of course not," she snapped. "But Lorraine had several glasses of wine with dinner. But don't worry," she hurriedly added, "I was driving."

I ran a hand through my hair. "Okay, so Lorraine was suggestible because of the booze, but you could have stopped her."

Instead of an answer, Mom looked at the closed door. For a minute I wondered if she was going to try to make a run for it, or more like a shuffle for it, considering her age. She looked back at me. "I know, Odelia. I should have tried to stop her, but I didn't." She started tearing up again. "If anything had happened to Lorraine, it would have killed me." She mopped up new tears.

Seeing Mom's distress, I put an arm around her shoulders and gave her a hug. She leaned into me for comfort, something she rarely did, so I knew her despair over what might have happened was genuine. "Lorraine's okay, Mom. Scared and might be in a spot of trouble, but other than that, okay."

"Did they tell you who the poor woman was in the house?" Mom asked between soggy sniffs.

"Yes," I told her. "Her name was Cydney Fox. She knew Shankleman back during the band's heyday and could have been working as his band's current manager." I pulled back and looked at Mom. "Did you ever see her with Shankleman?"

She shrugged. "Sometimes I saw him with a woman, not always the same one, but it's not like he was a ladies' man, with women running in and out of his place. You know what I mean?" I did and nodded. "But I never saw the body in the house," Mom continued. "The police wouldn't let me, so I don't know if it's one of the women I saw with Boaz."

NINE

THE SUN WAS UP and morning rush hour just beginning by the time the police let Mom and Lorraine go. They'd both been soundly questioned by Detectives Mack and Gonzales, who knew about my past, especially the situation involving the body that had been found in the trunk of my car in February, since that happened in Long Beach. Neither were amused to be dealing with anyone in my family, and before letting us go, they admonished us to keep our noses out of Cydney Fox's murder. As for being charged with breaking into Shankleman's place, Fehring had worked some sort of magic. The police didn't charge them but gave both Lorraine and Mom stiff warnings, with a footnote that Shankleman might decide to file a complaint against them himself, so they weren't out of the woods yet.

"What about Boaz Shankleman?" I asked Fehring when the other detectives had gone. She'd stuck around and must have witnessed the questioning from behind a two-way mirror or something because she showed up right before we left, knowing everything. Steele had headed home to properly clean up before going into the office, and Mom and Lorraine had gone to the restroom. Fehring and I were alone.

"We'll be locating him, Odelia," she told me. "Looks like Grace is going to get her wish after all, so you folks just stay out of it, you hear?"

"You'll get no argument from me," I told her. "I've got better things to do, like get some sleep."

"Don't you have to go to work?" she asked.

"Steele told me I could take a couple days off." When Fehring gave me an odd look, I added, "What can I say, he has a soft spot for Mom, and marriage has mellowed him. Not a lot, but a little around the edges."

When we got back to Seaside and pulled in front of Mom's, my mother said, "Drive by Boaz's before parking. I want to see what's going on."

"Really?" I shot at her. "Spending all night at the police station wasn't enough excitement for you?"

"Please, Odelia," Lorraine said from the back seat with the first note of life in her voice since being released. "I want to see it too."

"Really?" I repeated, but this time I was looking in the rearview mirror at my niece. "A few hours ago you were scared snotless."

"Just drive by, Odelia," Mom ordered. "If you don't, we'll simply walk over and check it out for ourselves as soon as you leave." It was more than a threat, so I caved and asked for directions to Shankleman's. I figured it was close since they'd walked there in the late evening, but I was wrong. Shankleman's place was on the other side of the complex, closer to Art's townhouse than to Mom's. Seeing the distance made me even angrier. Mom had had tons of time to talk Lorraine out of her boozy foolishness.

When we got close, I didn't need directions. The place looked like opening night of a blockbuster Hollywood movie, only early in the morning. The townhouse was surrounded by yellow crime tape, and on the sidewalk clusters of senior citizens, many in lightweight colorful track suits and knee-length shorts, had gathered to gawk and gossip. As we drove by, a few turned to look at the car. One woman pointed at us, causing most of the others to check us out. Instead of ducking, Mom gave them a slightly cupped wave, like a queen greeting the common folk of her realm. A tiny elderly woman holding a small white dog waved with enthusiasm.

"Isn't that Teri Thomson, the woman who does the lovely knitting?" I asked.

"Yep," Mom answered as she gave the woman a special wave.

When we finally returned to Mom's place, I parked curbside in front of it, behind a compact car. Mom's assigned covered carport was across the street with a bank of other slots. We were almost to the front door when a white golf cart zipped up, made a sharp U-turn, and parked behind my car. Mom and I groaned in unison. Lorraine would have too, had she known it was Mona D'Angelo swooping down on us. Mona stomped up the walk, a clipboard clutched in one of her hands.

"Hello, Mona," my mother said in a flat tone. "Kind of early for you, isn't it?"

"I've been up all night, Grace, thanks to you," the complex manager said. Mona D'Angelo was about my age, with a decent figure, lovely shoulder-length auburn hair, and a face that would have been considered very pretty if not for its perpetual pinched look, like her face had frozen after she'd tasted something rotten. She was dressed professionally in a pantsuit, but the dark circles under her eyes told me she hadn't lied about being up all night.

Mona turned to greet me. "Odelia." She eyed Lorraine with the type of disdain usually reserved for the criminally insane. "Is this your granddaughter, Grace? The one who broke into Mr. Shankleman's home last night?"

"One and the same," Mom answered, her voice filled with challenge.

I took a step forward. "This is my niece, Lorraine Littlejohn. She'll be visiting Mom for a little while."

"Oh, no, she won't," announced Mona.

"According to the rules and regulations of this place," Mom countered, "I am allowed to have guests under the age of fifty-five for up to sixty days. Lorraine has only been here one day. She has fifty-nine days left to go." Mom turned and put her key in the lock.

"I'm not talking about length of stay, Grace Littlejohn," Mona said, unwilling to be dismissed so easily. She shook the clipboard at us. Well, she shook it at Mom. Lorraine was starting to shrink into the shrubbery, and I was not Mona's target. "According to these same rules and regulations, the management office of Seaside Retirement Community has the right to deem a guest unfit for occupation and expel him"—she stopped to give Lorraine a withering look—"or her from the premises. We feel breaking into another resident's home is definitely grounds for expulsion." She made it sound like Lorraine was being kicked out of school for smoking in the girls' bathroom.

Mom looked from Mona to Lorraine, then to me, clearly stumped for words. But I wasn't. "Lorraine is coming home with me," I said. "My mother also." Mom started to protest, but I held up a hand to stop her. "We're just picking up a few things."

Deciding I might be the more reasonable of the family members, Mona turned to give me her attention. "Good. You might even consider thinking about relocating Grace. It might be best for all concerned."

I stepped forward again, closing up the short distance between Mona and me. "If my mother chooses to sell this place and move elsewhere, it's her decision, and it will be for security reasons."

"But Seaside is completely secure," Mona protested. "Your mother is the problem here."

"My mother did not kill Cydney Fox," I pointed out. "Nor did Lorraine. That murder took place right under the nose of your security guard. Not to mention, what was a non-resident doing inside Shankleman's home in the first place? Did the Fox woman have permission to be in there? Did Shankleman put her on your guard's list to allow her access when he wasn't around? Did she have the passcode to the security gate?"

"We…um…we're looking into all of those questions," Mona sputtered. "We're taking steps to make sure our security wasn't breached."

Just then another golf cart drove up to the curb. In it was a guard named Milton. I didn't know his last name, but I did know that Milton usually manned the guard shack on the graveyard shift, so I seldom saw him. He climbed out of the cart and shuffled up to us, his shoulders sagging with exhaustion. Milton was in his late sixties, medium height with a slight paunch and a shock of white hair that matched his short beard. He approached but didn't say a word until Mona acknowledged him. He was wearing the uniform all the Seaside guards wore.

"Yes, Milt," Mona snapped at him with impatience, "what is it?"

"Ms. D'Angelo," he said slowly, "I was wondering if I could go home now. I've been here all night talking to the police, and I'm about done in."

"We were just talking about the front gate, Milton," I said to the guard. "Maybe you can help. Do you recall if Cydney Fox had permission from Mr. Shankleman to be here or do you know if she had the code to the gate?"

"He's my employee," Mona said, barely containing her anger. "You have no right to question him. I told you we were looking into it."

"Forgive me," I said to her with a half snarl, "if I don't exactly trust you to do a proper job of it." She had attacked my family and I wasn't going to stand for it, no matter how annoyed I was with them myself. "You're looking into it, Mona, because the homicide detectives want to know what happened, and because your residents are nervous about a murder taking place just yards from the bocce ball court, especially since it happened a couple of days ago. If not for my mother and my niece, no one would have noticed until that body turned to stinky goo in this heat."

I turned back to Milton, crossing my arms to let him know I was waiting for his answer. Nearby, Mom and Lorraine were also waiting to hear what he had to say, but they both hung back.

Avoiding Mona's glare, Milton finally answered me. "The police asked me the same questions. I don't recall seeing Ms. Fox come onto the property recently, but in the past when she's visited, she's always had the code for the gate."

"The code is digital, isn't it?" I asked, my eyes moving between him and Mona. "I mean, it records whenever a resident's code is used to open the gate, right?"

Milton clearly deferred to Mona to answer. "Yes," she said grudgingly. "It keeps a record of which codes are used and when. The police asked to see the records for the past few weeks." She paused, then added with emphasis, "You, however, are not entitled to that information."

"And what about the security camera?" I asked, ignoring her dig. "Did it show anyone unauthorized entering the property recently?"

"The camera's been down," Milton answered. "For a few days now."

Mona whipped around on him, outraged about the disclosure. "You can go home, Milton. Get your rest. We'll expect you back at your post tonight."

With eyes cast down, Milton turned and headed down the walk to his cart. He might have shuffled from the cart to us, but for his retreat he picked up his step considerably. I would too if I worked for the dragon lady and I'd just been told to go home.

Mom had the door open, and I shuttled her and Lorraine inside. Right before I started to shut the door on Mona, I dug into my purse and pulled out one of my business cards. "If you have anything further to add, put it in writing and mail it to this address. My mother's attorney will handle it. His name is Michael Steele. Like the police, he's looking into the breakdown in security here."

Okay, that last part was a lie, but it felt good to say it.

Once the door was closed, Mom said, "That was great, Odelia! You really called her bluff."

Lorraine was in the kitchen getting a drink of water. She drank down a glass, then refilled it and drank half of that one. Nothing like having a cottonmouth the day after too much hooch and a whole lot of police interrogation.

"It wasn't a bluff, Mom. You and Lorraine get your things. You're coming home with me."

"But I don't want to go to your house," Mom whined, jutting her chin out at me.

"Just for a day or two, Mom." I looked toward Lorraine, but she'd disappeared. A minute later she came out from the hallway. She was still wearing Fehring's workout clothes but was rolling a suitcase behind her. There was no question that Lorraine wanted to get out of Dodge as soon as possible.

"I'm ready to go, Odelia." She looked at Mom. "Come on, Grandma, just for a few days, until this cools down. Then you can come back."

Mom pursed her lips and remained silent for almost a full minute. Finally, she slapped her keys down on the table in the entry hall in surrender and went to pack a bag.

On the way to my house, Mom fidgeted with her phone. "Dammit," she cursed. "I keep calling and texting Art, but he doesn't answer."

"After what's happened," I said as the light turned green, "his daughter probably changed his number. I didn't tell you this, Mom, but yesterday morning I had coffee with Shelita Thomas. She told me she didn't want you spending time with her father. She said you're a bad influence."

"What?" Mom turned sharply in her seat to look at me. "We're not kids. We can spend time with whomever we want."

"That's exactly what I told her, but after last night she has a pretty strong argument for her position."

We arrived in Seal Beach in minutes. I checked the rearview mirror to make sure Lorraine, who was driving Mom's car, was behind us. I didn't want the two delinquents to have their own wheels while staying with me, but it was the only way Mom would agree to go to my house. I asked Lorraine to follow us in Mom's car because in spite of her bravado, Mom seemed a little shaky. It could be she was tired and hungry. Except for many cups of coffee, she hadn't eaten a thing.

Greg's van was in the garage, but we had room for two cars in the carport. Originally our home was built as a duplex—two small homes built side by side, with a common wall. When Greg bought the place, he gutted it and turned it into one very spacious three-bedroom house outfitted with wide doorways, lower counters, and every other convenience for someone in a wheelchair. The bigger garage and large carport were also part of the renovation.

We were barely through the back gate when Wainwright came through his doggie door and hopped around the backyard with excitement over seeing company. That, and he hadn't had his breakfast yet either and was thrilled to see me. When we got inside, I directed Lorraine to our home office, where we also had a pull-out bed for guests. Mom could have the more comfortable bed in our guest room. While they got settled, I fed our cat and dog and started whipping up eggs, bacon, and toast for us. After breakfast, the three of us turned in for much-needed naps.

When my cell phone woke me, I was doing a face plant in my pillow in the middle of a great dream. Still half asleep, I reached for the phone. It was Clark. Crap. "What?" I answered with a thick voice.

"Did I wake you?" he sounded surprised.

I looked at the clock on the nightstand. It was almost ten thirty. "Just taking a little nap. I was dreaming that Ben & Jerry's named an ice cream after me."

"What flavor?" he asked.

"Burnt sugar vanilla with tiny chunks of English toffee, dark chocolate, and kitty kibble."

"Kitty kibble?" He was laughing—a good mood that was about to change.

"Don't knock it. It was delicious." I was fully awake now and surprised that he was so calm. I figured somehow he would have gotten wind that his eldest daughter and mother had been dragged to the police station in cuffs.

"Why aren't you at work?" he asked, the observant retired cop in him coming to the surface. He knew I usually worked Mondays, Wednesdays, and Fridays. If my memory served me, today was Wednesday. "Are you sick?"

From the casual question, I was pretty sure he didn't know yet about the family crime spree. "No, but Steele gave me today off." I paused, thinking I should have told him I was a little under the weather. It would have been less suspicious than Steele giving me a day off. "I had a bunch of personal errands to take care of, and we aren't that busy at the office right now. What's up?"

"Have you talked to Mom yet today?"

"Yes," I answered truthfully. My brain kicked to full alert. "Earlier. Why?"

"Just that I'm having trouble reaching her. I've been trying both the landline and her cell phone."

"You know Mom. Sometimes she just wants to be left alone. She was fine when I spoke to her. Is there anything the matter?"

He hemmed and hawed, a sure sign he was bothered by something. "I got a call from my ex-wife a little bit ago. Seems Lorraine and Elliot had a big fight, and Lorraine has taken off. Elliot thought she was heading for California. She's not answering her phone either. Lorraine has always had a special relationship with Mom, so I wanted to see if she showed up there."

I pushed my face back into my pillow and let loose with a strangled scream. There was no easy way around this. I might fib once in a while to Clark about some things, but about his daughter, there was no way.

"You okay, sis?" I heard him call from the phone.

I put the phone back to my ear, resigned to tell the truth, the whole truth, and nothing but the truth, even if it did mean Clark was going to go ballistic. I craned my neck to make sure the door that separated the master suite from the rest of the house was shut tight. "Don't worry, Clark, Lorraine is here with me. She arrived in California last night."

"Then why didn't you say something when Greg and I called you? Her mother and I have been very worried." Through the phone I could hear his blood pressure jiggling like a nervous tic, threatening to rise.

"Because I didn't know she was here then. She went straight to Mom's. Now she's here with me." I paused, took a deep breath, then tacked on for good measure, "Mom's here too. We're all at my house."

There was a long pause on the other end of the line—long, swollen, and sore, like a boil about to erupt. "So why didn't you tell me that when I first said something about trying to reach Mom?" he asked, his words measured and barely restrained.

"Because I was dreaming about ice cream?" I suggested. Yes, it was a lame answer, but it was all I had at the moment.

"What in the hell are you not telling me, Odelia? What is going on out there?"

I took a deep breath. "Why don't you sit down, Clark. I have a lot to tell you."

"I *was* sitting until you started lying! Now start talking."

I told my brother everything from the time I got the call from Mom right up until I brought Lorraine and Mom back to my place. When I was done, there was an even longer silence from Clark's end than before. I began to worry that he'd had a stroke. "Clark? You still there?" When I heard heavy breathing on the other end, I took a breath of relief.

"I'm grabbing the first plane out," Clark announced. "The three of you are to remain in that house until I get there. Do. You. Understand?"

Considering that Phoenix was a very short plane ride, with frequent flights to Southern California, I calculated that Clark would show up too late for lunch but in plenty of time for supper. "I understand, but you know Mom."

"I don't care if you have to hogtie the woman, Odelia. Keep her there—and Lorraine. I'll call Andrea Fehring and see if there's anything new on the case."

"Don't tell Greg about this, okay?"

"Of course I'm going to tell him. He's staying with me, and he should know."

"But it wasn't me that found the body, and I don't want him to come charging back home for no reason." I took a deep breath before I snapped at him and made him angrier. "Look, Clark, tell Greg what happened, but let him know I had nothing to do with it and that you'll be here handling it. He's been looking forward to this trip, and I don't want to ruin it for him."

More dead air, then Clark finally said, "Okay, I'll convince him I've got this. You weren't involved, were you? It will be an easier sell if you weren't."

"No, Clark, I wasn't. I just went to the police station when Mom called. Like I told you and Greg, all I was doing for her was checking out information about Shankleman on the web. It wasn't me climbing through that window."

"Not that you haven't done such stupid things and worse," he growled. "Put my daughter on the phone. If she won't answer her damn phone, I'll go through you."

Now it was my turn to pause before speaking. "Clark, the three of us were up all night and didn't finally get to bed until just about an hour ago. I really don't want to wake Lorraine just so you can yell at her."

"Dammit," he yelled, "I'm not going to yell at her!"

"How about I have her call you when she wakes up," I suggested. "You and her mother."

"I might be on a plane by then," he countered.

"Then you'll see her when you get here." I was determined to stand my ground. "Between her breakup with Elliot and this, Lorraine has been through a lot in a very short time. Let her rest before you come at her like a charging bull."

I expected him to bellow again, but he didn't. After another pause, he simply said, "Have her call her mother as soon as she wakes up. I'll call now and let her know that Lorraine has been found and will be calling. It will give her some comfort. I'll text you when I know my flight number and time."

"Are you going to tell Lorraine's mother about the police and the body?"

Instead of yelling, Clark barked out a short laugh, somewhere between a chuckle and a cough. "Not on your life, sis. I'll leave that dirty deed up to Lorraine. Frankly, I don't care if she does tell her. Lorraine's an adult."

Huh. That wasn't Clark's opinion on what *he* should know or not know, but I kept my mouth shut on that subject.

Before he hung up, Clark let out a string of swear words that scorched the air waves. They were said half under his breath, and I don't think they were meant to be aimed at anyone in particular—at least I hope not.

I couldn't go back to sleep after Clark's call, so after using the bathroom I decided to head to the kitchen and see what I could put together for dinner. I had planned on finishing up some skimpy leftovers tonight, but that was before dinner went from a party of one in front of the TV to a family gathering.

I was shocked to see my mother seated at the dining table reading. Wainwright was resting on his big bed located where the kitchen and dining area bled into the great room; he had a full view of both. Muffin was curled up on the kitchen chair closest to Mom. When I realized what Mom was reading, I wasn't happy at all.

Spread across the table were the printouts of my research on Boaz Shankleman and Acid Storm. I had been reading them last night and left them on the coffee table when I went to bed. In all the hubbub, I'd forgotten they were still out in the open.

"Boy," Mom said, looking up at me, "that Cydney Fox really caused a major ruckus back then, didn't she?"

"What are you doing up, Mom?" I asked, stopping at the table, hands on my hips. "You need to get your rest."

"I slept a little, but my inner clock is all whacky. Not to mention, I drank a gallon of coffee at the police station. I thought a cup of herbal tea might help." She put her eyes back on the paperwork. "I checked on Lorraine. The poor kid is totally zonked out."

"Good." I continued on to the kitchen, which was separated from the dining area by a short, low counter. I knew that scolding my mother for reading through the papers I left in full view in the living room would fall on deaf ears. Since it was about Shankleman, she'd consider herself part owner.

I opened the fridge. It was slim pickings. There were things in the freezer I could pull out and thaw, but I didn't really feel like cooking on a hot summer day. We had a side-by-side refrigerator-freezer combination so it was easier for Greg to reach both. I stood in the coolness escaping from the freezer and considered the possibilities. Clark would be here for dinner, and he would be huffing and puffing about Mom and Lorraine. I also knew my big brother loved a good surf and turf on the grill. Greg was the real grill master in the family, but I could char a mean steak myself. Maybe a nice filet and some seafood would soothe the savage beast? And maybe if I put Clark in charge of the grill, it would give him something to do besides bellow about what had happened. However, that would mean a trip to the grocery store. I turned to look at Mom, who was soaking up the information she was reading, and wondered if I should tell her that Clark was coming or let it be a big surprise. Then I remembered that I'd promised to have Lorraine call her mother, so at some point I'd have to spill the beans that Clark had called. I closed the fridge door and took a seat at the table.

"Mom, why haven't you returned any of Clark's calls? He just called me and said he couldn't reach you. He's also trying to reach Lorraine. Her mother is worried about her after speaking with Elliot."

She never looked up. "Is that who you were gabbing with just before you came out of the bedroom?"

"Yes. I told Clark about last night. He's about to hop a plane to come here."

That got Mom's attention. "And that is exactly why I didn't call him, Odelia. I don't need Clark bitching and moaning about what happened. You shouldn't have told him."

"He would have found out some way or another," I said, getting a bit defensive. "He is friends with Andrea Fehring, you know."

Mom chuckled. "Don't you think they're more than friends by now?"

Clark had voiced an interest in Fehring a while back, then seemed to drop it. I think she's great, but given Clark's ties to Willie Proctor, a romantic connection might be tricky for everyone.

"I thought he'd dropped the idea about dating her," I told Mom, "but I know they're friends and go to dinner once in a while when he's in town."

"If they're sweet on each other," Mom pointed out, "it could explain why she came to the station in the middle of the night to look after us."

"Or maybe she did it because she's friends with all of us," I suggested. "She's been here many times in an unofficial capacity." Mom didn't say anything. Her tight-lipped smile spoke volumes. Then something odd scooted across my brain like a mouse scurrying across a kitchen floor. When Fehring saw me with Steele, she never asked about Greg. She didn't seem at all curious about why he wasn't with us. Did she already know he was out of town? Were Clark and Andrea Fehring closer that I thought, and she knew when she arrived at the station that Greg was with Clark in Arizona? I wrote *question Clark about his relationship with Andrea Fehring* on my mental to-do list.

"Where did you get all this stuff?" Mom asked, referring to the printouts she was reading. Fortunately, the Marigold web address wasn't present on any of the information.

"It's a research site I use for work," I told her, only half lying. "I thought it might be helpful when we were looking for Shankleman."

She looked up at me and leaned back in her chair. "What do you mean *were* looking for him? We still are, Odelia. Unless you have him tucked in a closet somewhere."

"Mom," I began, leaning forward. "You heard the police today. They are now looking for Shankleman. We're to get our noses out of this and keep them out."

She picked up her mug. Taking a drink, she snorted into its depths. "Yeah, like that's ever stopped us."

She was right, but for me this was over. I stood up. "Mom, if we're to eat tonight, I need to run to the store. Can I trust you here with Lorraine?"

"What do you mean by that remark?" she snapped, glancing up at me. "Are you afraid I'm going to drown her in your tub?"

I slipped my feet into my espadrilles, which I'd left by the back slider. "Just stay put, okay? I need to run to the store to get some groceries."

"Okey dokey," she answered, her eyes back to poring over the research information.

TEN

When I returned almost ninety minutes later, I was relieved to see Mom's car still in the carport. There had been a fifty-fifty chance that she'd be gone by the time I got back. I hadn't planned to be gone so long, but Greg had called me just as I'd pulled into the grocery store parking lot and we'd talked for quite a while. Well, in reality, he talked, yelled, demanded, and ordered, and I listened, once in a while making attempts to calm him. In the end I'd worn him down, pointing out that we were fine, Clark was on his way here, and Greg's annual trip was too important to interrupt. After all his fussing, Greg agreed to go on to Colorado while Clark babysat us.

Wainwright greeted me as I made my way into the house, my arms laden with two heavy canvas bags of groceries. I heard people talking and stopped short when I recognized the voices. From the back door I could see most of our living room, all but a chunk to the left where the kitchen wall jutted out. I had correctly matched the names with the voices. On the sofa, prim and proper and not at all happy, sat Shelita Thomas. She stood up, hands on her hips, when she saw me.

After putting the bags on the counter, I greeted her. "Shelita, what a surprise to see you here." Frankly, I didn't realize she knew where we lived, then remembered that our address, along with our phone number, was on Mom's emergency card at Seaside. *That damn Mona*, I swore to myself, guessing she was the source of Shelita's information. When this was all over, I was going to bring up to the owners of Seaside's management company my concerns about Mona being a leaky pipe of confidential information.

Without greeting me back, Shelita demanded, "Where's my father?"

"Your father?" I parroted. "I would imagine he's home. He's certainly not here."

"I tried telling her that I've been trying to reach Art, but he's not answering," Mom added.

"It's true," I said to Shelita. "Mom has been trying to reach him. Have you gone by Seaside?"

"Of course I have. I went as soon as Mona told me about what happened there last night." Shelita glared at Mom as if she were a serial killer caught with blood dripping from her hands. "Dad's not home. I assumed he was with Grace."

"Well, you assumed wrong," I told her, trying to not let her anger fuel mine. "We were at the police station all night, then came here after stopping at Seaside to pick up some stuff. Mom is staying with me for a few days. Art was not one of the things she packed."

"Well, where is he?" She looked from me to Mom, then kept her eyes on Mom.

"Believe me," Mom told her, "I wish I knew. I haven't seen him since yesterday morning when Odelia came to visit. Was his car there? Maybe he took a ride down the coast to San Diego. He loves to do that."

"He does?" Shelita seemed surprised.

"Yes. That man's a driving fool," Mom said, "especially in the summer. He often drives down to San Diego and visits the museums or walks around the harbor or Coronado Island. Other times he goes north and visits Santa Barbara. Sometimes he just likes to find a nice beach and sit and watch the ocean. I go with him sometimes, but mostly he prefers to go alone. He says it helps him relax and think. It's his happy place." Mom stared at Shelita. "He goes on these road trips at least once a week in the summer. Didn't you know that?"

From the look on Shelita's face, my guess was she didn't know that about her father. I did. In spite of the frequent friction between my mother and me, Mom mostly kept me in the loop as to her whereabouts, if only for safety reasons, and she usually told me when she and Art were heading out on one of these day trips. Once they'd even invited me to go along on a drive to Malibu. Once there, I had treated them to lunch at a seaside café. It had been a lovely day.

Shelita finally found her voice again. "Even if he is on one of these trips, why isn't he answering his phone?"

Mom shrugged. "Beats me. Best I can tell, maybe he was upset by what happened at Seaside and decided to take a drive to think about it. Maybe he turned off his phone to get some peace and quiet on the drive, or maybe he forgot to charge it? He's always forgetting to charge his phone."

"True," Shelita said in frustrated agreement. "It's why I wanted him to get a landline when he moved in there, but he refuses. He claims he only needs one phone." She narrowed her eyes at Mom. "So Dad wasn't with you last night at Mr. Shankleman's?"

Mom shook her head back and forth like a pendulum. "Like I told the police, it was just Lorraine and me there last night. Lorraine's my granddaughter."

"Give it some time, Shelita," I told her, my voice adjusted to calm her. "I'm sure Art will be back tonight. Just leave him a voice message to call you when he gets home."

Shelita picked her purse up from the coffee table, then turned back to Mom. "Does Dad ever stay overnight on some of these trips?"

Mom paused before answering. It was the kind of pause that made me study her closely, unsure if she was trying to think or thinking of a sidestep to the question. With Mom it's difficult to tell. She likes to play the forgetful old lady card to her advantage and does it often. "He has a few times," she finally answered. "It depends on how late it gets or how tired he is from all the walking when he's there. His vision isn't that good at night, so he doesn't like driving after dark."

Shelita snorted. "At least that I do know."

As Shelita started for the front door, I saw movement down the hallway that led to the other bedrooms. It was Lorraine, poking her head out of her room and listening.

Mom got up, and she and I walked Shelita to the front door. Just outside, she turned and faced Mom. "I don't know if Odelia told you or not, Grace, but I think it's best if you and my father stop spending so much time together. After your behavior last night, I just can't allow it."

"Art and I are adults," Mom said after squaring her narrow shoulders. "We will continue to spend time with whomever we wish, including each other."

Shelita and Mom stared at each other a long time, then Shelita said, her eyes narrowed and her jaw tight, "We'll see about that."

If I hadn't had such a firm grasp on the door, Mom would have slammed it in Shelita's face. She certainly tried, but my grip was stronger so it stayed put. Shelita was worried about her father. I understood that completely. At some point in life, the tables turn and adult children start looking after the welfare of their aging parents as if the kids were the parents and mom and dad were the kids. Whether Mom liked it or not, I did it with her, and Greg keeps an eye on his parents, although Ronald and Renee Stevens never get into situations like my mother. They're normal, and when they call for help, it's for routine day-to-day stuff or advice like which contractor they should use to remodel the downstairs bathroom, not which lawyer can meet them at the police station in the middle of the night. If I were in Shelita's shoes, I'm not sure I'd be wanting my father to hang around Grace Littlejohn either.

After watching Shelita go down our walkway to her car, I shut the door and questioned Mom myself. "Are you sure Art wasn't with you last night?"

"He wasn't," said a voice behind us. It was Lorraine, who'd finally decided the coast was clear enough to come out. "It was just Grandma and me. I haven't seen Art yet this trip."

I might not always trust my mother to not fudge the truth, but I didn't have that same misgiving about Lorraine.

"Okay, then," I said, heading back to the kitchen to put away groceries. "I'm sure Art will turn up when he's ready."

I took a package of steak out of one bag, then remembered my promise to Clark. Lorraine had followed me into the kitchen and was helping by unpacking the other bag. "Lorraine," I said to her, "you need to call your mother. She talked to Elliot and is worried sick about you. She called your dad, who called me."

"Yeah, I know," Lorraine answered. "She's left me a million voicemails and texts. So has my father."

"Your dad called me," I continued as I put the steak and the salmon I'd bought to go with it into the fridge, "and I told him you were here. He said he'd call your mother and let her know where you are, but you still need to call her yourself."

Mom had drifted in and taken a seat at the table, watching us. "Your father's on his way here," she announced.

Lorraine froze. In her hand was a bottle of salad dressing. Fortunately, she didn't drop it on my clean floor. "Dad's coming here? Why?"

"Because of what happened last night," I told her. "You didn't think he'd find out and not come running, did you?"

She was quiet as she worked to empty the bag, placing items on the counter for me to stash in cupboards. "I don't want to talk about Elliot. It's over, and that's that."

"Honey," I said to her, "I'm sure your parents are very concerned about you and Elliot, but your father is mostly worried about what happened last night. He wants to make sure you're just a witness and not a suspect."

Lorraine stared at me with the wide eyes of a tired raccoon. "I'm not a suspect, am I?" She started squeezing the loaf of bread in her hand. I rescued it before it became gummy pulp. "The police said I was free to go."

"Everyone's a suspect until they catch the killer," Mom stated in her usual blunt fashion.

Lorraine turned to me. "Is that true?"

I shut my eyes, then opened them to tell her the truth. "Yes, Lorraine, pretty much. But don't worry," I told her before she panicked, "your flight times give you a solid alibi. You were nowhere near here when Cydney Fox was killed, and the police would never have let you go if you were at the top of the suspects list."

I went to Lorraine's side and slipped an arm around her shoulders. I didn't know her sister very well, but Lorraine had visited several times after Mom relocated to Southern California. We were in contact quite often and had become friends.

She turned and folded herself into my arms, looking for comfort. "Oh, Aunt Odelia, what am I going to do?" I smiled and gave her a tight hug. Clark's daughters seldom referred to me as aunt since they hadn't grown up with me in their lives. They were adults when Clark and I finally met. Greg's two nephews, on the other hand, always called me Aunt Odelia, and Zee and Seth's children grew up calling me Aunt Odie. In spite of the serious nature of the situation, my heart became as warm and gooey as a chocolate chip cookie upon hearing the words.

I pulled slightly away from Lorraine. "What you're going to do first is get more sleep," I told her, "especially if you're going to face your father later."

"I don't know," she answered, "I'm too jittery."

"Why don't you take a bath in Odelia's fancy tub?" Mom suggested. "That will help."

"Your grandmother's right," I told Lorraine. "Take a nice long soak in the whirlpool tub. There's a bottle of lavender bath gel on the ledge to add to the water. You'll be out like a light after."

After Lorraine left and I finished putting away the groceries, I sat down at the kitchen table with Mom. She had gone back to reading the information on the members of Acid Storm and now had her cell phone in her hand, punching numbers. "What's up, Mom?"

"I'm going to call some of the numbers for these guys and ask them about Boaz," she told me.

I took the phone from her hand and stopped the call mid-dial. "You heard the police; we're not to do anything."

"What harm is there in making a few calls, Odelia?" she asked, snatching the phone back out of my hands. "It's a free country, and Boaz is my friend." She started dialing again. "I'm starting with this David Oxman guy since he's known Boaz the longest and you've already called their manager." She looked from the Marigold print-out to her phone to confirm her fingers were hitting the right numbers. Done, she put the phone up to her ear.

"At least," I said to her, "put it on speaker so I can hear."

Mom did as I asked but added, "Let me do the talking." I nodded, knowing I'd never be able to stop her.

A man answered the phone. "Is this David Oxman?" Mom asked.

"Yeah. Who's this?" asked a very gruff, thick voice.

"My name's Grace. I'm a neighbor of your friend Boaz Shankleman," Mom said into the phone.

"Bo's no friend of mine," barked Oxman.

"But you're in that band together," Mom countered.

"That's business, old lady. That's all it is."

A cloud of stormy anger crossed Mom's face. "What makes you think I'm an old lady?"

"If you're a neighbor of Bo's, then you live in that old folks' place."

I found this conversation amusing since Oxman had to be in his sixties, like Shankleman, and more than qualified to live at Seaside himself.

Mom was about to say something snarky when I cut in. "Mr. Oxman, my name is Odelia Grey. Grace is my mother. She's concerned because she hasn't seen Mr. Shankleman in a few weeks. Do you happen to know where he is or might be?"

There was a pause, then Oxman said, "Hopefully in hell."

"Do you know about the murder yet?" Mom asked before I could shush her. I shot her a look that I hoped would stop her in her tracks, but it only garnered me a withering look in return.

"What?" Mom said to me in a stage whisper. "It has to be on the news by now." She had a point, but the police might not have released Shankleman's name or the victim's yet.

"Murder?" Oxman asked, his voice going up in surprise. Clearly the police hadn't reached him yet for questioning and he hadn't seen any news reports.

"A body was found in Boaz's home last night," my mother said, returning to the phone conversation and leaving out her part in the body's discovery. "Some woman named Cydney Fox. So now I'm really worried about Boaz."

There was a very long pause on the other end.

"Mr. Oxman?" I asked. "Are you still there?"

The line went dead.

"He knows something," Mom said, looking at the phone in her hand. She turned her eyes to me. They were sharp and bright behind her Coke-bottle glasses.

My Spidey sense was on alert too, but I tried to tamp it down so as not to feed Mom's excitement. I didn't know if Oxman actually knew something about Fox's murder, but his animosity toward Shankleman and his abrupt departure following the news about Fox had me more than just a little curious.

Mom started punching numbers into her phone again. "Now who are you calling?" I asked her.

"That Tuttle kid. The other member of the band."

We sat at the table and listened as the call went straight to voicemail. Mom tried again, and again the call was picked up immediately by voicemail.

"What do you want to bet that Oxman's talking to Simon Tuttle right now?" Mom said. "Could be a conspiracy." She tried calling Oxman again. "It went straight to voicemail," she reported. "See? A conspiracy."

I got up and went to the kitchen to get myself a glass of water. "I doubt that, Mom. They are probably just talking. Titan West said Cydney Fox was now the band's manager. If that's true, one band member telling another about her murder wouldn't be that odd." But even as I said it, my stomach pinched, telling me that it thought there was something else afoot.

Mom got up from the table and disappeared down the hallway. By the time I'd polished off the water, she'd returned with her purse. After straightening the papers on the table into a neat pile, she picked them up and headed for the back door.

"Where are you going?" I asked.

"I want to talk to that Oxman guy." She shook the stack of print-outs at me. "It says here he lives in Costa Mesa. That's just down the road."

Nothing in Southern California is just down the road. Costa Mesa was fifteen to twenty miles away, depending on which part of it you were talking about, and whether you took the freeway, which added miles but could save time if it wasn't jammed up, or took Pacific Coast Highway, which ran along the coastline. PCH was shorter but could have backed up traffic, especially in August, and only served the westernmost part of Costa Mesa. Before I married Greg, I had a condo in Newport Beach almost where it bordered Costa Mesa. The T&T office where I worked was in Santa Ana, almost where Costa Mesa, Newport Beach, and Santa Ana came together. I knew the way well.

"Mom, let the police do their job." Even as I said it, I was itching to go with her. Based on the vibes Oxman gave off, I knew there was more to the story, even if not connected to the murder. I'm usually not given to reading and listening to juicy tabloid gossip, but this was about a band I adored in my college days. The pull on my interest was strong and insistent, like a powerful magnet.

When she was halfway out the door, I said, "You're not going alone, and Lorraine needs her rest."

Mom turned, the door half open, letting out all the cool air. If Greg was here, he'd be barking about all the money flying out the door. "Lorraine is thirty years old," Mom reminded me, "and she's tired, not sick. I checked on her when I got my purse. She's soaking away in your tub, happy as a clam at high tide." She paused. "I'm going, Odelia, with or without you."

As tired as I was, my need to know more about this puzzle won out. I also knew my mother would probably get into less trouble with me there. She was the one who needed the babysitter, not Lorraine, and I could hardly put my mother in a straitjacket to keep her here. Knowing her, she'd slap elder abuse charges on me if I tried. "Close the door and hold your horses," I said to Mom. "Let me tell Lorraine that we're going out for a little while."

As Mom had said, Lorraine was soaking away in our whirlpool tub, fragrant bubbles up to her neck. She had earbuds firmly tucked in place, and her eyes were closed. It took me saying her name twice to get her attention. "Lorraine, Grandma and I are going out for a bit. Will you be okay?" In response, she gave me a dreamy smile and a thumbs up.

"If you get hungry, help yourself to anything you find," I added. In response, I got two soapy thumbs up.

ELEVEN

FROM THE ADDRESS ON the Marigold report, I knew that Oxman lived in the part of Costa Mesa farthest from the ocean and not far from my office. I plugged the address into my car's GPS. Along the way, I noticed Mom playing with her phone.

"You trying Art again?" I asked her.

"Yes, and I texted him. He's not much for texting, but he will use it from time to time."

I glanced over at her. "So what was it you didn't tell Shelita?"

Mom didn't look up at me. "I told her everything, smarty pants."

Mom only called me that when I hit a bull's-eye. "I'm betting you didn't," I pressed, my eyes back on the road. "I know that Art likes to take road trips, but I also sense that there's something else." I made a safe lane change before adding, "Why are you so worried about contacting him?"

"I can't tell you."

"Yes, you can, Mom. I won't tell Shelita."

Mom took several deep breaths before deciding to give in. "Art has a lady friend in San Diego. Her name is Tess—Tess Kincaid. That's why he goes down there so often."

I let out a short, sharp gasp of surprise.

Mom looked at me, pleased as punch with herself for catching me off-guard. "You've always thought Art and I were fooling around, didn't you?" She crossed her arms in front of her and looked out the windshield. "Art and I are just friends—best friends actually. He just didn't want his family to know about Tess because they get so weird whenever he has a girlfriend." She glanced at me. "Art really likes this Tess. I've met her a few times and think she's a doll. She's smart, fun, and attractive. She's been divorced a number of years and has grandchildren. Art and I let people believe that he and I are involved to keep his family off the scent. They've sabotaged a few of his other relationships."

"If you've met her, then Tess has come up here?"

"A few times," Mom replied, "and then she parked at my place and pretended to be visiting me. You know how nosy that Mona is about Art. We think she even has a few of the guards watching him. She's the one who squealed to Shelita before about Art having lady friends."

I shook my head, astounded at both the subterfuge of Mom and Art and the stupidity of Shelita at not letting Art live his own life. It made me wonder if she was this overprotective of her kids when they were growing up.

"So you're trying to reach him to let him know his family is trying to reach him?" I asked.

"Well, that, and I'm worried about him myself." Mom glanced at her phone, checking for a return text. "You see, Art always tells me when he's going to see Tess, just like I always tell him when I'm taking one of those casino busses or spending the night at your place. But he didn't say a word yesterday about going anywhere."

"Maybe," I suggested, "it's just like you told Shelita. Maybe he decided at the last minute that he needed to get away from all the hubbub at Seaside and forgot to charge his phone? That's why he couldn't tell you."

Following the snarky instructions called out to me by my GPS, I took a ramp off the freeway and started traveling surface streets. We were very close to our destination.

"Maybe," Mom agreed, but I could tell her heart wasn't in it.

"Mom, Shelita went to Art's place. He wasn't there, and his car is gone. He must have simply taken one of his road trips. If you have Tess's number, why don't you give her a call?"

"I do have it, but I don't want to bother them if he's there, and if he's not, Tess might get to worrying."

I shot a look at her. "If I were worried about your whereabouts and you were somewhere reachable, I'd want Art to track you down and let you know to call me."

For a change, something I said got through to her. She placed the call to Tess. It was answered quickly. "Hi, Tess," Mom began, "this is Grace Littlejohn. Is Art with you?"

"Put it on speaker," I told her.

She did as I asked just as a pleasant, mature voice answered, "No, Grace. I haven't heard from Art since Sunday night. What's going on?"

"His daughter is worried. Art and his car are both gone, and I thought maybe he went to visit you. He's not answering his cell phone, but you know how he forgets to charge it."

Tess laughed softly. "That I do, but I'm not home this week. I'm taking care of my grandchildren while my son and his wife get away for a few days. Art is probably on one of his drives. You know what a driving enthusiast that man is."

"Well, if you do hear from him," Mom said into the phone, "have him get in touch with his daughter, and have him call me so I know he's okay. I'm staying with my daughter for a few days, so I'm not home either."

After Tess promised to pass along the message to Art should he contact her and the call ended, Mom looked over at me, worry beaming through her glasses like spotlights. "I don't like this, Odelia."

"When we finish up with Oxman," I said to her, "why don't we put our heads together and try to find Art." She nodded, pleased with the idea.

The GPS directed us to a small mobile home park on the city's border with Santa Ana. The park wasn't fancy, but neither was it run down. It was older, with single-wide mobile homes neatly parked side by side, with parking spots and tiny strips of grass between them and in front of each. The grassy areas were so small, the miniscule lawns could have been mowed with a weed whacker. Instead of grass, some of the homes had landscaped with draught- friendly shrubs or covered the area with concrete.

Almost all of the homes we passed as we wound our way through the small community displayed a variety of lawn furniture and accessories, like garden gnomes. In fact, there was a large cluster of colorful garden gnomes present at every home, like a pint-size ceramic army guarding the residents. I had a momentary flash of Gulliver being tied up by tiny Lilliputians and broke out into a slight sweat that had nothing to do with the heat of the day.

Confession: I have a phobia about garden gnomes. It's one of the things Greg loves to tease me about, and only he and Zee know about it.

"Those things give me the creeps," Mom said from the passenger's side. "A few of the residents at Seaside have them, but nothing like this. This looks like a scene in a Stephen King novel. You know, right before everyone is slaughtered." Mom continued staring, keeping watch as we passed each house with its pack of gnomes waiting for us to let our guard down.

"I once had a dream," she said, still keeping watch, "that a bunch of garden gnomes attacked me and tied me down like those tiny people did to Gulliver in *Gulliver's Travels*. Damn dream nearly put me in my grave."

What can I say? The neurotic apple didn't fall far from the neurotic tree.

There were no sidewalks in the mobile home park, so I pulled over onto the shoulder of the road in front of our destination: a white older mobile home with dark green shutters at the windows. A silver SUV, about a decade old, was parked in the space next to the trailer with its back hatch open.

"So what do we say?" Mom asked, unbuckling her seat belt. "That we were in the neighborhood selling Girl Scout cookies and thought he might want a few boxes?"

I started to climb out of the car. "How about you follow my lead?"

"Talk about the blind leading the blind."

There were four steps and a small landing with a thin railing leading up to the door on the side facing the SUV. At the end of the carport was a small storage shed that matched the mobile home. Inside the back of the SUV were a couple of boxes and a large suitcase.

"Looks like he's heading somewhere," Mom noted, "and not just for a few days."

I nodded in agreement as I took the first few steps and rang the doorbell as soon as it was within my reach. On the ground level, Mom fidgeted with something in her handbag.

"What are you looking for?" I asked her. No one had come to the door, so I rang the bell again.

"Nothing," Mom said, but she kept rummaging.

The main door was open, with only a screen door between us and the inside of the trailer. I stepped closer, cupped my hands around my eyes, and peered in, only able to make out a small kitchen table and behind it a tiny kitchen. I rang the bell a third time, leaving my finger in it for several heartbeats.

A man I recognized as David Oxman came to the screen door and opened it. He was dressed in a black T-shirt, well-worn jeans with rips that had nothing to do with fashion, and a nasty scowl. His stringy, shoulder-length hair was streaked with gray. "Yeah?"

"Mr. Oxman," I began, "my name is Odelia Grey, and this is my mother, Grace Littlejohn. We called you earlier about Boaz Shankleman."

"I didn't want to talk to you then, and I don't want to talk to you now, so get the hell out of here," he snapped and slammed the screen door shut.

"It's very important, Mr. Oxman," I called into the house as I pressed my face against the screen again. "A matter of life and death."

"Oh yeah," he said returning. I stepped back just in time to avoid being hit in the face by the opening screen door. "Whose life and whose death?" The question was more of a sarcastic snarl. His face was gaunt and lined, his eyes deep set and slightly haunted. I knew that look. Dollars to donuts, Oxman had once struggled with a drinking or drug problem, maybe both. He didn't appear to be currently engulfed by the addictions, but the yearning in his eyes signaled his daily struggles. I knew that look because my mother and brother sometimes had the same look of faraway longing in their eyes, even after all their years of sobriety.

"Um," I began, searching around for an answer. Oxman had already said he didn't give a damn about Shankleman, and the mention of Cydney Fox had caused him to hang up on us earlier. "My niece's life," I finally said. "She found Cydney Fox in Mr. Shankleman's home and is now a suspect in her murder."

"And that's my granddaughter," added Mom with emphasis. "The one who found the Fox woman."

"I can't help you with that," he said.

"Wasn't Ms. Fox your manager?" I pressed. "Don't you care what happened to her?"

He snorted and cleared his throat. "Bo anointed Cydney our new manager. Simon and I had nothing to do with that decision. She came back into town a few months ago after being gone for years and got all chummy with Bo. Next thing we knew, Titan was out and Cydney was in." He snorted again, then cleared his throat. I was betting he was at least a two-pack-a-day man. I could even smell stale smoke wafting off of him. "Cydney Fox couldn't book shit. When Titan's gigs ended, we had nothing."

"I was a big fan of the band back in your heyday," I told him, hoping a little fan worship would grease the wheels. "Didn't Cydney Fox break up Acid Storm back then? Didn't she cheat on you with Kurt Spencer-Hall?"

The top half of him disappeared in a twisty movement I'd last seen in the one and only yoga class I'd attended. When the top half rejoined the party, Oxman had a cigarette between lips and was lighting it. "Ancient history, man."

"Or a motive," Mom said, still clutching her handbag.

"A motive?" Oxman took a step outside onto the small landing and stared at Mom, his eyes narrowed, smoke curling out of his nose like a dragon. "Are you saying I killed Cydney, old lady?"

Mom did not back down. It wasn't in her nature. "No, I'm just saying you might have a motive for killing her. She shows up and ruins your bookings. Didn't she send you all to the poor house years ago?"

I was impressed. Mom had not only checked out the Marigold report, but had read the printout I had of the old breakup of the band and the financial woes that followed.

"My mother is right, Mr. Oxman," I said. "Maybe you were looking for a little delayed revenge."

He took a step toward me, his lit cigarette held between his fingers like a pointer. It got so close to my face, I backed off the steps, out of range. "I'm not saying that Cydney didn't deserve some payback," he said, "but whatever happened to her, it wasn't me who did it."

"Where were you the night before last?" Mom asked.

"That's none of your business, old lady," he snapped.

"Who are you calling old?" Mom shot back, stepping closer until she was next to me. "You can't be that much younger than me, and at least I don't look like an old retread on its last bit of rubber."

He took a long drag from his butt before waving it in our direction. "Get the hell out of here, both of you," he said as he exhaled. "I don't have time for fatties and old ladies playing Columbo."

"My mother is just asking the same questions the police are going to ask you," I said to him, trying to keep my anger in check. "I'm sure they've linked Cydney Fox to your band and know how you were treated by her back then and now. You're going to be the first person they look for, Mr. Oxman. Not to mention you just might be a suspect in Bo Shank's disappearance."

"Yeah," Mom barked. "Maybe you killed him and Ringo."

"Listen," he answered, barely keeping his own anger on a short leash, "I have no idea where Bo is. I haven't seen or talked to him in a while myself—weeks at least. As for Cydney, sure, I was pissed off about what happened with her and Kurt. Who wouldn't be? But in hindsight, it was probably a good thing for me. She was bad news then and bad news now." He took a long drag from his cigarette. "But I'm more pissed off about the destruction of the band. I might not be living in this dump with these creepy gnomes if things hadn't gone down like they had. But it's all I have now. I inherited this place from my mother two years ago. We were getting steady gigs until Cydney came back and Bo made her manager without discussing it with us. I mean, we weren't getting rich and famous, but we were able to pay our bills and play our music. Now that bitch has screwed the band over again."

"Sounds like another motive to me," Mom pointed out.

Oxman started for Mom, but I blocked his way. "She's right, and it's another question the police are going to ask, so get used to it."

Oxman took another long drag on his smoke before dropping it on the floor of the small landing and snuffing it with the toe of his worn Nikes. With a swipe of his foot, he brushed the butt over the side to the driveway. "Since you two are so nosy, I'll tell you where I was two nights ago. I was with Simon Tuttle. We were going over some new stuff we've been tinkering with—songs we want to cut on our own, without Bo."

"Simon—that's the other member of the band, right?" I asked, even though I knew the answer. "Didn't he take over for Kurt Spencer-Hall?"

"Yeah. Titan had approached Bo about getting the band back together. He said nostalgia gigs were all the rage with the aging baby boomers. Kurt died of an overdose, so we needed a new bass player." He scoffed. "Not that we wanted that asshole back, but he was one of the best guitarists we've ever known. Over the years we've had a few different guys fill the spot. Simon joined us about two years ago. Bo found him somewhere, and he's pretty good. He's also not happy with the way things started going a few months ago." He glanced at the cheap heavy watch on his wrist. "Now get out of here. I got places to go." Without even a glance at us, he went inside and shut not only the screen door, but the inside door. We'd be getting nothing else from him today.

I started back toward my car. "Come on, Mom. Let's go."

I had reached the driver's side of the car before I realized Mom wasn't following me. I looked over at Oxman's home, worried that she would try to barge in on him and ask more questions, but she hadn't. She was bent over by the back tire. She straightened, and I figured she'd dropped something, but as I watched, she walked behind the open back hatch of the SUV and bent down near the other tire. After straightening, she scurried over to me on her rubber-soled shoes while putting something back into her purse. My eyes caught on the SUV, its back end slowly going down as if someone was lowering a jack.

Holy crap! Did my mother just slash someone's tires?

"Let's get going, Odelia," Mom said as she yanked open the door and lowered herself into the passenger's seat.

"What did you—" I began to ask, but she cut me off.

"Move it, chubs," she snapped. "We gotta get out of here before he comes back out."

Without a word, I jumped into the driver's seat, started the car, and took off, not even stopping to buckle up until we hit our first red light. Great. It was bad enough Mom and I were turning into some kind of hit-and-run gang, but did my street name have to be Chubs?

"Did you slash his back tires?" I asked as I finally pulled the seat belt across my torso and clicked it into place.

Mom stared out the window, watching a young woman cross in the crosswalk with a large German shepherd on the end of a leash. "Maybe."

"Maybe?"

She shrugged without looking at me. "We needed to slow him down. He was obviously making a getaway. One tire wouldn't work because he probably has a spare, but it's going to take time for him to get both tires fixed. By then the police will catch up to him."

"Okay," I said slowly as I wrapped my brain around all this information. "But first, what did you use to cut the tires?"

When Mom hesitated, the acid in my stomach bubbled like a cauldron. The light changed, and I moved forward through the intersection. "Well?" I prompted. I knew a knitting needle didn't rip through those tires, and Mom didn't knit. If she did, Teri Thomson at Seaside would lose a good customer.

Mom reached into her purse and pulled out a four- or five-inch black item shaped sort of like brass knuckles. It had rounded ends, a curved middle, and grip indents on one side.

"Holy crap!" I said, this time out loud. "Is that a switchblade knife?"

Mom quickly put it back into her purse and snapped her bag shut. "Maybe." She went back to looking out the window.

"'Maybe' nothing!" I shouted. "Aren't those illegal?"

"Maybe."

I was about to reach over and slap the maybes right out of her. And maybe she sensed impending physical danger because Mom turned to me. "An old helpless woman like me needs protection, especially with all the scrapes we get into."

My mother may look like a good wind could blow her over, but she was far from helpless. "Mom," I began, trying to get my anxiety under control, "did you have that thing with you at the police station?"

"Nah," she said, waving off my concern. "I didn't have my purse. They didn't give me time to go get it before they hauled us away.

Besides, even if they did, I'm smart enough to know to take it out first."

"When and where did you get that thing?" I had no idea where I was driving but kept moving down the street with the traffic flow.

"I got it after that incident with the body in your trunk," she answered. "From an online store." She fixed her eyes on me. "Aren't you going to call the police and tell them that Oxman is about to take off? That seems pretty suspicious to me."

"You're changing the subject," I said, gripping the steering wheel until my hands hurt.

"Just moving the conversation along, Odelia," she said. "There are more important things going on here than a little knife."

"Mom, we're not supposed to be anywhere near this, remember?"

"If you aren't getting involved, then why are we here? Why aren't we home playing canasta?"

I couldn't argue with that, except that I don't play canasta. We were here to help Lorraine and to find Boaz Shankleman, although I was pretty sure Lorraine was in the clear on the murder end of things, but better safe than sorry. If Shankleman hadn't been missing, my first thought would have been that he killed Cydney Fox and took off. But if he didn't, how did Fox get into his house? And why was she there? Had she and Shankleman started up some sort of affair after she returned on the scene, or was she there in her capacity as the band's new manager and stumbled upon something she shouldn't have? There was also the possibility that Shankleman came back, did the dirty deed, and took off again. And why did Shankleman dump Titan West after he'd built up steady bookings with steady income and then put Fox in his place? From just the little bit we got from Oxman, it did seem she was nothing but trouble for the band.

"I can smell the gears in your head burning," Mom said.

She was right; my mental wheels were turning and at a fast rate. After years of being a reluctant corpse magnet, I confess, working through these puzzles got my juices going. It was the same with Greg, and it was something we'd talked about a few times. While we didn't care for the danger end of things, we did find it exciting to talk to people and ferret out the truth, like playing a live game of Clue. We'd become murder junkies.

Without answering, I turned into the parking lot of a grocery store, pulling into a space on its outside edge.

"Did you forget something at the store today?" Mom asked.

"No," I said, putting the car into park. I turned the engine off, but left the AC running. "I pulled over because I need to think. I do want to find out what happened to Fox to make sure Lorraine is in the clear, and I want to find Shankleman because he's your friend and you seem to care about him. But, Mom, did you ever think that maybe he came back to kill that woman? Maybe that light you saw two nights ago was him back home, expecting Fox. Maybe they had a spat and he killed her."

"It was more than a spat that triggered the murder," Mom said, looking at me, her eyes narrowed. "You didn't see the blood. Lorraine did. She said it was everywhere."

Fehring had said that Fox had been killed by several vicious blows to the head, and that Lorraine had vomited a few times. I knew that blood spatter had a way of decorating a scene like a Jackson Pollock wannabe. I was sorry Lorraine had to see that, but glad I didn't.

"Bo's a great guy," Mom continued. "I can't imagine him brutally murdering someone like that. And what would be his motive?"

"Oxman said that Fox had killed all their paying gigs," I reminded her.

"True, but I don't think Bo had money problems," she countered. "Unlike Oxman back there, he seems to have saved for his future. Seaside isn't a grand place, but you do have to have good credit and a nice balance sheet to buy in and pass their resident standards." Mom was right. I remembered all the hoops we'd had to jump through when she bought her place. Seaside was a co-op, and they wanted to make sure the residents were solvent and could take care of their own needs financially.

"I think Oxman had other problems along the way, Mom. I don't think he's using now, but I'd bet he was heavy into drugs and alcohol in the past. Their friend Kurt died of an overdose."

"Yeah, I wondered about that myself," Mom said. "Boaz once told me that back when the band was riding high, they were all into booze and drugs. He went cold turkey on both after his pal died. I think it was that Kurt fellow."

"Besides money, there are a lot of other reasons to kill someone, Mom." I shifted the AC vent on my side to blow at my warm face. "From the way she was killed, it feels personal, so it could be Oxman on a revenge bender."

"How about that Titan guy? If he lost a lot of business because she came back, he might be pretty angry."

"I talked to him yesterday," I told her, "before you discovered the murder. I called to ask him if he knew where Shankleman might be."

Mom turned in her seat, waiting for more. "And?"

106

"And he didn't seem all that upset about losing them as clients. In fact, he pretty much said Fox could have Acid Storm."

"Did you believe him?"

"I'm not sure." I shrugged. "It might be interesting, though, to talk to him in person."

"Well, what are we waiting for?"

I glanced at the clock on the dashboard. We'd already been gone well over an hour, but it was likely Lorraine was out cold. I had no idea when Clark was landing, but if he got to the house before we got back, he and Lorraine could have a father-daughter chat. Plus Clark had a key to our place.

"Look at those printouts, Mom. I don't think Titan's office is that far from here. I remember the address as being in Santa Ana, and we're right on the border of that city now."

Mom pulled the pages out of her purse, which I now considered a dangerous weapons vault, and looked through them until she came to the one about Titan's company. "You're right, it is Santa Ana." She read off the address and I plugged it into the GPS. After the nasty woman inside the gizmo recalculated, it popped up that we were just three miles from Titan Entertainment.

"We're pretty close," I reported. "We can be there in a jiffy."

Before I could restart the car, my cell phone rang. It was in its hand-free holder on the dash, and both Mom and I could see the caller was Greg. "Hi, honey," I said, pushing the answer button that put it automatically on speaker. "I'm in the car with Mom."

"Good," he replied. "That saves me a call. This is for both of you."

"Now, Greg," Mom started, leaning toward the phone, "don't go getting your boxers in a bunch over what's happened. Clark's on his way here to help so you can stay on your trip."

"That's why I'm calling, Grace. There's been a change of plans. Clark's not coming. There's been an accident."

In tandem, Mom and I gasped and locked eyes, our mouths open slightly in fear of what was to come. "An accident?" I squeaked out.

"Clark slipped on a curb at the airport," Greg explained. "He's okay, but it looks like his ankle might be broken."

"Are you with him?" Mom asked, worry dripping from her words like melted wax.

"Yeah," Greg answered. "He called me after he was taken to the ER. Boomer brought me down and will take us back to Clark's when they're done." He sighed. "You know ERs, it could take hours, but even if Clark's ankle is just sprained, he's in no shape to travel."

"I'm glad you're with him, Greg," I said with relief.

"Not for long, Odelia. As soon as we get Clark settled and some help, I'm coming home. I can't have you running around on this thing involving Lorraine without me or Clark there. Who knows what trouble you'll get into." He paused. "In fact, Grace, Clark thought maybe you and Lorraine should fly out here. He could use your help for a few days."

"Help, my old ass," Mom sneered. "He just wants to keep me away from finding out what's happened to Boaz."

"Honestly, Mom," I said, thinking about Oxman's slashed tires, "I think that's an outstanding idea. You and Lorraine can fly to Arizona to help Clark. If the police need you, they can call or you can fly back super fast. Since they didn't charge you, it should be okay with the police."

"It is," Greg added. "Clark called Andrea Fehring just now about it, and she said it would be okay for Lorraine and Grace to come here, as long as they were reachable. Meanwhile, I'll fly home and help you, Odelia."

Help or hinder, I thought, unsure of his plan.

"No, Greg," I said, putting some oomph into my words. "You've been looking forward to this get-together in Colorado with your friends. You are not missing it. I'll be fine here." What I wanted to add was that with Mom not pushing me, I'd probably just sit back and let the police handle everything, but I knew I'd never get Mom out of town if I said that.

As usual, Mom read my mind. "I'm not going anywhere," she complained. "Lorraine can take care of her father. I'm staying right here. If I don't, nothing will get done." Mom didn't waste any time on maternal instincts, if she had any.

"Have you talked to Lorraine yet?" I asked Greg.

"Clark tried calling her, but she's not picking up," he told us.

"She was in the tub when we left the house," I told him. "She was dead tired. I'll bet after her bath she turned her phone off to get some sleep." I started the engine. "We're heading home now." As soon as I said the words, Mom shot me a dirty look. "We'll tell her, and we'll get her on a plane to Phoenix."

"But what if she'd rather stay here?" Mom asked.

"You're not helping, Grace," Greg said, his voice laced with frustration. "If you won't come to Arizona, then at least get your granddaughter on that plane. Otherwise, I'll come out there and do it myself."

I love it when my husband goes all gangsta on my mother. He's about the only one she'll let get away with it.

After a pause, Mom agreed to help. "Okay, we'll get her on the plane. What time is the flight?"

"I don't know yet," Greg said. "But get home and get her packed. I'll text you as soon as I know the flight information."

"Easy peasy," I said. "She hasn't had time to unpack."

TWELVE

"WHAT ABOUT GOING TO see that Titan guy?" Mom asked as soon as I ended the call with Greg. She'd pulled her iPad out of her vault of a purse and was poking her index fingers at the screen. My mother may be in her seventies, but she's pretty tech savvy and seldom goes anywhere without her tablet—and, it seems, her switchblade.

"We can always come back after we put Lorraine on the plane," I offered, feeling as disappointed as she sounded. I was really primed to pay a visit to Titan West, and I didn't want to say goodbye so soon to Lorraine.

"We need to strike now, Odelia, while the iron's hot. By the time we get there, that place will be closed for the day, even if Lorraine is on the first plane out." Mom's fingers kept working, jabbing at the screen.

"What in the world are you doing?" I asked her.

"Looking up flights to Phoenix," she answered. "There's one at four thirty and another around seven thirty. We can say she missed the earlier flight because we cut it too close and stick her on the later one. That will give us plenty of time to visit Titan before we get Lorraine."

I glanced at the screen. "Those flights are out of Long Beach. What if they book something out of John Wayne?"

"I didn't think of that." Her fingers went back to work. "No problem," she announced. "There are also two flights and at almost the same time. I doubt they'd make us drive all the way to LAX." She turned and gave me a sly wink. "And if they book her out of John Wayne for four thirty, there's even more of a chance that we could miss her plane, but we could make seven thirty at either airport."

I had stopped being surprised at how calculating and devious my mother could be. These days, I was simply frightened. But I was also pretty impressed most of the time. "I really don't want to see Lorraine go," I said as I put the car in gear and released the parking break. "And I do want to talk to Titan West, but I'm not going to lie to my husband."

I thought I heard a low, grumbling *wuss* come from the passenger's side, but when I shot Mom a sour look she was diligently punching her iPad.

"You can look at this two ways, Odelia," Mom said, still not looking up. "Lorraine's leaving can be considered collateral damage—a compromise we comply with so we can keep looking into this. Or we can ignore Greg and Clark completely and simply not put Lorraine on that plane." She finally looked up. "Whether you lie to Greg about it or not is up to you."

The car suddenly filled with a blast from the past as I recognized one of Acid Storm's biggest hits: "The Sweetest Death."

"Where did you find that?" I asked her.

"Pandora." She adjusted the volume so we could talk. "So, what's it to be? Are we sending Lorraine to Clark or keeping her here?"

"Don't you think we should ask her?"

Mom hit buttons on the device, and the music was replaced with the sound of a phone ringing. When the call went to voicemail, I heard Lorraine's voice telling the caller to leave a message. "Lorraine, it's Grandma. Call me or Odelia as soon as you hear this." As soon as she ended the call, Mom turned and stared at me. She was waiting for me to choose. Would I go on to Santa Ana or back to Seal Beach?

I spotted a favorite burger place on a corner of the parking lot. "It's well past lunchtime," I said, pointing at the fast food place. "I'm not sure we should face Titan with growling stomachs."

She gave it less than ten seconds' thought. "Good idea; I am rather peckish. But go through the drive-thru, and let's eat in the parking lot. It'll be faster. I'll keep trying Lorraine."

We devoured our food in fifteen minutes flat. I had a burger, and Mom had a grilled chicken sandwich. I'm not sure either of us chewed a single bite thoroughly as the food went down. We ate to a medley of Acid Storm's hits. As I finished my last bite, my phone lit up with an incoming call from Greg. Mom shot me a look that said it was time for me to make a decision. As she turned off the music, the greasy burger turned in my stomach.

"Hi, honey," I said into the phone that was still attached to the dashboard. "That was fast."

"We're putting Lorraine on an American Airlines flight that leaves Long Beach at four thirty," he said without a proper greeting. "Make sure she gets on it."

"Um…," I stuttered.

"'Um' what?" he asked sharply, knowing that tiny word meant I was about to say something he might not like.

"We've checked flights on our end," I said. "How about putting Lorraine on the one at seven thirty instead? I really don't want her leaving so soon, and it's going to be tough making that earlier flight."

"Tough? It's just after two. You have plenty of time to get her to Long Beach, especially if she doesn't need to pack." He paused. "Where in the hell are you, Odelia?"

"In Costa Mesa with Mom," I told him truthfully. "We just finished lunch."

"There's still enough time for you to get home, throw Lorraine in the car, and head for the airport."

"But Greg, can't we at least have a few more hours with her?" I begged. Next to me, Mom's phone rang. She stopped the call dead in its tracks and started texting something to someone. I switched my attention back to Greg. "Honey, have you even reached Lorraine yet?" As I asked the question, Mom showed me her phone screen. It had been Lorraine who'd called her and was now texting a reply. All I saw was a *HELL NO!!!* from Lorraine's side.

"Clark just got off the phone with her. It's all set," Greg said.

In response to that, Mom was shaking her head. She leaned forward and whispered, her face turned away from my phone, "Lorraine doesn't want to go."

All set, my fat behind. "Tell Clark we'll put Lorraine on the seven thirty flight," I told my hubs with finality. "A few hours won't hurt, and besides, you're going to be tied up at the hospital most of that time. I know how ERs work. Has Clark even been seen yet?"

"Um…," Greg began.

"I'm sorry, Greg, I didn't hear you."

"Um, no, he hasn't," Greg admitted.

"See?" I said, going in to close the deal. "So a seven thirty flight it is."

After a long pause, Greg gave in. "Well, I can't see the harm, Odelia. Go home and spend time with Lorraine. The ticket will be waiting for her at the airport. Boomer can probably pick her up when she lands. Give her his description."

"Okay." I gave Mom a thumbs up. She winked back at me.

"Nice going, Odelia," Mom said when the call was finished. "And you didn't even have to lie to the man."

I took several deep breaths. Lying or not, Greg and I would be discussing this later; I was sure of it. My husband is not one of those overbearing types by a long shot. He's wonderful and believes in equality in marriage, but he's also very protective of me. He doesn't mind the snooping if he's with me, but he hates it when I go solo. Maybe I should have told him that Mom was armed with a deadly knife. Nah, that would just make things worse. He worries more about me when I'm snooping with Mom.

"So what's up with Lorraine?" I asked as I started up the car. In response, Mom called Lorraine.

Lorraine was not a happy camper. "Look," my niece began, "I'm really sorry Dad is hurt, but I will not be ordered onto a plane like he owns me."

"Odelia bought you a stay of execution," Mom told her. "She negotiated a seven thirty flight instead of the earlier one."

"Hell no!" came a determined voice from the phone. A few hours of sleep had done wonders for Lorraine's spunk. "I came here to get away and think. If I had wanted to mope around at one of my parents' homes, I would have gone there, Grandma. I needed to go someplace where I could breathe. They would both ply me with happy-face pancakes while pumping me for information about my breakup with Elliot."

"Your father may have broken his ankle," I said. "Maybe he could use some help."

"Oh, *please!*" Lorraine snapped. "I've seen that man not miss his weekly poker game after taking a bullet to the leg."

I glanced over at Mom. "Lorraine's right," she confirmed. "The bullet tore through his thigh like one of those bulls in Spain. It was on a Tuesday, and he was playing poker with his buddies the next night." She paused, then added, "And that was after he'd stopped drinking."

"Don't get me wrong, if it was a heart attack or something like that, then I'd be worried," Lorraine clarified. "Very worried."

"So, Lorraine," I said into the phone, "what do *you* want to do?"

"I want to stay here and see what happens with that dead woman," she told her grandmother and me. "I'll bet that's where you are right now, isn't it? You're investigating—without me. *I* found the body. Don't you think I should be included?"

Geez. Was Lorraine really getting possessive about a corpse?

"She gets that pigheadedness from our side," Mom said proudly, without any attempt to whisper. "Marie is more like her mother. God knows I love Marie, but she can be a real snooze."

From the phone I heard laughter. I couldn't argue. Although I'd never met Clark's ex-wife, I'd met Marie a few times, and she was rather conservative and sedate. The phrase "stick up the butt" came to mind. It was her opinion that her grandmother belonged in a home with round-the-clock care and sedation. Some days I couldn't argue with that.

I glanced again at the clock and did some math in my head. It wasn't rush hour yet. If we went back to the house to pick up Lorraine before going to see Titan, we'd lose at least an hour. Or, we could go see Titan, then go back to the house. That seemed the most logical and wouldn't get Lorraine very involved.

"Lorraine," I said into the phone, "Grandma and I have an errand to run. We should be back at the house in about an hour or so. Get dressed and be ready. I'm thinking we should go back to Seaside to check on Art's place, but we'll swing by the house and pick you up first. How about that?"

"Why can't I go with you on that errand?" Lorraine complained. "I'm already dressed."

"Because we are across town right now and close to where we need to go," I explained.

"I have an idea," Mom said. "Lorraine, do you still have my car keys?"

"They're here on the counter where I left them," she answered.

"Then why don't you come to us?" Mom told her. "It's only about a thirty-minute drive, and we won't have to circle back to get you. After we finish up, you and I can go to Seaside to check on Art, and Odelia can go home."

I started up the car's engine again and pulled out of the parking spot. "Hang tight, Lorraine, we're on our way back to pick you up. Why don't you grab some lunch while you wait? Grandma and I already had ours."

Mom didn't say a word until we were back on the freeway heading for my house. "Why didn't you let Lorraine come to us?" she asked. "My car has a GPS. She would have found us."

I shook my head and stared out the windshield at the traffic ahead of us, which was moving along nicely. "Because, Mom, the last thing I want is you and Lorraine running around getting into trouble on your own." I glanced over at her. "Without your car, you can't do that."

"Humph," she said, hugging her purse to her. "Can't blame me for trying."

THIRTEEN

Titan Entertainment was housed in a two-story brick office building on 4th Street between Bush and Spurgeon, in the heart of a cute and historical business district. Most of the buildings on the street housed retail stores and small restaurants on the ground floor, with office suites above them. Most of the signage was in both English and Spanish. The first floor of Titan's building housed a taquería. We found parking on the street several buildings down from our target.

The second-floor offices in Titan's building were accessed via a small door on the left side. We entered a small portico that housed a couple of mailboxes, a wooden staircase with a polished bannister, and a miniscule elevator. A narrow hallway led to a door at the back with a lit exit sign. The floor was black-and-white tile, shiny and clean. The walls were unmarked and painted a soft gray, like the underbelly of a mourning dove. The building looked historical and well-maintained, and the entry smelled of cleaning solvent and tortillas, the latter complements of the taquería. From the names on the mailboxes, it looked like Titan Entertainment shared the top floor of the building with a law firm called Ortega and Escobar, P.C.

If Mom hadn't been with us, I would have opted for the stairs, but I knew her legs weren't good with stairs, especially steep ones. The three of us turned toward the elevator. As soon as the doors opened and Lorraine saw the size of the car, she said, "You go with Grandma, Odelia. I'll take the stairs."

"I don't blame her," Mom said with a shiver. "This thing is the size of a coffin."

Tiny or not, Mom and I arrived safely in the elevator at the top floor to find Lorraine standing in front of a doorway down the hall. The building was much deeper than it looked from the outside, and the hallway was long, with an emergency exit sign at the end. I hadn't noticed another staircase, so maybe that went to a fire escape in the back of the building. We joined Lorraine in front of a black lacquered door frame with a frosted glass pane. Stenciled on the glass was *Titan Entertainment.*

Once the three of us were gathered in front of the door, I tried the handle. The door was locked, but I thought I could hear someone talking inside. I knocked on the door. "Mr. West?"

"Someone's in there," Lorraine said, putting her ear to the glass. "I can hear someone talking." We all remained still while Lorraine went back to listening. "But I only hear one person."

"Maybe he's on the phone," Mom suggested as a well-dressed petite woman with long dark hair and striking dark features came up the stairs. She carried a briefcase and paused in front of the law firm's door on the other side of the hallway.

I knocked again. "Mr. West?"

"Titan should be in there," the woman told us as she opened the door to the other office and stepped halfway in. "His car's parked out back."

"Thank you," Mom told her. "We have an appointment, but the door's locked."

"He might be in the men's room," the woman offered. "I don't think Titan has had a secretary in a while, so he probably locks up when he runs down the hall." She pointed down the hall and I spotted two doors, side by side, on Titan's side of the hallway, across from the exit sign. "Or he might have run down the street to grab a quick bite or something like that."

"Thank you," I told her with a smile. "So you know Mr. West well?"

"Well enough," she told us. "He owns the building."

"You've been very helpful," I said, still smiling. "We'll just wait a bit and see if he returns." If we'd been three men, I doubt she would have been as forthcoming with information.

As soon as the woman was inside the law firm and the door shut securely, I said to Lorraine, "Keep listening while I check the bathrooms."

I scooted down the hall and gently tapped on the men's room door. When I got no answer, I opened the door and peeked in. The room was very small, containing a toilet, urinal, and small sink with a mirror above it. Paper towel and soap dispensers hung on the wall next to the sink. Like the rest of the building, it was sparkling clean. I next tried the ladies' room. It was also empty and the same as the men's room, except that it contained no urinal and was on the outside wall, on which was a closed window of frosted glass. A small glass jar of potpourri had been left on the window's ledge.

The small room smelled of citrus with slight undertones of savory herbs.

Quickly I made my way back up the hall. "No one in either bathroom."

"Good," Mom said, "because I have to pee."

"You went back at the burger place," I protested. "And again at my house when we picked up Lorraine."

"I'm old," Mom snapped, doing a quick two-step down the hall, "and so is my bladder."

"Grandma's a real piece of work, isn't she?" Lorraine whispered to me with a wink.

Instead of answering, I closed my eyes and took two deep breaths. "Can you still hear someone inside?" I asked her.

Lorraine put her ear to the door again and shook her head. I put my fingers to my lips, letting her know to keep quiet. I indicated for Lorraine to back off to the side, away from the door, so her shadow couldn't be seen. I did the same. "Guess we should go," I said toward the door. "No sense hanging around here all day." I motioned for Lorraine to cross in front of the door and start for the stairs. A quick study, she caught my drift and started for the stairs. I followed and together we tried our best to sound like we were leaving. It was a corny trick that shouldn't work, but it was all we had to work with outside of breaking down the door.

"Come on, Mom," I said to no one, happy that Mom was taking her usual sweet time in the bathroom, "we're leaving."

"Hold your horses," Lorraine said, doing an excellent impersonation of her grandmother's voice and crankiness.

After making the best retreating steps we could, I sneaked back to the door and stood against the wall. Lorraine did the same. We stayed that way, still as statues, until the handle turned on the other side and the door was pulled inward a few inches, just enough to permit a round bald pate to pop out like a curious prairie dog. First Titan West looked straight ahead, then he looked toward the stairs, and that's when he caught sight of us in his peripheral vision. He tried to slam the door shut, but I heaved my 200-plus pounds at it before he could shut and lock it. Lorraine followed. The little man was stronger than I'd imagined possible, and it took the two of us to force it open.

Once we were inside, Titan ran for an inner office, and again we raced to prevent him from slamming that door and locking us out—or I should say Lorraine raced to that door. She sprinted across the room with an agility I'd never had, not even in my younger days. All we wanted was to get inside and have a conversation with this man, but we got carried away and went at him like a seasoned SWAT team. No wonder he ran.

"We just want to talk to you, Titan," I said as we spilled into that second room together like clowns tumbling out of a cramped tiny car.

Instead of listening or replying, Titan, huffing and puffing, scrambled to his desk, yanked open a drawer, and pulled out a gun.

OMG—a freaking gun! I nearly wet myself. It was a small handgun, but a gun just the same. It also wasn't the first time a gun had been pulled on me, but, trust me, it's not something you get blasé about.

I froze in my tracks, except for my right hand, which reached out and grabbed Lorraine by the back waistband of her jeans to keep her from going after Titan. It was clear she hadn't seen the gun yet. Like a hunting dog retrieving a fresh kill, she was focused on getting to him. When I pulled her up short, she came out of her frenzied state and gasped when she noticed the gun. Seeing that her father had been a cop for a couple of decades, I'm sure it wasn't the first gun she'd ever seen, but I was pretty sure it was the first time she'd had one pointed directly at her chest.

I pulled harder on the back of Lorraine's jeans until she started retreating backwards. When she was shoulder to shoulder with me, I took a slight side step forward, putting my body in front of hers. My niece was not going to get shot today unless the bullet went through me first. As for my mother, I could only hope she had the runs from her lunch and would remain in the bathroom, where she'd be safe.

Seeing us stopped, Titan took a deep breath and wiped sweat off his shiny forehead with the back of his free hand. He was dressed in nice gray slacks and a white knit shirt with a polo player over his heart. The shirt pulled slightly over his round belly and was tucked in, secured by a leather belt. I guessed him to be in his sixties, like Oxman and Shankleman. On his left hand, the one not holding the gun, was a wedding ring. "Who in the hell are you?"

"We just came to talk to you," I told him, keeping my voice calm. "My name is Odelia Grey. This is my niece Lorraine. I called you yesterday about Boaz Shankleman. Do you remember that, Titan? My mother is a friend of his."

His eyes seemed to retreat into his fleshy face, red from exertion, as he dug through his memory bank, but the gun never wavered. "Yeah, I remember." The eyes focused on us again. "So are you here to take me out?"

"Take you *out*?" Lorraine asked. "You mean like on a *date*? Ewww-www." Both Titan and I looked at her like she'd just put a finger in a light socket.

"Really?" I said to Lorraine. "That's where your mind went? Even your grandmother would know better."

She looked puzzled for a nanosecond, then her brain caught up to the situation. "OMG," she said to Titan in horror, "you think we're here to kill you?" She pointed from me to herself. "Seriously, do we look like hit men?"

If not for our precarious situation, I'd take Lorraine out for coffee and ply her with stories about Mother, the notorious leader of a gang of hit women, who could pass for anyone's granny. But that was for another time.

"Titan," I said instead, "no one has sent us. We really do just want to talk to you about Boaz Shankleman and Cydney Fox."

"I told you on the phone," Titan answered, "I have no idea where Bo is. As for Cydney, she can rot in hell."

"She's halfway there now," Lorraine said. I turned in surprise. In seconds Lorraine had gone from thick skulled to the queen of snappy remarks. Mom was right: Lorraine was more like our side of the family.

"And what does that mean?" he asked, still not putting down the gun.

"It means that Cydney Fox is dead," I told him. "She was found in Shankleman's house beaten to death, but he's still missing."

"Good riddance," he barked after recovering from his initial shock. "Cyd was nothing but trouble." For all his bluster, his skin had gone ashen at the mention of Fox being found dead.

"Why would you think Shankleman sent us to kill you?" I asked, wondering in the back of my mind where in the hell Mom was lurking. "We're just trying to find him to put my mother's mind at ease. They're friends at the retirement community, and she's worried about him."

"I never said I thought Bo sent you," Titan snapped, his eyes shifting, alert and wary.

I rewound my brain back a few seconds. "You certainly inferred it," I told him. "We were talking about Bo, and you asked if we were here to kill you. I'm not sure how else to interpret that." I paused and waited, but Titan said nothing. "If you weren't talking about Bo, then who is it you thought sent us to kill you? Could it be the one who killed Cydney Fox? Is it David Oxman?"

"That burnout?" Titan scoffed. "Don't make me laugh. If not for me and Bo, he'd be living on skid row in downtown LA or dead."

He started moving away from his desk. He kept the gun on us, forcing us to rotate with him. As he got closer to the doorway to the outside room, we pivoted until we were facing the doorway. For the first time I noticed his office walls were covered with framed posters of old bands, mostly from the '70s and '80s, many of which I remembered seeing on his website as available for bookings. Some of the posters were signed. Otherwise the office was pretty basic. There was a very large wooden desk, an oversized leather desk chair, and two visitor chairs. Against the outside wall, set between two small windows, was a leather sofa. On the desk sat an open cardboard document storage box, and next to it, an array of files. An old-fashioned leather-edged desk blotter covered the middle of the desk and matched the half-full pencil cup and business card holder. The office was very tidy and the furnishings of good quality. Like the bands in the posters, the office was a throwback to an earlier time. Only a horizontal file cabinet against one wall and an open laptop on the desk were modern.

As if reading my mind, Titan started to edge back toward the desk, forcing us to rotate again like flowers following the movement of the sun. With his free hand, he closed the laptop and tucked it close to his body. With small jerks of the gun, he indicated for us to reverse our direction again as he edged back to the door.

"You two stay right where you are," he warned, "unless you want to get shot. I'm leaving now, and if you try to follow me, I'll shoot you both." He was trying to play a tough guy, but his roly-poly physique and doughy features weren't backing him up. If not for the gun, I felt certain that I could easily take him, even without Lorraine.

I put my hands up in the air, as if I was being robbed. I nudged Lorraine and she did the same. Titan edged backwards, the gun still pointed at us, until his backside was halfway out the doorway. He reached for the door handle, then realized he didn't have a free hand to pull it shut. He rolled his eyes at his own predicament before deciding to just continue backing up.

"You two stay right here," he ordered. "You follow me and I'll shoot you both, I swear." Titan didn't seem the violent type, so I felt there was only a fifty-fifty chance that he'd make good on that promise, but I wasn't about to gamble with my life or Lorraine's. And I've learned that even nonviolent people might shoot a gun under duress.

What happened next happened so fast it took me a moment to realize what went down. Just as Titan lowered his gun to turn and flee, he yelped in pain, dropping the gun to the floor. I ran over and kicked the weapon out of his reach and shoved him, knocking him against the doorjamb. He slid to the floor, yelping again. The door to the office suite was still open. Quickly, I crossed the room, closing and locking it just in case someone from the other office heard anything, and also to slow Titan down should he manage to get to his feet. Titan turned slightly on his side and clutched his right buttock with his right hand. The laptop was still in his left hand. It was then I noticed Mom standing off to the side holding her knife like one of the Jets from *West Side Story*.

Still inside Titan's office, Lorraine's legs buckled and her butt hit the floor with a muffled thud, her bravado of a few seconds ago melted away like ice.

I didn't want to be the type of person who sneered *I told you so*, but I couldn't help myself. "You're the one who insisted on coming with us," I told Lorraine as I grabbed the laptop from Titan and indicated for him to get to his feet. "But since you're here, now would be a great time to pull up your big girl panties."

As Titan slowly found his legs and stood up, I turned to Mom. "And you—put that damn thing away before you really hurt someone!"

Mom sniffed at me. "Just let me wash the blood off first." A small kitchenette was built into the side wall, along with a tiny sink, microwave, and compact fridge. A folding door was half opened across the front of it. Mom pushed the door wider and turned on the faucet.

Blood! For the love of…

"And bring some towels for Titan," I snapped at her as he limped into the inner office. "Who knows how deep you got him."

"Aw, it's only a flesh wound," Mom said. "He'll live."

I knew that and Mom knew that, but I wasn't sure Titan did. Whimpering like a little girl who'd lost her balloon, he was standing by his desk, half bent forward, his left hand gripping the edge, his right hand still clutching his right butt cheek. I put the laptop back on the desk and bent to examine the damage. There was a small tear in his pants and some blood, but not much. It didn't look like Mom's knife had gone very deep.

"It was just a poke," I told him. Mom came in with some towels, one of them wet. I took them from her and dabbed at the spot with the wet towel first.

Titan yelped again. "Should I drop my pants?" he asked.

"You do," I warned him, "and I'll set my mother on you again." Not only did he not drop his pants, but he stopped whining. Dabbing at the wound again, I noticed very little blood. "It looks like the bleeding is stopping already, but you might want to wash it with some antibacterial soap and dress it after we leave." I handed him the dry towels. "Here, put these down on your chair and take a seat. We have some questions for you."

"No," Mom said, stepping forward to stop him from moving. "Make him stay bent over like that. If he's uncomfortable, maybe he'll talk more and not dawdle about it. And kick his feet apart like they do on TV."

I looked at Titan, still slightly bent forward, both hands on his desk. He did look like he was bent over the hood of a car after police found dope in his vehicle. Mom had a point, although I did not kick his feet apart.

"Where did you pick her up?" Titan snapped. "Guantanamo?"

I glanced over at my mother and said under my breath, "Sometimes I wonder."

Once again my I-told-you-so side came out. "If you had simply answered our questions," I told Titan, "this never would have happened."

"Well, you have my attention now," he barked. "So get on with it, then get the hell out of here." He lifted one hand off the desk to point at my deceptively frail-looking septuagenarian mother. "Just keep her away from me. She's a menace."

Mom stepped forward. "Me? You're the fool with the gun." Lorraine had taken a place on the love seat and was watching intently, as if she was in the orchestra section of the Ahmanson Theatre.

"We're trying to find Boaz Shankleman," I said to Titan.

"And I told you," he answered firmly, "I have no idea where he is." He shot Mom a sneer. "And stabbing me isn't going to make him appear out of thin air."

I wanted to ask again about who he thought had sent us to kill him but felt I'd hit the same brick wall. I went in another direction. "You've been Acid Storm's manager a long time, haven't you?"

Titan nodded. "Since the very beginning. In fact, I discovered them in a little club in Oxnard."

I took a seat in a chair in front of his desk. No sense we should all be uncomfortable. "Are you the one who got them back together several years ago?"

"Yes," he said, indicating the posters with a swing of his chin. "Some of my other old bands were finding a second life on the fair and summer circuit. Lots of baby boomers flock to those concerts. I approached Bo, and he jumped at it. They've done well," he said, pausing briefly, "until recently."

"By 'recently' do you mean when Shankleman fired you and replaced you with Cydney Fox?" In answer, he shifted his stance, obviously uncomfortable and not just because of his injury. "And why did Shankleman do that?" I pressed.

"We heard he did it without consulting the other band members," Mom added. She'd taken a seat next to Lorraine. "Is that true?"

Titan hemmed and hawed. He was a short man. Bending at the waist to lean on the desk made an almost right angle out of him. "Bo was unofficially in charge of the band," he finally said. "It was like that in the old days, too. Oxman and Spencer-Hall were too busy shagging groupies and getting high to care about the business end of things. Bo was the only one with any sense."

"He's always struck me as having a good head on his shoulders," Mom noted.

"If he was such a good businessman, then it sounds as if he might have had a reason, a good one, for canning you," I noted.

"Artistic differences," was all Titan said.

"And Cydney Fox just happened to be waiting in the wings to take the job?" I asked, remembering our chat with Oxman. "Has she been in the picture all this time or did she show up a few months ago and talk Bo into hiring her?"

"I haven't heard a word about her since all that mess back in the day, so I was just as surprised as everyone else." Titan shrugged. "But who knows? Maybe Bo's kept in touch and just didn't say anything."

"Is she qualified to manage the band?" asked Mom.

This question prompted a snort from the bent man. "Not that I know of. Back then, all she knew how to do was party and look good doing it. I haven't even seen her since she's come back, so who knows what she's been doing."

"So one day," I asked, "Bo announced you were out and Cydney Fox was in? Just like that?"

"Pretty much," Titan answered. "No warning or explanation or anything. Bo showed up here a couple of months ago yammering something about her needing a job and about us owing her. He said the bookings were easy to do, so she was going to start doing them with Bo's help. He gave me a thirty-day notice, pursuant to our contract. I booked the band through the Fourth of July, then dropped them."

I leaned forward. "What did he mean by the band owing her? Wasn't it Cydney Fox who brought down the band in their heyday?"

Titan lifted a hand off the desk and pointed a sausage finger at me. He was a nail biter. Not a bad one, but it was still a sign that he was a nervous type. It went along with a few of my other observations. He was like a jittery cat, ready to bolt under the bed at any perceived sign of danger. But what danger? We'd just told him that Fox was dead, and he'd seemed genuinely surprised, but he'd been on the watch for someone when we arrived. He was already afraid, and I didn't think it was because three generations of women showed up at his door. He was expecting someone, and he expected that someone to want to harm or kill him. Was it Shankleman or was there another danger lurking in the shadows? Perhaps one that caused Shankleman to pull a disappearing act, one that Fox did not escape? And had she been a target or merely in the wrong place at the wrong time when the murderer showed up to take out Shankleman?

"That's exactly what I told him," Titan said, jabbing his stubby, gnawed finger in the air in my direction. "If anything, *she* owed *us*. The band lost everything because of her."

"And what did Boaz have to say about that?" Mom asked, leaning forward to not miss a word.

Titan didn't answer right away. Instead, he shifted his eyes and his body, rotating them in opposite directions. He might have been uncomfortable or he might have been trying to remember his conversation with Boaz or he might have been trying to think up a lie. My money was on door number three.

"Hey, have a heart," he finally said. "How about letting me sit? I can think better if blood isn't rushing to my head. And there's some water in the fridge in the other room," he added. "I could sure use some."

"Lorraine," I said to my niece, keeping my eyes glued to Titan, "would you please get him some water?"

Lorraine popped up from the sofa and headed for the outer room. "Sure."

"Bring two," Mom told her. "I'm quite parched myself."

"Go ahead and take a seat, Titan," I told him. He straightened and started to move to his chair behind his desk. "But keep your hands flat on the desk at all times," I added, remembering how he'd pulled the gun from one of the drawers before. I didn't want any surprise second weapons. Just to be safe, I moved the pencil cup out of his reach after noting it also contained a very sharp letter opener.

"Yeah," Mom said, "don't even so much as think about scratching your butt or we might have to really mess you up."

I turned and quickly shot Mom a look of mixed disbelief and annoyance. I made a mental note to myself to insist, when this was over, that she have a full physical, mind and body.

Titan gingerly settled in his chair just as Lorraine returned with four squat bottles of water clutched against her body with her left arm. In her right hand was the gun that had been kicked to the side in the scuffle. I sighed with relief when I saw that she'd had the good sense to pick it up using a paper towel; that was all we'd need to have her prints on a weapon. That gun might have been sitting undisturbed in Titan's desk for years or it might have been used in any number of crimes. It was bad enough our prints were probably all over this place without them being on a gun too.

"What should we do with this?" she asked, holding up the gun.

"Give it here," Mom replied, quick as a bunny.

"No," Titan and I snapped in unison. Mom rolled her eyes at us like we were spoiling her fun.

"Give it to me," I told Lorraine. "I'll think of something."

Using the paper towel like a pot holder, Lorraine transferred the towel and the gun to me, then handed Titan one of the bottles of water. She put one bottle on the desk by me and took the other two back to the sofa and took a seat again. I wasn't sure what I was going to do with the gun, but I sure as hell didn't want it anywhere near Titan. Getting up, I said to Titan, "You stay right where you are. I'll be right back." The look he gave me broadcast that I had a 50/50 chance that he'd listen.

I glanced over at the love seat. Lorraine was sipping her water and looking nervous. Mom had also just wet her whistle and looked alert. "Mom, pull out your knife and come stand next to the desk. If he moves, turn him into Swiss cheese. I'll be right back."

"That old lady's batshit crazy," Titan protested.

I waved the gun in his direction, not that it posed any threat being held like a hot pot pie. "That batshit-crazy old lady is my mother, and it's genetic." He clamped his mouth shut fast, like an alligator seizing his meal, and watched with worry while Mom took

134

out her knife. She deftly snapped the blade open and moved closer to the desk.

Taking the gun into the outer office, I looked around for a good place to stash it. For the same reason I didn't want our prints on it, I didn't want to take it with us. Well, not the only reason. Guns make me nervous, and if we were stopped for any reason, I sure didn't want one in my possession. I studied the desk but dismissed it as too obvious. I turned my attention to the kitchenette, looking for a good but improbable place to store the gun. There were cabinets above the small counter. I opened one and found various disposable goods such as paper plates, a couple of bowls, napkins, and cups, and a couple ceramic mugs. In the next cabinet were some handy food items like soup and cereal. One of the cartons contained packets of instant oatmeal in various flavors. It was the large economy size. We kept boxes of the same stuff in our office. I took the box down. It was almost empty. Fortunately, Titan's gun was small and compact, like him, and I was able to stick it into the box, cushioning it with the remaining packets.

"Good grief," Mom said when I returned to Titan's office. "We thought you'd abandoned us, you took so long." While Mom seemed annoyed, Titan looked relieved. I had only been gone a few minutes, wanting to get back before Mom mistook a simple thing like Titan passing gas as a threat, but I had also taken a minute or two extra to stop and run some ideas through my head without distraction.

"So," I said to Titan, ignoring Mom and getting the questioning back on track, "what did Shankleman say when you reminded him how Fox had brought down the band years ago?"

He shrugged, obviously more comfortable in his chair in spite of his puncture wound. "He said some BS like the past is the past, and we should move on."

I narrowed my eyes at the small, round man. Something wasn't adding up. Evasion wafted off of Titan like cheap aftershave. "Forgiving for the past is one thing, but replacing a successful manager with someone who tanked the group years ago doesn't seem like a smart move to me."

"And Boaz is a very smart man," Mom underlined again with conviction. She gone back to join Lorraine on the sofa.

"I could see," I said to Titan, "giving her something else to do but not handling the bookings, which meant income to the group." I paused as the gears in my head started to mesh like teeth on a zipper. "Unless the real point here wasn't about giving her a job but taking one away from you." My eyes met his in time to see a flicker of something. Was it surprise at the idea or surprise that I was getting closer to the truth?

"Nonsense," Titan finally said, forcing casualness into his voice. "He wasn't taking anything away from me. I'd told Bo shortly after New Year's that I was thinking of retiring at the end of this year, but I expected him to stick with me until then. Maybe he jumped the gun and decided to transition to someone new now." Titan shifted his body and winced. "At least that's what I'm thinking, but I sure didn't think it would be her."

"So that was a complete surprise?" I asked.

He nodded. "Yes. I met with Bo and tried to talk him out of using Cydney, but he was adamant—about her and about doing it as soon as possible. So we agreed that I'd book through the Fourth of July. After that, they were on their own."

Something still wasn't adding up, but I didn't have enough information to call Titan out on his story. "Do you have any idea who might want to kill Shankleman or Cydney Fox?"

Titan's eyes bulged like he'd been squeezed tight. "I thought you said it was Cydney who was dead."

"We did," Mom confirmed. "But it seems to me whoever killed her might have been looking to do harm to Boaz and found her instead." Mom had voiced exactly what I was thinking. "Maybe Boaz grabbed Ringo and left because he'd been threatened."

"And whoever did the killing, they were very angry. Cydney Fox was killed by repeated blows to the skull." Out of the corner of my eye I saw Lorraine shiver at the memory. I turned my eyes back to Titan, trying to imagine the short, portly man bludgeoning anyone with such viciousness, but couldn't. "Maybe it was someone who lost income because of her and Shankleman."

"What about the other members of the band?" suggested Lorraine, shaking off the bloody scene now burned into her memory.

Titan considered the possibility. "I can't see David Oxman mustering that much energy for anything. He's a very competent musician, but he has the personality of dirty laundry. He'd be more likely to bitch about it, not take revenge."

"And Simon Tuttle?" I asked.

Titan considered the question a moment. "He's a young guy." He aimed a finger at a poster on the wall of the current Acid Storm group to make his point. "And strong enough, but I've never seen him lose his temper. Oh, he gets mad enough once in a while, but he sloughs it off quickly, and he has a lot of talent. Simon Tuttle could be doing a lot more with his music than playing backup with these old guys, but it seems to suit him for some reason. I know during the off-season he does a lot of freelance gigs and studio work."

"What about Oxman and Shankleman?" I asked. "Do either strike you as the violent type?"

"Definitely not Boaz," my mother protested. "He's sweet as a lamb."

"The old lady's right," Titan said.

"Watch who you're calling an old lady, Humpty Dumpty." Mom patted her handbag where she'd once again stored her knife.

"Madam is correct," Titan said with heavy sarcasm. "Bo is a lot like Simon, but even more reasonable—positively Zen at times. He gets angry but gets over it quickly, and I've never known him to hold a grudge. If he killed Cydney I'd be totally shocked. And like I said, Dave is more the type to stew and rant but not take action. If anyone in Acid Storm was the type to beat someone to death, it would have been Kurt."

"You mean Kurt Spencer-Hall?" I asked.

"Yeah," Titan confirmed. "He was a mean SOB. I could never understand how he got so many sweet young things with that nasty personality, but it could explain why none of them stuck around for long."

"But he's the guy who died, right?" asked Mom.

Titan nodded and briefly shut his eyes tight. "Yeah. Drug overdose. I identified the body myself. Had to fly to Mexico to do it. Nasty business."

Mexico wasn't mentioned in the Marigold report, just that Spencer-Hall was dead. I hadn't read much after hitting that piece of information. "Mexico?"

"Yeah," Titan said. "After the shit hit the fan all those years ago, Kurt disappeared into Mexico. Besides the group's financial troubles, Kurt had several charges of rape hanging over his head from several of the groupies. He still had me listed as an emergency contact, so I got the call when he was found dead. It was several years after all the scandal."

A lull filled the room like heavy humidity. Something told me if we left, we might never see Titan again. He was spooked when we got here, and hearing about Fox's death had rattled him more. There was a good chance he might disappear the minute we were gone. I needed to get from him everything I could now.

"Who were you expecting to show up today?" I asked him.

"I wasn't expecting anyone."

"Don't give us that," Mom said, sounding like a tough cop from a movie.

"You were definitely afraid of something," Lorraine pointed out. "You had the door locked, and you ran when you saw us."

"You can't be too careful in this neighborhood," he answered. He lifted a hand to his mouth and gnawed at the end of a thumb.

"You were afraid of something or someone when we got here," I noted, "and now that you know about Cydney Fox, you're as jumpy as a squirrel crossing a highway." Immediately Titan stopped chewing his nail.

"I'm not afraid of anything," he said, but his darting eyes gave away his lie. "I just heard noise outside in the hallway and checked on it. You two rushed me, and I panicked."

"And you still haven't clarified who you thought had sent us to kill you," I pointed out. "If not Shankleman, then who?" At this question Titan clammed up, his jaw tight as a vault. He locked his small, beady eyes on me, letting me know even torture by my mother wasn't going to unlock that answer.

"Shankleman has a sister, doesn't he, in Syracuse, New York?" I asked, moving to another topic. "Do you think he might have gone there?"

"But Boaz told us he didn't have any family," Mom said.

"I'm not surprised," Titan said, looking at Mom. "Bo and Harriet have been estranged for years. I doubt he went there."

Titan fidgeted again and glanced at his wristwatch without taking his hands off the desk. Unlike Oxman's, Titan's watch was an expensive timepiece. "Look," he said, looking up at me, "I've told you all I know, and I need to be somewhere. My wife's expecting me. As it is, I'm going to be late." He narrowed his eyes in Mom's direction. "And I'm going to have to change my pants before I go. Fortunately, I keep extra clothing here."

FOURTEEN

BACK IN THE CAR, Mom huffed and puffed at me. "Odelia, you know darn well that little pipsqueak knows more than he's saying. Why didn't you go after him?"

"Because," I answered as I buckled my seat belt, "I could tell he'd dug in his heels and wasn't going to say anything more."

"So we're done?" Lorraine asked from the back seat. "That's it?" She sounded as disappointed in my efforts as Mom.

"Not entirely," I said as I pulled out of the parking space and started down the street. At the first cross street I made a right-hand turn, then another right when I spotted an alley entrance. The alley ran behind the buildings on Titan's side of the street. I drove slowly. The alley was narrow, with just enough room for two cars to pass side by side if the drivers were careful and clung to the sides. On trash day only a disposal truck would fit. I hoped Titan was taking his sweet time changing his trousers.

"Smart thinking, Odelia," Mom said, catching on quickly. She glanced into the back seat. "I'll bet she's going to check out his car," she told Lorraine. "Maybe tail the guy."

I checked out the backsides of the various businesses until I came to a stop behind one. "This looks like his building, doesn't it?" I asked my posse.

"I think you hit the jackpot," Mom said. She pointed at the row of cars neatly parked behind the building. There was only room for four vehicles and an area for the dumpster that served the building. A back door with the name of the first-floor restaurant stenciled on it was on one side. Another back door was on the opposite side with no stenciling; that had to be the back door to the lobby. On the outside of the second floor was a fire escape landing, as I expected. Even the back of the building looked in excellent shape, and the area was clean. Titan definitely took care of his building; contrary to what he'd said, the neighborhood seemed peaceful and well maintained.

"That thing has to be his wheels," Mom said. All four parking spaces were filled, but Mom was pointing at one car specifically. It was a charcoal gray Mercedes SUV with a personalized plate that made no mystery of who owned the vehicle.

We were out in the open. The minute Titan came out, he'd spot us. I looked into the rearview mirror and then both side mirrors. The narrow alley held no place to tuck into and wait him out.

"He doesn't know your car, does he?" asked Lorraine.

"No," I responded.

"It looks like there might be a parking space on the street just past the alley," Lorraine pointed out. "Maybe if we park there, we'll be able to see him without him seeing us."

I barely looked at the space, but it was enough to see that Lorraine was right. It was the first one on the curb just beyond the alley to the left. It was ideally located for keeping an eye on Titan's car, but not for getting into since we'd be going the wrong way to nab it. I moved the car forward anyway. At the end of the alley, after making sure the coast was clear, I pulled out onto the street, heading right, then put my car into reverse and started backing into it. A car came down the street behind me and stopped, waiting for me to make my awkward backward parallel-parking effort. Parallel parking is not one of my talents, and I will avoid it at all costs. Seeing how lopsided the job was, I pulled ahead and started backing up again for another try, the urgency of the situation adding to my frustration.

As I eased into the space, a young guy hung out of the driver's window of the car behind me, an older black sedan. He made a rude gesture and yelled, "Come on, lady, get the car in there or move on. A blind man could park it better."

I hoped Titan didn't choose that moment to come out and look down the alley to see what the shouting was about. I also hoped my mother would hold her tongue and not cause more of a scene. Instead, she asked with heavy sarcasm, "Want me to do it for you?"

"No," I snapped. I took a deep breath and gently put my foot on the gas while I turned the wheel. This time I made a smooth job of it, which was amazing with all the performance pressure. At least Lorraine had the good manners to button her lip. As soon as the car was out of his way, the kid in the car sped off, only to be stopped by the streetlight on the corner a few yards away turning red. Served him right.

Parked and settled, I looked over toward Titan's car. His building was the third one down, but the buildings were small so we could see the tail end of his car from our vantage point. There was no way he could get into his car and drive away without us seeing him.

Even though the street ahead was busy with midday traffic, the alley was quiet and few cars came down the side street we were on. The three of us waited and watched, three sets of eyes on the back end of the Mercedes. Occasionally we took swigs from the small bottles of water we'd gotten from Titan, which my mother had had the presence of mind to snag on the way out the door.

"He's taking a long time," Lorraine said, breaking the silence after a few minutes.

"Maybe he's packing up more than just his laptop," I suggested. "Now that he knows Cydney Fox is dead, he might be worried that whoever he thinks is after him might step up their game, so he's planning on taking off."

"He could also go out the front," Mom added. "He might think his car with those vanity plates would be too easy to spot, so he called a cab or one of those Uber cars."

"That's a very good point, Mom. So how can we check?"

"How about I go to the front and see if he comes out that way?" Lorraine offered.

It was a good suggestion, but I didn't want Lorraine to tackle him in broad daylight. She swung between going ninja and being a wilting flower. Who knows which side of her would pop up if she saw Titan making a getaway? Mom must have been thinking along the same lines because she turned in her seat and said to Lorraine,

"Okay, but if you see him, get the info on the car he gets into. Do *not* try to stop him. Got it?" With some reluctance, Lorraine agreed.

Lorraine had her back door open when I stopped her. "Hold up. There's Titan."

All our eyes turned to watch as Titan emerged from between two cars and made his way to the rear of his vehicle. Before he got there, the back lift of the SUV opened upward. He was carrying the document storage box, now covered with a lid, indicating he had taken the time to finish packing up. Over one shoulder was slung a laptop in a carrying case, and he'd changed into jeans and a light-colored knit shirt.

I was about to start my car's engine and put it into drive when Mom put a hand on my arm. "Wait," she told me. She was pointing down the alley.

While we watched, Titan put the box and laptop into the back of the vehicle, but what had caught Mom's attention was just beyond Titan's location. The nose of a black car could be seen easing forward, not driven at a normal speed but crawling a few inches at a time like a lion about to jump its prey. Titan saw it too, but it was too late. As soon as the car moved closer to Titan, his head snapped back and he slumped to the ground right before our eyes. Someone jumped out of the car, grabbed the laptop and box, and tossed them into the vehicle. The car sped off—in our direction. The car was the same one that earlier had been stopped by my sloppy parking.

"*Get down,*" I said in a loud whisper, full of urgency. Mom, Lorraine, and I all ducked, getting our heads down and out of sight. With any luck the driver didn't see us as he barreled out of the alley and headed left up the street.

Once we were sure they'd passed, we lifted our heads and glanced over at Titan. He was still on the ground. Yanking open my door, I jumped out and made a beeline for him. After shaking off her initial shock, Lorraine did the same, her long stride getting her there just after me. Mom took up the rear. By the time she'd arrived, I'd confirmed that Titan was dead. He'd taken two bullets to the chest.

"We need to call 911," I said. "I'll go get my phone from the car."

"Way ahead of you," Mom told me, holding up her phone. "I've already called them and said there'd been a shooting."

Lorraine looked down at the second corpse she'd seen in two days. Her face was ashen. "I didn't hear any gun shots; did you?"

I shook my head. "Nothing. They must have used a silencer or else we definitely would have heard something, as close as we were. So would the people in these buildings. Gun shots are loud."

My first instinct had been to flee the scene. After all, Titan West was dead, so there was nothing we could do to help him, and I sure didn't want Lorraine and my mother mixed up in another investigation. But leaving the scene would only make the police search us out as suspects. We'd been seen by the woman from the other office, too; while she didn't have our names, I'm sure she could give the police decent descriptions. Also, our fingerprints were all over Titan's office. Better to stay and tell them the truth: that we'd come to Titan's office to ask him about Boaz Shankleman, my mother's friend, and while we were getting ready to drive off we saw Titan get shot in the parking lot. Nothing more, nothing less, along with a description of the car we saw drive away. For good measure, we could throw in that Titan was nervous when we had arrived and that his door had been locked.

That's the rundown I gave to Mom and Lorraine as the police and an ambulance roared into the alley in answer to the call that there had been a shooting.

There was no way Lorraine was going to make any flights today.

FIFTEEN

WE DIDN'T GET BACK to our place until almost nine o'clock. All of us were exhausted, especially Mom and Lorraine, after all of the questioning by the Santa Ana police.

None of us was hungry, and when I suggested stopping for a quick late dinner or going through a drive-thru, no one seemed enthusiastic.

"You need to eat something, Mom," I said to my mother. "You've hardly eaten all day. You too, Lorraine."

"I'll have some tea and toast when we get home," Mom said in a small, weary voice. "Nothing else sounds good."

"Will you let me put some peanut butter on that toast to give you a little protein?"

She nodded slightly. "I like peanut butter," she said, perking up a tiny bit. "Got any jelly?"

"PB&J it is, Mom." I looked over and gave her an encouraging smile. "Tomorrow we'll look for Art. I'll bet that's what you're worried about, isn't it?"

"Yes, Odelia," she said. "I sure am. There's still nothing on my phone from him."

"After we get a good night's rest, we'll look into it with fresh eyes." She returned a weak smile. I knew Mom was all done in because she didn't fight me on this plan. If she were fully rested, she'd be insisting that we look tonight, no matter how late.

I looked into the rearview mirror at Lorraine. She looked barely awake. "You okay with PB&J?"

"Yeah, or some soup," she answered. "But not much else."

Mom perked up a little more. "Soup does sound good. Chicken noodle, or tomato soup and grilled cheese. Too bad Greg isn't here. He makes the best grilled cheese sandwiches."

I smiled to myself. My husband did make kick-ass grilled cheese sandwiches. Even when I followed his routine to the letter, mine came out acceptable but not great like his. He had the magic touch when it came to melting cheese and my heart, although I was worried at the moment that he was thinking about calling a divorce attorney.

When we pulled into the carport, Wainwright came rushing out his doggie door into the backyard. We could hear him whining and pacing on the other side of the fence as he recognized the car and our scents.

"Hold on, boy," I told him in a low voice as I unlocked the back gate.

Poor Wainwright. He'd been left home most of the day, something he's not used to, even though he had Muffin for company and a doggie door to use at his convenience. Muffin used the doggie door too, and even though she's a cat, she showed no signs of wanting to hop the fence and explore the neighborhood, as we had originally feared she might. Guess she knew a good gig when she saw it.

I opened the back gate, then pushed the big, excited dog back so that Mom and Lorraine could come in before shutting and locking the gate again. When I saw how excited the dog was to see me, guilt weighed on me like an anvil. Not only was Greg gone, but Wainwright hadn't even gotten his usual morning walk today. It made me even more glad we'd taken one the night before.

"Odelia," Mom whispered as she entered the backyard, "there are lights on in the house."

"Yes," I confirmed as I made sure everything in the back was buttoned up for the night. "I left the light over the stove on, and one of the lamps in the living room is on a timer."

Then I heard Mom and Lorraine gasp. Turning back to the house, I saw them huddled together and shuffling back toward me as a solid unit. Then I gasped too. Framed in the doorway, backlit by the low light from the house, was a man. It certainly wasn't Greg, since he was standing. And whoever it was, was much smaller than Clark and didn't seem to be suffering from any ankle injury.

While we were waiting to be interviewed by the Santa Ana police as witnesses to the murder of Titan West, I'd called Greg and gave him a synopsis of what had gone down and how there was no way we could put Lorraine on a plane today. To say he wasn't pleased would be a gross understatement. He was still at the hospital ER. Clark had indeed broken his ankle. It wasn't a bad break and the doctor was hoping it would heal without surgery. He was expected to be released soon. If Greg hadn't been in a public place, I'm sure I would have gotten a loud and colorful earful. Actually, two earfuls, the other from Clark, but Greg said he was pretty groggy from painkillers. As soon as Clark was released, Boomer was going to take them back to Clark's place. Poor Greg. What should have been an easy annual trip was turning into a nightmare with him at the center, the hub of a wheel trying to micromanage broken spokes. Still, I convinced him that we were all okay here and were merely witnesses in Titan's murder, not suspects. The latter didn't mollify him much because he kept arguing that we had no business in Santa Ana in the first place. The call ended with him saying Clark was being released and they would call later. That was five hours ago, and I hadn't heard a word since. The silence worried me more than the arguments.

Staring at the person in the doorway, it struck me like a lightning bolt that Wainwright wasn't barking at him. In fact, Wainwright seemed right at home with this stranger's presence. I relaxed, realizing it wasn't a stranger and thinking it must be Chris Fowler, Greg's right-hand man from the print shop. Greg might have called him to look in on us, and Chris had a copy of our house key since he housesat for us when we traveled. Wainwright loved Chris, who wasn't a big guy. "Chris, is that you?" I asked tentatively.

"Wrong, little mama."

I gasped again and took several steps forward. "Willie?"

"In the flesh." He chuckled. "I hear you three have been busy, so come on in and relax."

Mom put a hand out and grabbed my arm. "Is that Mr. Carter?"

When Mom first met Willie Proctor, we'd palmed him off as Willie Carter, Greg's cousin and the black sheep of his family that no one talked about. But my mother is no dummy. Earlier this year she'd pieced it all together and had researched Willie Proctor, discovering that he'd stolen millions from investors in his company years ago. Willie had paid the money back, but he was still a criminal hunted by the authorities.

"That's Willie Carter," she told Lorraine without waiting for an answer from me. "A distant cousin of Greg's." I saw Lorraine relax considerably as we made our way across the patio to the back door where Willie waited with a warm smile for them and a big hug for me.

"Is Sybil with you?" I asked after our embrace.

"No, she's at home," he answered as he got us bundled inside the house and closed the vertical blinds on the back slider. We usually left them open, but, as always, Willie was being cautious. I didn't even know where home was for Willie and his wife, Sybil. "I was in Phoenix on business," he continued. "Clark told me Greg would be in town, so I thought I could visit with him at the same time."

It was no surprise to me that neither Greg nor Clark had mentioned this to me on the phone earlier. It was an unspoken rule that we mentioned Willie on the phone as little as possible because these days you never knew who was listening. Early on in our nutty relationship, Willie had wanted to make sure we never knew how to reach him directly or where he was or lived so that when the police asked us, which they often did, we wouldn't have to lie. Before Clark went to work for his company, Willie just showed up, like a genie without us having to rub a magic lamp. Now Clark conjures him up when he's needed.

"So they sent you when Clark couldn't come?" I asked. I had put my tote bag down and was busying myself in the kitchen. Mom and Lorraine had opted for chicken noodle soup. I opened a couple of cans and poured them into a saucepan to heat while Willie stood at the counter. Lorraine was helping by getting out bowls, utensils, and crackers. Mom was seated at the kitchen table. She looked long past exhausted; as soon as she ate, I was going to try herding her into bed. Once the soup was heating, I tossed both Muffin and Wainwright some treats for being so good today and set out fresh water and kibble for both of them.

"I offered," Willie said, "and it eased their minds. Aren't you happy to see me?" He grinned. He looked good. I hadn't seen Willie in a while. His hair was thinner and he was just as wiry as ever, but there was less of the hunted animal look about his eyes. He was tan and not wearing his usual glasses. Agewise he was somewhere between Clark and me, making him in his late fifties or on the brink of sixty.

"No glasses?" I asked as I stirred the soup.

"Laser surgery," he answered. "I'd wanted to do it for years but never got around to it. Last year Sybil gave it to me as a birthday gift." He smiled. He'd met Sybil while helping me get my mother out of a pickle, the first of many since she'd come back into my life. Sybil was divorced, and Willie was a widower. Both like to color outside the lines, making them well-suited to each other. About a year ago Clark had insisted on taking Greg and me to a luxury cabin in the mountains as a treat. When we got there, we found Willie and Sybil already unpacked and enjoying a cocktail. We had a lovely four-day weekend together, although I felt guilty that we had lied to Mom about Clark going with us. She might have wanted to come along otherwise, but we had sold it as a romantic getaway. We had taken Wainwright with us but shuffled Muffin off to stay with Mom.

"Sybil's well?" I asked.

"Very well," he said. "She says we need to plan another trip soon. Maybe someplace like Hawaii or Mexico."

I smiled. "Sounds good." I ladled soup into the bowls. "You joining us for dinner?"

"Thanks, but I already ate. I will take a beer, if you don't mind." Willie ferried the full bowls to the table while I snagged a beer from the fridge.

When the four of us were all settled at the table, we filled Willie in on what we knew about everything that had happened. When we were done, Willie announced, "Titan West was trouble—or rather, he was in a lot of trouble. But I don't think you're surprised by that, considering he was gunned down."

The three of us stopped eating and stared at him, waiting for more. Lorraine asked, "How do you know that?"

I was wondering what to say to her when Mom said, "Willie does a lot of security work, Lorraine, like your father. He's got all kinds of connections." I saw Willie and Mom exchange glances. She winked at him. He winked back. Now that Mom knew the truth about him, she was obviously enjoying all the cloak and dagger.

"That I do," Willie said. "My sources tell me that he was laundering money through his booking agency for a guy he met years ago when he needed to borrow money. The word on the street is the guy who took him out is not only a loan shark but a drug dealer who uses his debtors to launder money, even long after they pay off their debt."

"Titan didn't look like he was strapped for cash," I said, remembering the nice building and car.

"He may not have been now," Willie told me, "but once these guys get their hooks into you, they don't let go."

"So the police know this?" asked Lorraine.

"I doubt it," he answered dryly. He took a sip of his beer.

"Then we need to tell them," Lorraine insisted.

"No, we don't, Lorraine," he told her. "The police will discover it on their own once they dig into Titan's books and dealings. But even then it may not lead them directly to the guy who took him out, especially if they took the laptop and box of documents when they killed him. This has nothing to do with you, and the more distance you put between yourselves and this matter, the better." He turned to me. "Did you get a good look at the gunmen?"

"Just the driver of the car," I said. "He was young, with brown skin, but I don't think he was Latino or black—maybe Middle Eastern or something like that. His hair was thick and black. That's about it."

Willie nodded. "The people Titan was mixed up with are Armenian, based out of Glendale, so that fits."

Mom had been quietly downing her soup. As the food hit her system, the color was slowly returning to her lined cheeks and the spark to her eyes. Ah, the powers of chicken noodle soup. "Do you think maybe it was this Armenian gang who killed Cydney Fox?" Mom asked as she finished and pushed her bowl away from her. "Maybe Boaz found out about them and took off before they got to him. That poor Fox woman might have gotten in the way."

"Could be," agreed Willie. "That Shankleman fellow could have gotten wind of the problem and took off before he got caught in the crossfire." Willie looked at me. "Didn't you say that Oxman was about to run?"

I nodded and played with the puddle of soup left in my bowl with my spoon. "Yes, it looked like he was heading out, and fast."

As I said the last word, I glanced at Mom. Our eyes locked briefly. I'm sure she was thinking of Oxman's slashed tires too. She looked down into her soup, pale again. She'd only wanted to slow Oxman down for the police, not make him a sitting duck for killers.

"And Titan also asked if we were sent to kill him," I continued. "I'm now assuming he meant this gang kingpin and not Shankleman, as we originally thought."

"Humph," Mom snorted. "Boaz would never kill anyone, and he's certainly not a drug guy." Color returned to her cheeks.

"Grace is right," Willie agreed. "My contacts came up clean on him and on the Fox woman. Oxman came up clean, too, except for a few old arrests for being drunk and disorderly, but that's about it." Willie took a drag from his beer. "It looks like the trouble was all on Titan, and when the others found out, they took off rather than get caught standing too close to him."

Lorraine stared at Willie. "How could you have checked that out when we just told you all this?"

I wanted to tell Lorraine that Willie had magic powers, so just go with it, but before I could, Willie told her with a patient smile, "Your father and Greg told me everything when I saw them earlier, not just about Titan West being killed. I had my people check into everyone." Muffin hopped up into Willie's lap and settled in for a nap. He stroked her gently. Wainwright was on his bed having his own nap.

"Okay," Mom said, placing both hands on the table, "so let's say that the boys in the band found out about the trouble Titan was in and decided to take off. Cydney Fox went to Shankleman's to see him. Maybe she had a key. Maybe they were seeing each other or something like that, and she ended up in the wrong place at the wrong time."

"That sounds feasible," Lorraine agreed.

Mom sighed and reached for her tea. "Too bad we never reached Tuttle. I'd like to know if he took off too."

"Tuttle?" Willie asked.

"That's the third member of Acid Storm," I told him. "The young guy. We tried calling his number but just got voicemail."

I got up from the table. "Would anyone like more soup? There's some left."

"I would," Lorraine said, holding out her bowl like Dickens's Oliver. Mom shook her head. I turned the flame on under the saucepan while I retrieved Lorraine's bowl. While the soup reheated I ran information around in my head. Something wasn't clicking. I stirred the soup, watching the fat noodles and sliced carrots swirl in the remaining broth. When it was heated, I poured what was left in the pan into Lorraine's bowl, splattering some on the counter in the process. I stared down at the drops of broth scattered on my kitchen counter as a lightbulb went off in my tired brain.

"I don't think Cydney Fox was killed by the Armenian gang," I said as I placed the bowl back in front of Lorraine. The three of them turned to me, waiting for an explanation for my theory. Instead, I cleared my bowl and my mother's from the table and placed them in the sink, giving myself time to gather my thoughts into a tidy explanation.

"And?" Mom asked with her usual impatience.

I turned, leaned against the counter, and faced them. "I don't think she was killed by the gang," I repeated. "I think she was killed by someone else. Her murder seemed more personal. Titan's was business."

Three sets of eyes stared at me, waiting for me to make my case. "Why is that?" Willie asked, encouraging me to lay out my reasons.

"Detective Fehring told me that the Fox woman had been killed by several vicious blows to the head." I looked at Lorraine, wondering if maybe the conversation would be too much for her.

Blood drained from Lorraine's face at the memory. "It looked that way, yes," she confirmed. "Blood was everywhere, even on the walls." She pushed her second helping of soup away and slumped in her chair like a rag doll.

"Okay," I said, "vicious blows to someone's skull seems like a very personal thing to me. If she was killed by someone who had snuck in to take out Shankleman, wouldn't she have been killed cleanly, like with a gun fitted with a silencer, as Titan had been?"

"Excellent point, little mama," Willie said, giving me a wide grin. "You go to the head of the class."

Mom was holding her mug of tea between her hands. "Let me get this straight," she said. "If your theory is right, then there are two murderers? One for Fox and one for Titan?"

"Yes." I went to the table and reached for Mom's mug. "Do you want a refill, Mom?"

"Just some more hot water," she said, handing me her mug.

I turned on the hot water kettle that sat on the stove. It was still warm from making Mom's tea earlier, so it wouldn't take long to bring to another boil. "So if the Armenian gang took out Titan, who killed Cydney Fox?" I turned to look at everyone, hoping someone had some ideas. They all looked as blank as walls.

"But what about Art?" Mom asked, her voice shaking with new fear. "You don't think he was killed like Fox, do you? You know, collateral damage?" She seemed about to cry.

The kettle started chirping, getting ready to whistle. I took it off the stove, poured fresh hot water into Mom's mug, and took it back to the table, joining everyone again.

"Mom, I really don't know what happened to Art," I told her kindly, "but I sure hope he was nowhere near that place that night. The thing is, usually, but not all the time, when someone bludgeons another to death in that manner, it's an emotional thing. Either the murderer was angry at Fox or they wanted to kill Shankleman and got angry because he wasn't home and took out their frustration on that poor woman."

"What about the idea that Shankleman killed Fox?" Willie asked.

Mom nearly flew out of her chair in a rage at the idea. "Boaz would never do such a thing! He's not violent at all."

"Grace," Willie said in a soothing, practical voice, "even the calmest of people can become irrational and dangerous at times."

Out of the corner of my eye, I caught Lorraine watching my mother, a puzzled look on her face. "Grandma," Lorraine finally said, "are you and this Boaz guy a thing?"

"Huh?" my mother said, turning wide owl eyes on Lorraine in surprise. "What do you mean by that?"

Lorraine might be on to something—something that never occurred to me in spite of all of Mom's defensive behavior on Shankleman's behalf. "Mom," I said, "Lorraine's asking if you and Boaz Shankleman are seeing each other. You know, are you dating?"

"Or maybe," Lorraine said with a smug smile to her grandmother, "you have a crush on him. Are you an Acid Storm groupie?" She giggled.

Okay. Lorraine obviously didn't know her grandmother like I did. Asking Mom if she and Shankleman were seeing each other was one thing. Asking Grace Littlejohn if she was a rock groupie was quite another, and the remark garnered the response I expected at the end of a long, tiring day: a meltdown, right at my kitchen table.

"A groupie?" Mom asked in a terse, strained voice, not taking her fiery eyes off of Lorraine. "Is that what you think of your grandmother?" Her look was withering, and it was working on Lorraine. She shrunk in her chair like a small child who'd been caught coloring on the walls. Willie had leaned back in his chair. His arms were crossed and his lips tight as he fought the urge to laugh. To him, this was good TV.

"Mom, calm down." I put a hand on her arm, hoping to ease the tension. "Lorraine was just wondering about your constant defense of Boaz, that's all. I was wondering about it myself. Even when Titan suggested something about him, you got all huffy."

Mom dragged her eyes off of Lorraine and fixed them on me. The outrage was gone, replaced by sadness. "Boaz was the very first friend I made when I got to Seaside," she told us. "A lot of those old folks, especially the old biddies who rule the place like high school divas, have never cared for me and are always running to Mona with gossip."

I sat up straight in my chair. "But why?"

"Don't look so surprised, Odelia," Mom said. "We both know I'm not exactly Miss Congeniality. But Boaz and I hit it off from the start. We met at the AA meeting they hold there. Since then, he's always had my back. Because of him I was finally able to make some good friends and settle in there." Her voice cracked a little, like a fine fissure in a china cup. "He and Art—both of them—have been my friends from the beginning, and now they're both missing." A strangled sob escaped from her lips. "If you'll excuse me," she said, getting slowly to her feet, "I'm going to bed. It's been a long day."

Willie, Lorraine, and I stood up with her. I held Mom's arm in support. Lorraine came to Mom's side. "I'm so sorry, Grandma," she said to Mom in a small voice, giving her a short hug. "Let me help you." I let loose of Mom's arm as Lorraine took it. Without protest, Mom let Lorraine guide her down the hallway to the guest room. Usually my mother is full of piss and vinegar. Tonight, watching her shuffle down the hall with help from Lorraine, I noticed how small and vulnerable she really was, with or without a switchblade.

Willie and I sat back down and remained silent for a few moments. He drank his beer while I thought about Mom's revelation at Seaside. I'd known it had been rough when she first moved in there. Mom didn't make friends easily because of her prickly nature and rough edges, but I had no idea how tough it had been. If I had, I would have intervened. But that's probably why she didn't tell me. Mom liked to fight her own battles.

I got up and started to clear the table. "Would you like another beer, Willie?"

"No, thanks, I'm good." He was peeling the label off the bottle. I smiled. Greg did the same thing when he was thinking. "We need to find Boaz and Art, at least for Grace's sake," he announced.

I nodded my agreement. "Honestly, I don't care who killed Cydney Fox or Titan West, as long as it wasn't Shankleman, again for

Mom's sake." I paused, thinking about sweet Art Franklin. "I'm worried too that Art was collateral damage. Maybe Fox's killer crossed his path and took him out."

"There's no body, though," he pointed out. "The killer wouldn't have killed Art, then dragged his body off. If he got in the way, as I imagine Fox did, he'd have been left where he dropped."

"I still think we're looking at two different killers."

Willie was quiet while he contemplated my theory again. "I tend to agree with you, Odelia. If it were the Armenians, they would have just shot her. Not to say drug gangs don't beat people to death, but not people who are simply in the way."

He put the bottle down on the table and started going through the Marigold printout. When we were telling Willie about our busy day, Mom had taken it out of her purse, where she'd stashed it while we were on the road. "I think I'm going to pay this Simon Tuttle a visit tonight, as well as see if I can dig anything up on him that's not on this." He got up. "You ladies okay here without me for a few hours?"

"What do you think?" I asked with sarcasm.

Willie winked at me. "I was sent to watch over you, but I think I'd be of more help following up on this stuff."

I winked back. "I won't tell if you don't."

I had just shuttled dinner dishes to the sink when Willie's phone vibrated softly. He pulled it out and read the display. "You expecting anyone?" he asked me.

"At this hour?" A glance at the clock on the microwave told me it was after ten.

"My guy outside said a middle-aged Asian guy is heading up your walk." Just then our doorbell rang and Wainwright charged the door, barking.

Of course Willie would have brought a bodyguard. He always traveled with one. When I first met him years ago, his constant companion was Enrique, a handsome and smart young Mexican. But I knew that since then, Enrique had gotten his master's degree in International Finance and was working for Willie in an executive capacity. He was also married now, with a young family.

Willie indicated for me to see who was at the door while he slipped into the kitchen area, out of sight but within earshot.

"Wainwright, down," I said to our dog, grabbing him by the collar while I looked out the door's peephole. It was indeed a middle-aged Asian man, small and trim, with gray streaked hair and a familiar face, angular and wearing thick-framed glasses. I turned toward the kitchen and saw Willie peeking out from around the small divider wall. "It's okay," I told him in a loud whisper. "I know him."

Mom and Lorraine came into view from the hallway. Mom was in her nightgown and robe, but Lorraine was still dressed. "Who's at the door at this time of night, Odelia?" Mom asked.

"It's Kevin from Seaside," I told her.

"Oh no, something's happened to Art," she said, slightly staggering. Lorraine put a supportive arm around her.

"We don't know that, Mom," I said to her as I unlocked the door. "And I doubt they'd send someone here to tell you."

"Evening," Kevin Wong said apologetically as soon as I opened the door. Kevin was one of the guards at Seaside. He usually manned the front gate for the second shift.

"Kevin, what are you doing here?" I asked. "Is something wrong at Seaside?"

He sighed deeply and shifted from foot to foot in discomfort. "Is Grace here? I was told to come here to look for her."

"What's the matter, Kevin?" Mom asked, stepping forward as she clutched her robe tighter together. Willie was out in the open now but still remained near the back door.

"Please come in, Kevin," I said, opening the door wider.

He hesitated, looking down at Wainwright, who was now quietly standing guard.

"It's okay," I assured him. "Wainwright won't bother you." I pulled Wainwright away from the door and told him to go lay down. As soon as I let loose his collar, he trotted back to his comfy bed.

But Kevin Wong still didn't step inside, and I didn't think it was because of the dog. His eyes were cast down as he continued his two-step on the landing. I thought about Milton and how he behaved the same way in front of Mona. Kevin wasn't in his Seaside guard uniform. He wore light khakis and a blue knit shirt. Reaching into a back pocket, he pulled out a business-size envelope and held it out in Mom's direction. "I'm sorry, Grace, but Mona said I had to deliver this to you tonight on my way home." I could see that the envelope bore the logo for Seaside Retirement Community.

Mom didn't make any move to take the envelope from Kevin. Instead, she said to me, "Would you see what in the hell that woman wants now?"

As soon as I took the envelope, Kevin apologize again and made to leave, like the missive contained a bomb. "Wait a minute, Kevin," I said to him. "I want to ask you something. It won't take long."

I could tell he didn't want to linger, so I got right down to it. "I saw Milton this morning, and he said he was the guard on duty last night and the night before; is that true?"

Kevin nodded. "Yes. He has third shift. Our shifts overlap by about thirty minutes every evening. Same with the morning shift and mine—there's always a small overlap so that one of us can do a quick walk of the property while the other's there."

"Who did the walk of the property last night and the night before?" I asked.

"I did, both nights," Kevin answered. "Usually it's the one going off shift who does it. I like making the rounds," he added. "It gets the kinks out before I go home."

"Is that the only time you leave the booth?"

"Pretty much," he answered. "The guard shack is a decent size, with its own small bathroom and mini fridge, and we have a TV. Some of us will leave it to walk around the front of the property, but we don't go far in case a visitor or a delivery comes up."

I leaned against the door and again thought about Greg and his ranting about cooling the great outdoors, but it was obvious Kevin had no plans to come in. With each question he was edging back inch by inch. "I understand the security camera at the front gate is on the fritz. Is that also true?"

He nodded and shifted back a baby step. "Yeah." He paused, then added, "A complete upgrade has been in the works for quite a while, but between the homeowners' association and management it's been bogged down for a few months—over cost, I think."

"They want to put cameras all over the place," Mom chimed in, "and a lot of the residents feel it's an invasion of their privacy."

Now that there'd been a murder on the property, I wondered how many of the dissenting residents would line up to welcome a more extensive security system.

I smiled at the guard. "One more question, Kevin. Did you see Cydney Fox come to Seaside the other day, the day of her death? Or weren't you on duty when she arrived?"

He gave this question some thought as he scooted back again, ready to make his escape on the promise it was my last question. "I remember her coming through the gate. It was about my dinner time. She must have Mr. Shankleman's passcode or someone else's because I never had to call and announce her like a normal guest whenever she visited."

"Thank you, Kevin," I told him. "I really appreciate you answering my questions."

"You're not going to tell Seaside I talked to you, are you?" he asked with worry. "We were told not to talk to anyone but the police."

"Don't worry," I assured him. "No one in this house will squeal on you. We're not exactly fans of Mona's." I glanced back at Lorraine, Mom, and Willie. All of them nodded their agreement of silence, including Willie, who hadn't even met the woman.

Kevin went down our walk at a good pace and climbed into a small sedan parked at the curb. I looked up and down the street, trying to spot Willie's bodyguard but couldn't, so I shut the door.

Envelope gripped in my hand, I returned to the kitchen. Lorraine and Mom had resumed their spots, and so had Willie. I ran a fingernail under the sealed flap, and everyone gathered around as if it was a notice that we'd won something. But if this was from Mona D'Angelo, then, if anything, it was a booby prize.

My eyes scanned the neatly printed formal letter, signed by Mona in her official capacity at the bottom. As I read, my blood pressure spiked, rising with each concise word.

"What does it say, Odelia?" Mom asked.

"It says," I began, then stopped to take a deep breath, which I held and let out slowly. "It says that the management of Seaside Retirement Community, and I quote, 'in the interest of the safety of its residents, held an emergency meeting and determined Lorraine Littlejohn, granddaughter of resident Grace Littlejohn, to be a threat to the well-being of the community.'"

"It says that about *me*?" asked Lorraine, her eyes wide with disbelief.

"It does," I confirmed as I skimmed the letter again. "Furthermore, it says that you are banned from stepping foot on the property of Seaside, even as a day guest."

Lorraine put her elbows on the table and buried her face in her hands. "I've never even been thrown out of a bar, not even in college. Or from a movie theater for talking."

"Don't you worry, Lorraine," Mom said, giving Lorraine's arm a comforting pat. "I've been thrown out of a lot of places. Think of it as kind of a badge of honor—like that Hawthorne fellow's scarlet letter."

Willie and I stared at Mom, then at each other. He was clearly amused. I was not.

"Mom's right," I said, folding and stuffing the letter back into the envelope with righteous huffiness, "at least about the not worrying part. We'll straighten this out, and you can stay here as long as you want. You too, Mom."

My mother poked the envelope that now lay on the table. "Does that thing say I can't live there anymore?"

"No," I answered, "it doesn't. And as I recall from the regulations of the place, they can't outright evict you since you own the townhouse, but they can take you to court and try to force you out." I paused. I didn't want to worry Mom, but we did need to be realistic in case Mona became that nasty. "I'll have Steele look over the regulations for you."

"I'm sorry, Grandma," Lorraine said. The poor thing was near tears. "I shouldn't have climbed through that window."

"Oh, honey," Mom said to her gently, "it's not your fault. I should never have encouraged you." Now that was something I could get behind, but I kept my mouth shut.

"You two look beat," I said to Mom and Lorraine. "Why don't you turn in?"

With a tired nod, Mom got to her feet. Lorraine followed, and the two of them wandered back down the hallway. Once they were out of earshot, I said to Willie, "I'm going with you."

"When?" he looked surprised.

"Tonight."

"Like hell you are!" His voice might have been barely above a whisper, but there was no mistaking the force behind it. "What happened to you not caring about those murders, just with finding Grace's friends?"

"I changed my mind. I'm a woman; it's what I do." I got up and finished putting the dinner dishes into the dishwasher. "If you're going to see Simon Tuttle, I want to be there. I want to see for myself if he acts all squirrelly like Oxman did." I turned, pointed a finger at Willie, and shook it to make my point. "And I think we should stop by Seaside and check out Art's place. Nighttime would be best for that since apparently their guards are asleep at the wheel during that time. Mom has a copy of Art's key. I'm pretty sure I know where she keeps it."

"And if I say no?" he asked, leaning back in his chair casually, as if I'd just said I wanted him to go shopping with me.

I wiped my wet hands on a dishtowel. "Then I'll just go without you."

"And what about them?" He pointed in the direction of the hallway.

"They'll be fine here by themselves," I told him. "Both will be out like lights in ten minutes after the day we've had, but if you're worried, you can always leave your bodyguard here to watch over them." I moved over to the table. "Like we agreed earlier, I won't tell if you don't."

Willie got to his feet and entered my personal space. I'm only five foot one or five foot two, depending on my slouch. Willie was only a few inches taller and probably fifty to sixty pounds lighter, but he was still intimidating. He wasn't a killer like my friend Mother, the hit woman, but he did work in and understand dark underground circles. Still, I did not back up. I held my ground, turning to grab my bag and car keys from the counter. "Ready?"

"And what if Grace and Lorraine discover you're gone and decide to go out on their own?" he asked. "You know that would occur to Grace in a heartbeat."

I spied Mom's car keys on the counter and scooped them up with the hand that held my own car keys. "Not if I take their wheels." I held my key-filled hand out to Willie with pride.

Too much pride, because in a swift grab of his own, he'd cleaned my hand of both Mom's car keys and my own and shoved them into one of his pockets. "Go to bed, little mama. I'll give you a full report in the morning." He gave me a small crooked grin. "I promise."

"But what about Art's place?" I asked, tamping down my frustration. "Aren't you going to look there?"

"We are, but don't worry, we'll get in without the spare key." He stepped forward and gave me a brotherly peck on the cheek. "I promised Greg and Clark that I'd look after you, and that does not include allowing you to run all over town with me."

Instead of going out the back, Willie headed for the front door. Wainwright got up and followed him, tail wagging, to say goodbye. At the door, Willie bent down and gave the friendly dog a healthy rub behind the ears. "Keep an eye on her, Wainwright. If she tries to leave, bite her."

SIXTEEN

Simon Tuttle lived in an ordinary apartment building in Newport Beach. What made it extraordinary was that it was right on the beach. It was about fifteen miles south from Seal Beach, where we lived. Unlike Oxman, Tuttle must be doing okay moneywise. Although the building wasn't fancy, its location would demand a pretty sizeable rent. It was a tidy two-story building with just four apartments, two upstairs and two downstairs, painted seashell pink. A carport with slots for four vehicles faced the street, giving all of the apartments an ocean view.

Peeking between Tuttle's building and the one next to it, which was similar but painted a soft seafoam green, I could see that a wide public walkway separated the building's miniscule front area from the public beach, and a low fence delineated the end of the building's property, which was a small front patio. It was the same with the building next door. It seemed to be a common setup. During the day it must be very noisy with all of the summer beach foot traffic, but at least public access to the beach didn't run past the building on either side. I had noted when I arrived that the public access was a few buildings down. The public beach was closed for the night, so there were few people around to compete with the calming sound of the waves. I stopped and breathed in the warm, salty air. We live near the beach, but this was the beach, one of my favorite places.

I knew Tuttle's apartment was unit B and hoped that meant it was downstairs. It would be easier to sneak around and check it out if it were, but first I went back to examine the car port, where there were only two cars parked. I had no idea what Tuttle drove and looked for some sort of identifier linking the individual spots to specific apartments. There were none. Crap!

I started back down the narrow walkway between the two buildings, then stopped halfway, just before a downstairs window, and listened. Next to it but a little higher up was a tiny window of frosted glass. These were most likely bedroom and bathroom windows, but of which unit I couldn't tell. Both were dark, and the bedroom window had the blinds drawn shut. A soft light came through the corresponding windows on the next building, and I could hear someone taking a shower. I'd keep my blinds shut too if I were this close to my neighbors. I stretched my arms out and could easily touch both buildings with my palms flat against them. I made a mental note to be super quiet. Not only were the buildings closer together, but being this close to the beach it was probably a good guess that none of them had central air and relied upon open windows and sea breezes for relief from the August heat.

There was no way I could identify unit B without going to the front. It could even be on the other side of the building, which would make the dark apartment window I was under unit A. But once I knew which apartment was his, then what? I wasn't sure. Should I just knock and start peppering him with questions when he opened the door? Or would he, like Oxman, have already taken off? Or maybe he was out somewhere kicking back a few beers, oblivious to the disappearance of Shankleman and the murder of Titan West, although the murder had been splashed across tonight's news, along with the murder of Cydney Fox and the disappearance of Shankleman, who was being sought for questioning.

Many possibilities scurried across my mind, including that of finding a dead body inside. Decisions. Decisions. My heart told me to turn and go home. My nosiness and determination to get to the bottom of things kicked me in the ass and got me moving forward again, foolhardy or not.

From the moment I arrived, I had been on the lookout for any sign of Willie or any car doing surveillance on the building, including the bad guys. I'd spotted nothing but didn't think Willie and his people would be out in the open waving flags. Finding no one at home, Willie already might have come and gone. Finding Tuttle at home, Willie might already be inside pumping him for information. As for anyone sent to pop Tuttle, well, I didn't want to think about that beyond hoping they would just wait for him to leave and not come to the apartment. I thought about watching Titan being gunned down in broad daylight and shivered even though the night was warm. Outside of using silencers, they weren't that subtle.

Go home, Odelia, my inner voice pleaded. *Go home, curl up with Muffin and Wainwright, dream pleasant dreams. Let Willie handle this.* I was still debating this when a hand clamped over my mouth, and I was grabbed from behind.

I struggled to break free. Kicking back with my legs, I connected with flesh and bone but not hard enough to make a difference. My efforts didn't even produce so much as a grunt from my attacker. Another arm from behind wrapped around my body, pinning my arms to my torso like a boa constrictor. I tried to scream through the tight fingers. It came out like a soft sexual moan. Not the sound I was trying for. *Oh gawd!* The Armenian gang had come for Tuttle and found me lurking instead. If it was the same guy as the driver in Titan's hit, he'd recognize me for sure—and a bullet would be put in my brain for sure. I almost fainted in fright.

My assailant turned me around with a small two-step so I was facing Tuttle's building, but he stayed behind me, still holding tight. Another man stepped in front of me. In the narrow space, the three of us were cozy, sandwiched between two stucco buildings in the dark. I shivered and felt tears starting to well in my eyes. The man in front of me leaned forward like he was going to sniff me.

"If Buzz lets you go, little mama, will you be quiet?" he asked in a barely audible whisper. My legs nearly turned to jelly in relief and I nodded up and down with fast, short jerks, my eyes wide as they tried to focus in the dark to confirm the voice's identity.

The hand slipped away from my mouth, and the vicelike grip relaxed from around my torso but kept hold of my upper arm. Another silent gesture from Willie, and the man behind me started guiding me out of the walkway and back toward the street, using the hold on my arm like a rein on a horse. I tried to jerk away, but he only tightened his grip and urged me forward. I half expected him to gently kick my flanks.

"I didn't see you," I whispered to Willie. "I thought you'd come and gone."

"Shhhh," Willie said.

The three of us quickly exited the space between the buildings and headed across the street to an older black SUV. I was deposited in the back. Willie climbed in after me. The guy named Buzz took the driver's seat.

"I told you I should have asked for her spare key too," Willie said to Buzz. From my spot behind him in the dark vehicle, the driver's hair appeared black and thick, his skin dark. Instead of turning around, Buzz looked at me in the rearview mirror and chuckled in agreement. From the little I saw in the reflection, I guessed him to be young, in his late twenties to early thirties, and with sharp, dark eyes.

"FYI," I said with sarcasm, "when you took my keys, you also took the spare keys I had to Greg's van and my mother's car. My car's spare key is with Greg in Arizona. Believe me, more extras will be made and hidden in the house, starting tomorrow."

Both Buzz and Willie chuckled, but it was cut short when a car coming down the street slowed down near Tuttle's place. They watched the vehicle, the inside of the SUV thick with anticipation, until it turned into a carport a few buildings down. Then the air lightened as the tension deflated.

"So how did you get here?" Willie asked. "I know you didn't walk. Did you enlist Mike Steele or your friends the Washingtons?" He glanced out the window, expecting to see my ride waiting for me.

I shook my head. "I took Uber."

The air inside the SUV grew tense again, then both Willie and Buzz broke into soft laughter. "You took *Uber* to get here?" Willie asked with surprise.

I slipped a hand inside my purse, which was a small cross-body style I'd grabbed out of my closet at the last minute, choosing it over my usual big tote for convenience. It was just big enough to hold some cash, ID, and my cell phone and keys, if I had them. And when it was worn cross-body, it kept out of the way of any movement and even deterred thieves. I used it whenever we went places with large crowds, like concerts or amusement parks. Considering how I was grabbed, it was a good thing I had it or else my belongings would have ended up strewn all over the walkway.

The small bag even held a small canister of pepper spray—something Greg had bought me ages ago for my safety but which I seldom carried, much to his dismay. Whenever I did have it in my purse, I was always worried that I would spray it accidentally and end up doing my purse or me more harm than a bad guy. But tonight I thought it might come in handy and grabbed it from my nightstand drawer on the way out. I fingered the pepper spray, thinking about Mom and her switchblade. I guess we all have our security blankets. If the guy who grabbed me hadn't pinned my arms or snuck up on me, I might have managed to nail him with it. Or not.

Instead of the pepper spray, I pulled out my cell phone, I held it up to show its face. "See," I said to Willie, "the app is right there on my phone—easy peasy. But I will take my keys back." I held out a hand to Willie. "You also took my house keys." When Willie hesitated, I wiggled my extended fingers. "Come on."

Willie handed me both my keys and my mother's, then glanced at the guy in the front and said, "How rude of me. Let me make the introductions. Odelia, this is Buzz, one of my employees—and

Enrique's cousin, by the way. Buzz, this is the infamous Odelia Grey."

"I've heard a lot about you," Buzz told me, his eyes in the mirror flashing with amusement, clear even in the darkened vehicle. His voice, unlike his cousin's, was free of any Hispanic accent.

"From Enrique?" I asked.

Buzz laughed. "From everyone. Enrique, Willie, Clark, even Enrique's mother, my *tía* Esmerelda." He laughed again. "Even your husband."

I had once saved Enrique's life. As a reward, his mother, Esmerelda, had put me on her annual tamale gift list for life. Between her and my cleaning lady, Cruz, Greg and I never bought tamales. I had the pleasure of meeting Esmerelda once. She was a lovely woman, fiercely loyal to her family and to Willie. The fact that Buzz knew Clark didn't surprise me, but Greg?

"You know Greg?" I asked him.

Willie answered the question instead. "Of course." It was all he said, giving no further explanation of when or how many times they'd crossed paths. His words could imply many things, like it happened often or maybe just recently while Greg was in Arizona visiting Clark. But this visit wasn't the first one Greg had made to Arizona without me. What in the hell were Clark and Greg doing when I wasn't with them? My husband had some explaining to do when he got home.

"So," I said, changing the subject back to why we were all there in the first place, "what's going on with Simon Tuttle?"

"Nothing yet," Willie told me. "His apartment is the one on the left, downstairs. You were right under his windows. He left on foot shortly before you got here, and it doesn't look like anyone else is there. He could have just walked to the store or was meeting someone. He wasn't carrying anything that we could see." Willie paused, then added, "We were about to let ourselves inside when you showed up."

"So let's get going," I said as I reached for the door handle to get out of the SUV. "Before he gets back, just in case he did just go to the store."

"Not so fast," Willie said, grabbing my shoulder and pulling me back. "You're not going anywhere." He pointed at the phone in my hand. "You have your house keys now, so just call Uber to come get you." He fixed me with a steely eye. "We'll wait."

"No," I said with defiance. "I'm staying."

"No," Willie volleyed back. "You're not."

I took a deep breath. "Look, we can do this all day, Willie, or I can pretend to go home and just circle back."

"Or," Willie countered, "I could have Buzz bind and gag you and leave you here while we check out the apartment."

I looked at him with wide eyes of disbelief. "You wouldn't dare."

"Not only would I do it," Willie said with a half-smile, "but Greg would probably buy me a bottle of good scotch if I did."

I stared into the eyes of the wanted felon and weighed my possibilities. Willie wasn't the sort to make idle threats for fun, and he was right about Greg. He and Clark had sent Willie here to protect me, so they'd probably reward him for trussing me up like a turkey. Quickly, I weighed my options and found few.

"What about Art?" I asked as a diversion. "We need to find out what happened to him. I can get you past the guard at Seaside and show you the way."

He thought about that. With a deep sigh, Willie gave in a tiny bit but not without a compromise. "If you promise to keep your ass here while Buzz and I handle this Tuttle guy, you can come with us to the old folks' place."

While I considered the deal, Buzz perked up. "Boss," he whispered to Willie. "He's back."

All three of us turned our heads to watch a young guy come down the street and turn into the walkway we'd just vacated. He was skinny and had longish hair. His walk was a bit drag-ass as he carried a six-pack of either soda or beer in one hand and a grocery bag in the other. My money was on the beverages being of an alcoholic variety.

"Is that him?" I asked. From across the street and with only weak streetlights to help, I couldn't tell if the guy we were watching was Simon Tuttle or not, but next to me Willie nodded.

"You stay here," he ordered, and with another nod, this one in Buzz's direction, they both quietly exited the SUV and started across the street toward the apartment building.

I started fidgeting with impatience the moment they left. As I watched them slither between the two buildings, staying close to the walls, my desire to join them ramped up until I nearly levitated out of my seat with electricity. Or maybe it was caused from the buzz you get when you head into a second night without much sleep.

They were both dressed in dark tee shirts and jeans, and as soon as they melted into the darkness, I quickly eased myself out of the passenger's side of the SUV and stayed low, just in case one of them glanced this way. I was going to catch hell from Willie, but I didn't care. I duck-walked along the curb, staying behind the SUV, then waddled toward the parked car ahead of ours, using it as further cover. Once out of sight, I stood and crossed the street, dodging a Mini Cooper that nearly clipped me because I wasn't paying attention to traffic.

Instead of the wider walkway, I took the one on the right-hand side of the house. It was very narrow, barely wide enough for me to pass through without my shoulders touching the buildings. It seemed to be a service walkway for the gas and electric meters for Tuttle's apartment building and the one adjacent to it. As I started down it, I walked in a zigzag pattern to avoid making contact with the meters jutting out from both buildings. Lights were on in both buildings but, as with the other side, all the blinds were drawn.

I was halfway down the side of the building when a figure surprised me at the far opening, running toward me at a high speed. In such a small space, we collided before I could even make a peep of protest, tumbling in a heap to the ground. I let out a small cry as the concrete bit into one arm.

The guy scrambled to untangle himself from me, but before he could, someone pulled him off and rendered him unconscious. Another figure filled the walkway behind that one, and in the hazy light that leaked into the walkway from the upstairs windows I recognized Willie and Buzz. Buzz still had a hold on the guy who'd crashed into me. Willie squeezed past them and reached out a hand to help me up. With his other hand, he held a finger to his lips and glanced upward.

"Did you hear something?" we heard a voice say from one of the windows above us from the other building. A blind pulled back and a woman's face appeared briefly. Quickly, we squeezed ourselves flat against her building.

"Probably just someone taking a shortcut back to the street," a man's voice answered. The blinds closed.

Once I was on my feet, Willie said nothing but steered me down the walk toward the front, his grip a painful vice on my upper arm, testing my ability to remain quiet. He directed me to the open door of one of the downstairs apartments, most likely unit B, and dumped me on a modern sofa of black leather. He dashed out and returned with the unconscious guy between him and Buzz. They dropped him into an armchair next to the sofa. After one final look out the door, Willie shut it. It was quite late now, and there were no people around. The blinds on the large front window, the one with the spectacular view of the ocean, were already closed.

Willie looked from me to the unconscious man, who was starting to come around, letting out small mews and moans, his head thrown back and mouth open. Normally good natured, I could see that I was pressing Willie's patience and he wasn't sure who to deal with first. Buzz stood next to the guy, ready to render him unconscious again should the need arise.

"You promised to stay behind," Willie growled in my direction, deciding to take me on first.

"Not exactly," I told him, but my eyes were on the guy sprawled in the chair. "We hadn't gotten to the promise part yet," I reminded Willie. He growled again. In all my years of knowing Willie Proctor, he'd never gotten angry at me. Usually he handled tense situations with glib remarks and casualness. I studied him, wondering what had changed. He was married now but still on the run and operating from the underground. Even so, his enterprises were above board, or so Clark told us. Probably the one Clark worked for was, but I'm sure Willie still had other projects that weren't so straight and narrow. He knew people—people who didn't attend PTA meetings and squeeze tomatoes at the local grocery store. I needed to keep that in mind, kind of like I always had to remember that Elaine Powers, as nice as she seemed in person, had been a scary killer in reality. Willie wasn't a killer, but he knew killers, and Elaine had been wary of him, which said a lot. Not for the first time I wondered how I'd managed to dip a toe into this shadowy part of life that went on well out of sight of those PTA meetings and squished tomatoes.

"We are more than capable of handling Tuttle ourselves," Willie pressed. "Don't you think?"

"Of course, but that's not Simon Tuttle." I cut my eyes from the guy to Buzz, then to Willie.

"This is apartment B, and this is the right place," Willie said with emphasis.

"Maybe," I said, "but that's not Simon Tuttle. He's about the right age, and the hair and build are about the same, but I'm sure that's not him."

I reached into my bag and retrieved my phone. I had saved a photo of the current Acid Storm band to it. I thumbed my way to it, enlarged it, and presented the screen to Willie. He took the phone from me and studied the photo. Walking over to the chair, he showed the photo to Buzz. The guy's head was now drooping, chin to chest. Buzz grabbed him by the hair and yanked his head back so they could get a better look. The guy who wasn't Simon moaned and his eyes fluttered.

"It could be him," Buzz offered.

"Yeah, on a bad day," Willie snapped, "after being dragged behind a truck. Check him for ID."

While they did that, I got up and started inspecting the place. "Don't touch anything," Willie ordered. I nodded that I understood.

The place had a weird vibe to it. Not the apartment itself, which was sparsely furnished and decorated with a young, hip masculine feel, but the atmosphere in the place. It was a one bedroom apartment with the living room in the front with a galley kitchen separated by a counter. At the counter were two leather bar stools. The kitchen sink held a few dirty dishes, but none looked gunky with slime or moldy food, letting me know they hadn't been there long.

Stepping past the kitchen, I passed through a dressing area with a sink and vanity and linen closet. A small door led to a bathroom that held the toilet and a decent size stall shower with a glass door. In the shower area was a high small frosted glass window. The shower was dry, so neither Tuttle or the guy out front had used it recently. Certainly not the guy out front judging from his odor, which was pretty rank. The vanity in the dressing area had a cut out beneath one half of it, the half not directly under the sink. It contained a small trash can that held nothing but a few tissues and an empty toilet paper roll. I knelt down and examined the floor in the cut out section, then got up and continued my exploration.

Passing through the dressing area I came to an average size bedroom. On the walls in both the living area and bedroom were framed art posters and music memorabilia. The place wasn't squeaky clean, but it wasn't dirty beyond normal use. Simon Tuttle wasn't a neat freak, but he did take care of his place. The guy out in the living room was unkempt and raggedy. Also, the front area smelled faintly of cigarette smoke; the back area did not. Tuttle didn't appear to be a smoker, but the guy out front smelled like he was. I knew that the minute he plowed into me. Even without a photo for comparison, there was enough evidence to set off identity alarms.

The closet was partially open. Using the toe of my foot, I pushed the sliding door back more to reveal that half of the closet had been cleared out, leaving behind discarded empty hangers and some holding miscellaneous clothing. At the bottom of the closet were some scattered shoes but nothing that looked like favorites. I opened the dresser drawers using my shirttail to cover my fingers and found them mostly empty.

"Simon is long gone," I announced when I came out of the back. I did a quick check of the kitchen floor before moving on to the living area. "And I'd say he left today. This place is clean except for this pile of dirty clothes in the living room." I indicated a backpack in a corner of the room that spilled gray wrinkled clothing like an old lava flow. "I'll bet this stuff belongs to this guy. A lot of Tuttle's clothing and personal stuff has been cleared out, and probably in a hurry. And there's no musical stuff left behind. A guy who works as a musician would have guitars and stuff, right? He's a guitarist in the band."

Willie was examining a wallet. The guy in the chair had come to and was sitting nervously, watching Buzz and Willie, fear radiating from him like a space heater. I didn't blame him. Buzz was now holding a gun, and it was pointed right at him.

"You looking for Simon?" the guy ventured in a weak voice. "You know, the guy who lives here? I ain't him." He swallowed hard. "I don't know where he is. You've got to believe me." Fully conscious now, he fidgeted with rattled nerves. Close up he didn't look one bit like Tuttle. His face was too narrow and his nose too long, with a bump halfway down his bridge. His hair was about the same and so was the short growth on his chin, but that was where the similarities ended.

Willie glanced at the ID in the wallet he held, then at the guy in the chair. "So, Craig Buck of Council Bluffs, Iowa, what brings you to Newport Beach?"

"Ever been to Iowa?" Buck answered with a half grin. He glanced at Buzz and his small effort at humor disappeared. "Hitched my way out here a couple of months ago hoping to find work. A new start. You know?"

"He's homeless," I said to Willie. "Lots of them around the beach areas."

"I'm not homeless," Buck protested. "It's just a temporary hiccup in my relocation plans."

"How do you know Simon?" Willie asked him.

"He sometimes lets me sleep on his half of the patio out front," Buck said, "or at least he does when his bitch neighbor isn't around. She calls the cops when she sees me, but she's been gone for a few days. A vacation, I think." He snorted. "Who needs a vacation when you live at the beach? The people upstairs pretty much leave me alone. I do odd jobs for folks around here for work, but it doesn't pay enough to put a roof over my head."

"But how did you get inside if Simon's gone?" I asked.

"He told me to watch the place for him," Buck answered, turning to look at me. "Said he would be out of town for a bit, and I could sleep on the couch." He straightened up and squared his shoulders, trying to muster confidence and legitimacy. "Lots of break-ins around here."

Something about his story wasn't adding up. If Simon Tuttle was worried about gangsters finding him, why would he encourage

185

a house sitter, knowing the killers might come here looking for him? And then there was the matter of what I had discovered on the floor of the vanity.

I held out my hand to Buck. "Let's see the house key."

"What?" Buck asked. He fidgeted some more and glanced around, not making eye contact with anyone.

"The house key," I clarified. "If Simon had you housesitting, he would have given you a key."

Catching on to where I was heading, Willie leaned in close to Buck. "You heard the lady: where's the house key?"

"I...I..." he stammered. "I think it dropped out of my hand when I ran. It's probably out on the patio along with the bag of stuff I bought."

"You're a squatter, aren't you?" I asked. "You saw Simon leave with his stuff and decided to break in and have a little vacation of your own."

"No. No," he protested, raising one skinny arm to swear. "He invited me to stay."

I turned to Willie. "Simon Tuttle has a cat," I explained. "There's cat litter on the floor in the vanity area. That's probably where he kept the litter box, which is gone. There's also a placemat on the floor in the kitchen with some kibble scattered on it but no bowls. That's where he would have fed the animal. If he were only going away for a few days and had a housesitter, he would have left the cat behind. Cats generally don't like to travel. But just like Shankleman, he took his pet with him. Also, this guy smokes, and I don't think Tuttle does. Most nonsmokers wouldn't ask a smoker to housesit for them."

"Nice work, little mama," Willie said to me before turning back to Buck. He said nothing to the man, just fixed him with a stare that could melt stone.

"Okay. Okay." Buck admitted in record time. "I saw the guy leaving with a couple of bags and his cat." He glanced at me and rolled his eyes. "It didn't look like he'd be coming back soon. I managed to jimmy the bedroom window open and crawled in that way." He shrugged, his bony shoulders flexing up and down. "What's the harm? I'd look after the place for him and get out of the heat and sun for a few days."

"Did you see any guys show up here looking for him?" Willie asked. "Before or after he left?"

Buck shook his head. "Nothing, man. Simon left early this afternoon. I waited until it got dark before I broke in. I've only been here a little while."

Willie turned and paced a few steps back and forth. He stopped, gave the situation some thought, then looked at Buzz, giving him a sign. Buzz put away his gun and moved away from Buck. Willie tossed the wallet into Buck's lap, then came over to me and took me by the arm, gently this time. "Let's go."

"What about me?" Buck asked. "You're not calling the cops, are you?"

Willie pivoted to the man who still sat in the chair like a sack of unwashed, unpeeled potatoes. "I don't care what you do, Buck. Stay. Go. Makes no difference to me. But you should know that some really bad guys might be coming after Simon and his friends. One is already dead and another is missing. That's probably why he took off. So if I were you, I wouldn't stick around. These guys are the type who shoot first and check ID later."

Buck's eyes widened, then narrowed. "But what about you? You look pretty badass to me." His eyes cut to me. "Except maybe her."

Willie laughed. Letting go of my arm, he dug into his pocket and pulled out a money clip. He peeled off several twenties and offered them to Buck. "Son, if we were anything like the other guys, you'd be dead already."

SEVENTEEN

As soon as we were back in the SUV and moving, Willie read me the riot act. "What in the hell were you doing, Odelia? I told you to stay put."

I curled my lip. "You're not the boss of me."

"I am when I'm sent to look after you," he shot back. He was in the front passenger seat, and I was in the back. Buzz was driving. Willie ran a hand through his hair. "Jesus, no wonder Greg and Clark thought you needed a keeper."

"Boss," Buzz asked, "we taking her home?"

"Damn straight," Willie said, the words quick and sharp as a snapped twig.

"But we need to check out Seaside and Art's place," I protested. "We need to find out what happened to Art."

"And we will," he said, turning around in his seat to fix me with a glare, "as soon we drop you off at home. You can't be trusted to keep out of trouble."

"All the more reason to keep me with you," I countered.

Willie turned from me and fixed his eyes on Buzz, who said something in Spanish. I couldn't understand the words, but I did hear my name, the word Uber, and the suppressed chuckle in his tone.

I slapped the back of Buzz's headrest with the palm of my hand. "It's rude to talk about someone when they can't understand what you're saying." This time Buzz didn't hide his laughter.

Willie turned his head toward me again. "Buzz said unless we tied you up, you would just call Uber again." He paused. "He has a point." He turned back to Buzz, and they continued a discussion in Spanish in spite of my protests.

"You know," I interrupted, "I have the gate code to the front gate at Seaside." They stopped talking and began listening, so I continued to plead my case. "I know you two are pretty adept at skirting walls and security, but wouldn't it be easier and save time if you simply rolled in through the front?"

"So just give us the code," Willie said.

"Fat chance." I leaned back in my seat and fiddled with my seat belt, which had gotten tight when I'd leaned forward. I heard another deep chuckle coming from the driver.

Willie shook his head. "If you were an adversary instead of a friend, we'd probably just slap it out of you." He jerked his chin toward Buzz. "Buzz here has lots of ways to make people talk."

I leaned forward again, and again the seat belt tried to choke me as I got closer to the driver's seat. "By the way, just how did you get the name of Buzz?" I asked. "It hardly sounds like a nickname given to a Hispanic kid—more like a white kid in the fifties."

In response, Buzz raised his right hand to show that one of his fingers were missing, the middle finger, leaving nothing but a one- to two-inch stump. "Buzz-saw accident when I was eleven. My brother started calling me Buzz, and it stuck."

"Are you sure it wasn't punishment for flipping off the wrong people?" I asked as I shuddered at the sight of the amputation. I hadn't even noticed it before, maybe because it had been holding a gun.

"Nah, I was using my dad's power saw. I was making him a Father's Day present and wasn't paying attention." He laughed. "But when I do flip someone off with this hand, they get the message."

We drove a few more miles in silence. I was busy lining up more reasons why I should tag along, each mile mentally preparing my case, ready to throw it at Willie as soon as we pulled up in front of my house, which would be in about five minutes since traffic was light. I'd also decided that unless they tied me up and locked me in a closet, I would use my recently liberated keys and go there on my own, just as Buzz had predicted.

When we were almost to Seal Beach, Willie reached out and tapped Buzz on his shoulder. "Change of plans. Go straight to the Seaside place."

Buzz reached over and tapped on a GPS screen built into the dash. It came to life. He stabbed the screen again, and it immediately blossomed into a colorful map showing the way to my mother's place.

"You already had the address?" I asked with surprise.

"Buzz looked it up and plugged it into the GPS while we were waiting for Tuttle," Willie explained.

"You mean the guy I identified as *not* being Simon Tuttle, right?" When Willie turned to look at me, I fixed him with my own lethal one-eyed stare.

"We would have identified him as soon as we looked at his wallet," Willie assured me.

"Sure, but would you and Buzz here have noticed the missing cat box?" I sniffed, my nose pointed upward in a salute to the world of insufferable smuggery. Neither man replied.

When we were almost to Seaside, I said, "I should be driving."

"Why's that?" Willie asked. "You can tell Buzz the code, and he'll punch it in."

"There's a guard at the front gate," I explained. "It will look less suspicious if I drive up, especially alone. They know me."

"And how do you propose to get us in?" Willie asked. "Is there a back gate you can open?"

"I was thinking that maybe you two could climb in the back and stay low." I could tell from the looks they shot back and forth that neither of them were sold on the idea. "Look," I said, "the guards are used to seeing me alone or with Greg, and even if the security camera is on the blink, the guard might still remember you and what you look like. And who knows, there might even be a cop stationed at the gate because of the murder." I looked around the back of the SUV. "It won't be so bad. The windows are tinted, and it won't be for very long."

After a few seconds Willie asked Buzz, "About how far are we from the place?"

Buzz consulted the GPS. "Less than a mile."

"Okay," Willie said to him, "pull into this empty lot."

It only took a couple of minutes to get both men comfortable. They laid out as best they could in the back cargo area, pulling a tarp they found back there over themselves.

I rolled up to the main gate at Seaside and lowered my window so I could punch in my mother's security code. It occurred to me that stinky Mona might have changed it or put my name on some sort of no-fly list, but my mother hadn't been tossed out, so Mona had no right to do either. But I doubted that would stop her. On duty in the guard shack was Milton, and, as I had hoped, he was nodding off. Mom always said Milton did his best sleeping on the job since there were very few comings and goings late at night at Seaside. He stirred as the gate opened to let me pass, blinked several times in my direction, then gave me a sleepy wave when he recognized me. I wondered if any of the guards outside of Kevin Wong knew about Mom's current status as an undesired resident. If Milton did, he didn't seem to care. I glanced one last time into the guard shack as I moved slowly through the open gate. Milton's chin was already on his chest.

Willie popped his head up when I came to a stop in front of my mother's. "Isn't there a less conspicuous place to park?" he asked.

"Not really," I answered, "but at this hour most of the residents should be asleep. Remember, these are people who eat dinner at four thirty."

Quietly, the three of us got out of the SUV and headed up Mom's walk. I let us in with my key and went straight to a small catchall drawer in the kitchen where I knew Mom kept extra keys to her car and to my home. She'd said Art's key was in the same place. I found a key ring with several keys on it. One key was an obvious car key. The other two looked like house keys. Affixed to the face of each was a small label, one with an O and the other sporting an A. Bingo! Holding the keys aloft, I said to the men, "Let's roll."

I debated on whether we should take the vehicle or leave it in front of Mom's. "Art's place is on the other side of the complex," I told the guys before leaving the house. "I'm not sure if we should drive or walk. Walking is quieter. What do you think? It's not that big of a place."

Willie and Buzz exchanged glances, then Willie said, "Let's walk. No need for lights or noise."

Buzz agreed. "I noticed plenty of ground-level lights and scattered streetlights outside, so we should find our way easy enough."

"Even though it's out in the open, I think we should stick to the paths," I suggested. "If we get too close to the houses, we might get noticed by someone with insomnia. If someone does notice us, we can always say I'm checking on Art. Everyone knows Art and my mom are close friends."

"Good idea, Odelia," Willie said. "We'll hide in plain sight."

"Boaz Shankleman's place is in that direction, too," I noted. "That's where the murder took place. It's just a few houses down from Art's."

Walking quickly and quietly but without any outward sign of urgency, the three of us started toward Art's house, crossing manicured greenbelts and passing the club house and pool area in the middle of the complex. I had never walked the property at this hour. Usually when I visited, the walkways and common areas were filled with senior citizens getting their exercise or visiting with each other in pleasant camaraderie. Now the houses were completely dark, except for a scattered few where dim lights seeped out from behind blinds. There was a peace about the place. Peace and serenity, like being tucked into a safe, warm bed for the night. I wondered if I'd ever see my bed again.

Art's place was a two-bedroom townhouse tucked into one of the few cul-de-sacs. Shankleman's place was on the corner of the entry to the cul-de-sac, just two small buildings down. I pointed to Shankleman's home, which had crime scene tape wrapped around it like a birthday present. "That's Shankleman's place," I whispered to my companions. I pointed just ahead into the cul-de-sac. "And that's Art's place." We moved forward.

Unlike my mother's home, which had a small entry hall, when you walked into Art's home you walked directly into the living room. The focus of the room was a large recliner in rich caramel leather. It was pointed at a huge flat screen TV way too big for the room. It must be a guy thing. If Greg had his way, one whole side of our living room would be a wall-to-wall TV. There was also an upholstered sofa in a subtle print that coordinated with the recliner, a coffee table, and a good-size end table wedged between the sofa and the recliner. Besides a lamp, the table held an assortment of books, mail, an open bag of chips, and a half-full bottle of beer.

Although Art had only been gone for a day or two, the place felt abandoned. Not rush abandoned like Simon Tuttle's apartment, but it felt lonely. There were a few dishes in the sink and a half pot of coffee in the very cold coffee maker. I'd been in this home several times and it always had a very friendly, warm vibe.

We moved into the back of the place. Here it was similar to Mom's with a master bedroom, a smaller guest room, and a bathroom between the two. The only difference was that Art didn't have a washer and dryer set up in the hall closet, and the rooms were a bit smaller. I did a thorough search of the bathroom, looking in cabinets. The three of us quickly covered the small place, looking for any indication of Art's whereabouts, then met up for a pow-wow in the kitchen.

"Wherever Art is," I said, "I don't think he planned the trip."

"Did you find another missing cat box?" Willie asked.

"No," I replied, my word snappy with return sarcasm. "But Art doesn't strike me as the type who'd go on a trip with dirty dishes in the sink and a half bottle of beer and bag of chips hanging open on the table. There's not even a chip clip on the bag. Also, his bed's unmade but not slept in, like he pulled back the covers to get ready for bed but never made it."

"You should be a PI, Odelia," Buzz said to me with a smile. "You have an eye for detail."

"And a nose for trouble," Willie added, looking straight at me.

Ignoring him, I went to the recliner and turned toward the TV. "It almost looks like he was watching TV, enjoying a snack, when he was interrupted."

"Wouldn't the TV still be on?" Buzz asked.

I shook my head. "His daughter came to check on him earlier today. If it was on, she would have shut it off." As soon as I said the words, I thought of something—something that could be important. "Funny, when Shelita came to my house looking for Art, she said she'd been here but said nothing about the TV being on. If I walked into my mother's and saw the TV on and she was gone, I'd be convinced something had happened to her. Shelita, though, was easily persuaded that her dad might simply be on one of his road trips."

"You think this Shelita might be lying?" Willie asked, quickly catching my train of thought.

My head swayed side to side in the negative. "No. I think if she had found the TV on when she checked on her dad, she would have mentioned it and been more upset. It's an important detail, and although she's rather uptight, Shelita is an honest and good person. She wouldn't have lied about something like that." I paused and looked around the place, wishing the walls would tell me what had happened to Art Franklin. "But I don't see any sign of Art's cell phone, and Shelita did say his car is gone, which feels like he left on his own." I walked from the recliner to the door and turned around, looking at the place from that view.

"He could have run to the store and got into an accident," Buzz suggested, "but the car registration would have told them who he was even if he wasn't carrying his wallet. Even if he had a heart attack or something like that, he would have had ID on him, wouldn't he?"

"True," I said with a nod. I went into the bedroom to recheck something and came back out in two shakes. "And I'm betting his wallet is with him because I don't see it anywhere. If he didn't have it with him, you'd think it would be on the dresser or the table or a counter out here, so if something awful happened, he would have ID."

"Old men simply don't disappear," Willie said. "And you say he went missing the night of the murder up the street?"

"As far as we can tell," I said. "I saw him yesterday at my mother's." I paused and glanced at the time displayed on the microwave in neon green. It was now definitely after midnight. "Correction: I saw him *two* days ago at my mother's."

"That was the day the Fox woman was murdered, right?" asked Willie, confirming the timeline again.

"Yes," I replied. "Although it feels like a lifetime ago." I slipped down onto the recliner and was sorely tempted to flip the lever to lean it back. But I knew if I did, I'd be a goner until morning. "What now?"

Willie and Buzz exchanged questioning looks, then Willie said, "In spite of the dishes and chips, I think it looks like the old guy decided to go for a drive and then decided to make it longer. It is odd, I'll agree, but there's no sign of foul play at all."

"And what would be the motive for someone grabbing him?" asked Buzz.

"Exactly," I answered. With great reluctance I hoisted myself from the comfy chair. "Art is a sweet man and well liked." When I got to my feet, I took another look around. "Now I'm worried he went for a drive and got disoriented or sick along the way. He might be holed up in a motel room with a dead cell phone. Mom said he's notorious for letting the battery die."

Willie patted me gently on the arm in comfort. "Sounds like you need to have his daughter put out a missing person report so the police can be on the lookout for him."

I nodded. I didn't relish speaking to Shelita about that, but if she hadn't already gone to the police, I needed to suggest it. "I'll call her first thing in the morning." Again I glanced at the clock and rubbed my eyes, happy I wasn't wearing mascara. "Or rather at a decent hour later this morning."

EIGHTEEN

WE HAD BARELY CLOSED Art's door when we saw a lone figure walking along the sidewalk just past the Shankleman home. When they passed under one of the soft-lit streetlights I saw it was a woman, tiny and slightly bent. Just ahead of her, a small white dog trotted along on the end of a leash.

"That's a friend of Mom's," I told the guys. "What's she doing out here at this time of night?"

I started walking fast to catch up to Teri Thomson. I didn't want to run and risk startling her or her dog, causing it to bark. "Teri," I called out in a hushed whisper. A few more feet and I called out again, my hushed voice sounding like I had a bad cold. "Teri."

The men had held back so not to alarm the woman. She heard me the second time and turned. As I got closer I could hear a low growl coming out of the tiny animal. She said something to it, and it quieted at the command.

"It's me, Odelia, Grace's daughter," I whispered as I approached her. "Please don't be alarmed."

She'd gathered the dog protectively under one arm instead of letting it protect her. Nice guard dog.

The elderly woman relaxed and nuzzled the dog by its ear, whispering, "It's okay, Lucy. It's a friend." Lucy was a toy poodle resembling a bag of cotton balls. One look at Lucy's face told me she was blind.

"What are you doing out here at this time of night?" I asked. It was then I saw the knitting needle, long, sharp, and lethal, gripped in her other hand. It seems my mother wasn't the only armed and dangerous little old lady at Seaside.

"I should be asking you that, shouldn't I?" Teri asked, eyeing me with suspicion. Touché.

"Mom's at my place and couldn't sleep," I told Teri. "She was worried about her place and wanted a couple of things, so I dashed over to get them to ease her mind." People say I'm not a good liar. I beg to differ.

"But Grace's place is over on the other side," Teri pointed out. Teri Thomson appeared to be pulling eighty, rather than pushing it. She was tiny and slightly bent, with puffy white hair like her dog's, but there were clearly no flies on her when it came to her faculties. In a show of comfort, she slipped the knitting needle into the deep right pocket of the pants of her lightweight blue tracksuit. I could just see the top of it jutting out.

"Mom also wanted me to check on Art's place," I quickly answered, keeping to a whisper and holding up Art's key as evidence. "He's been gone a day or two, and Mom wanted to make sure everything was good over here." I glanced back at Art's. Willie and Buzz were nowhere to be seen. "Mom thinks he took off on one of his little jaunts, but he didn't say when he'd be back."

"Did you check with his girlfriend?"

I looked at Teri with surprise, which caused her to chuckle. "Please," she said with a sly smile, "my dog may be blind, but I'm not. I know there's a woman who pretends to visit Grace but who spends the night at Art's."

"Yeah, Mom told me about that. Seems Mona D'Angelo keeps tabs on Art for his daughter."

"Mona's a fool," the old woman quipped without hesitation. "Treats us all like naughty, out-of-control children, then wonders why we don't respect her." She leaned closer. "That woman has her own secrets, believe me."

Do tell!

I looked around, worried that even whispering might catch the attention of someone in one of the nearby homes, someone who was a light sleeper. Across from us was a greenbelt with a bench. It was far enough away from the private homes to give us some privacy if we continued to keep our voices low. "Would you like to sit down, Teri? I'd like to ask you a few questions about all this, if you don't mind."

She nodded and put the dog down. The three of us walked across the quiet street to the bench. Lucy, blind or not, trotted along happily, letting her nose guide her.

"I love this place at night," Teri said once she was seated with Lucy in her lap. "Especially this time of year after the heat of the day cools off. Lucy and I often take walks when there's no one around. Makes no difference to Lucy if it's night or day." She stroked the animal's ears as she spoke, and Lucy snuggled into her. "I can only sleep a couple of hours at a time," she explained, "so often we come out for a short walk at night, sometimes two."

As tired as I was, my senses went on alert. "Did the police speak with you about the night of the murder?"

"Yes," she replied. "I believe they spoke to all of us who live in this section, but I had nothing to tell them."

"Were you out walking that night?" I asked her. "You know, the night of the murder?"

She nodded and stopped petting Lucy as she thought back. Not to be denied, the dog nudged her hand with its muzzle, and the hand continued the petting on autopilot. "Yes, I was." Teri turned to me, her lined face full of sudden brightness, as if she'd turned on a lamp. "Goodness, can you believe that happened just two nights ago? It seems like a lifetime ago." I nodded back. It did to me too.

"Like I told the two policemen who talked to me," she continued, "we did go for a walk that night, but it was a very short one because I was a little tired. So we came back and sat on the patio for a while. I didn't see anything or anyone unusual when I was walking or sitting."

No one unusual. "Did you see any of the other residents or maybe one of their guests? You know, someone like yourself who is up at night." I glanced over at Shankleman's home. "What about Boaz's neighbors on either side?"

She gave it some thought. "No, the Whites live in the home that's attached to Boaz's place on the right, and they've gone gallivanting in their RV. They do that every July and August." She pointed to another home, one to the left of Shankleman's. "Kenneth Lowe lives in the one on Boaz's other side, the one not attached, but he hasn't been well lately and is deaf as a post."

She stopped petting the dog and brought the hand to her lips. "But I did see someone last night—I just remembered now! I forgot to tell the police."

My brain snapped out of its exhaustion. "Someone who didn't belong, like a stranger?"

She shook her head. "No, I saw Art Franklin. I remember thinking how strange because he's not much of a night owl like I am."

"Did he see you?" I asked with interest.

"No, I don't think so. He was fussing with his car. It was out in front of his place, not in his assigned car port, and he was putting something into it—a bag, I think. I couldn't see well because he was fiddling with the passenger's side, the side facing his house, not me." She shrugged. "I'll bet he was getting ready to go on one of his little trips."

"What happened after that?" I encouraged.

"Why, nothing. I went inside. I was barely in bed when the whole place started buzzing with police."

"What time do you think it was when you saw Art?"

Again she gave my question thought as the memory returned. "About the same time as now." She paused and scrunched her brows together. "Actually, I believe it was a little earlier, maybe around eleven or so. Around the time I usually take my first walk."

My tired brain did some math. It would have been shortly before Mom and Lorraine went on their fact-finding mission. Mom had said that they had gone to Shankleman's after the news, and I knew Mom always watched the eleven o'clock news. "And you didn't tell the police about Art?"

Teri shook her head slowly. "No. I just remembered I saw him this very minute, and the police were more focused on the night before, the night that poor woman was murdered." She looked at me with eyes full of horror. "You don't think Art Franklin killed that poor woman, do you? I can't imagine such a thing myself. He's so sweet and always concerned for others." She laughed softly. "Grace once called him a wussy because he wouldn't kill a big spider we found in the game room. He gathered it up on a piece of paper and took it outside instead."

I couldn't imagine Art killing Cydney Fox either, although I could easily imagine my mother calling him a wussy. So Art wasn't a night owl, but he had taken off in the middle of the night. What would have made him do that, especially without telling my mother or even leaving her a message the next morning? Did he see the murder and the murderer? But Art disappeared last night, the night *after* Fox was supposedly killed. He disappeared the night my mother and Lorraine broke into Shankleman's.

"Teri, I can't imagine Art doing such a thing either—or anyone around here. Did you by chance see my mother or my niece last night? They were at Boaz's about the time you would have taken your walk or maybe a little later."

She shook her head. "No, but according to the scuttlebutt, they entered by the back bedroom window. In that unit's case, that window faces the back wall of the property. Once they were back there, no one would have seen them from the street. And Kenneth certainly wouldn't have heard him."

Between Lorraine and Craig Buck, it seemed a lot of people were shimmying through bedroom windows in the dark these days. I turned my attention back to Teri. "What about strangers hanging around, day or night? Certainly if a stranger entered the front gate, the guard would have seen them?"

Teri let out a very unladylike snort, causing her to quickly cover her mouth with her free hand out of mild embarrassment. In her lap, Lucy lifted her sleepy head. "Not if Milt was on duty, which he probably was. He works every night during the week." She shook her head. "It's a wonder we're not all slaughtered in our beds with him out front." She leaned in and dropped her voice even more. "Fortunately, the bad people don't know he's incompetent."

"Is that why you carry a knitting needle?" I asked.

"I've never had to use it in all the years I've lived here," she said with a smile, "but you never know. Lucy isn't much protection. Even her hearing isn't great now that she's gotten older. She's as bad as Kenneth some days."

"Tell me, if Milton is so incompetent, why does Seaside keep him on duty?" I asked. "Maybe he'd be better on day shift?"

"Because he's Mona's uncle, and the night shift doesn't include much work." When she saw my surprise, she added, "Didn't you know his connection to Mona? I would have thought Grace might have told you. His name is Milton D'Angelo. A couple of months ago the late-night guard left, and Mona brought Milt in to replace him. A mercy job, if you ask me. All any of us know is that he'd been gone for a long time and had just returned." She leaned in closer. "Some think he was in prison. Others think he was in some sort of home, like an asylum. Mona simply said he'd been traveling overseas for a long time and finally came home."

I shook my head. "Mom didn't tell me any of this." I filed the information away to be used later, in case it was needed when defending my mother against eviction, and wondered if this was the secret Teri had referred to earlier.

I took a moment to take several deep breaths of night air and caught the scent of night-blooming jasmine. Teri was right: it was pleasant sitting outside in the middle of the night. The complex was quiet and peaceful, like sitting in your own private garden. Dotted around the property were small stylish streetlamps that gave off warm yellow light. It was enough to light your way without blinding nearby homeowners. I took another deep breath and held it a few seconds. It was much cooler than during the day, and I was starting to get a little chilly. That's one of the great things about Southern California, especially near the ocean. It can be hot as blazes during the day in the summer, but it usually cools down at night. I wanted to stay on the bench until morning, the dew settling on my body until the sun came out to burn it off.

My moment of Zen over, my brain skipped back to a short time earlier and how Milt barely gave me any notice when I entered the gate. "So it would have been easy for both Cydney Fox and her killer to slip in unnoticed after dark the night of the murder?" I asked Teri.

"If they have the front gate code, Milt wouldn't care," she told me. "The only time he pays attention is if it's a guest without the code. But I'm pretty sure the Fox woman had the code."

My tired brain snapped to attention. Kevin Wong had said something similar. "Do you know if she was a frequent guest?"

"I saw her here quite often in the past few months," Teri reported, "especially in the evening. I think she and Boaz were an item because sometimes her car was here overnight."

"Are you sure?" I asked. "I know they were friends a long time ago."

"She wasn't around during the day that I could see, just at night. And I live just over there." Teri pointed to the right of us. "Just two doors down. I have a pretty good view of this entire area from my patio. Sometimes Lucy and I don't walk at all but sit outside enjoying the evening." She hesitated a heartbeat, then tacked on, "Not that I'm nosy or anything, mind you."

I gave her a warm smile. Of course not. No nosier than me or my mother.

I looked over at Shankleman's house. From where we sat I could see one side of it. From where Teri lived, she would have a better view. "I'm surprised the police don't have anyone posted at the house since the murder happened so recently."

"They did until just after suppertime," she answered. "Maybe they thought no one would go near it." She continued stroking the small dog, who'd woken up enough to wag her tail. "There was even a small crowd of reporters out front earlier, but they're gone now too. Probably everyone is focused on that horrible incident in Los Angeles."

Nosy reporters had been a concern of mine when I'd arrived earlier with Buzz and Willie, but when we got here there was no sign of anything. Earlier this evening there had been a report on the news of a bomb going off in an empty warehouse on the outskirts of Los Angeles. No one, thankfully, had been hurt, but there were rumors of an ISIS connection—that the warehouse was being used as a bomb-making center by locals connected to the terrorist group, although so far there was no hard evidence of either the ISIS link or that bombs were being manufactured in the place. Still, in a global, fast-paced news cycle world, terrorists always trumped missing aging rock stars, even if murder was involved. Even Willie had made a comment about it when we easily entered the property without notice.

"Odelia," Teri said, her sweet face clouding over, "should I call the police and tell them about Art?"

Now there was a million-dollar question. I ran it around in my tired mind, quickly weighing the options. "No," I answered quickly, "at least not yet. I don't believe he killed Cydney Fox any more than you do. Let's give it a day or two for the police to do their digging. If nothing comes up, you can say you just remembered seeing Art that night."

"And I did just remember," she assured me.

"Did you see anyone else that night?" I asked her. "Try to remember. Something might come to you, like remembering about Art."

She screwed up her face and closed her eyes. "No, just Art. I didn't even see the Fox woman, just her car parked in visitor parking." She pointed to the left of us to an area with about a half dozen visitor parking spaces. Visitor parking was scattered throughout the complex. None of these were filled tonight. "The police towed it away after her body was found."

"Did you tell the police that you thought Boaz and Cydney were seeing each other?"

"Yes, I did. I'm sure they now think that Boaz killed Cydney, and I feel bad for that. He isn't sweet like Art, but he's always very considerate and fun to be around. He doesn't strike me as a killer." She sighed. "But you never really know, do you?" She paused, then shook her head. "My mind really is slipping."

"Do you remember something else?"

"Yes, but not about that night. It's nothing really, just something about Mona D'Angelo."

"What about Mona? You know, she's suggesting that my mother move out of Seaside."

Teri looked surprised. "Why?"

"Because of last night," I told her. "Because Mom and my niece entered Boaz's home without his permission. Mona and Seaside's management have already banished my niece from the property."

"But they were just checking on him," Teri said, coming to my mother's defense. "He's been gone quite some time without a word to anyone."

"That's what my mother told me. She and Art are quite concerned."

"Seems like that Mona should be more concerned herself, considering, except that she's a hard-hearted one." Teri said the words with barely disguised anger.

"Why did you say *considering*?" I asked as my curiosity rose again. At this rate I might stumble upon something juicy to use on Mona as blackmail to get her to back off on Mom.

"It's what I just remembered that I forgot to tell the police." Teri looked both ways, as if expecting to see eavesdroppers hiding in the bushes. "She's had a big crush on Boaz—probably something left over from when she was a star-struck teen listening to rock and roll. I don't know if the interest was ever returned. I never saw anything to indicate that it was. But Mona was always making excuses to go over there."

This news woke me up fast, like cold water flung into my face. "Teri, think hard. Did you see Mona around here the night of the murder?"

The old woman closed her eyes and thought about my question. A full minute must have passed, and I wondered if she'd dropped off to sleep. The dog had and snored gently on her lap. Just as I was about to touch her shoulder, her eyes popped open and fixed on me like two blue clouds. "I'm sorry, but I never saw Mona that night. I went back over every move I made, but I only saw Art last night and Milt the night before."

Milt? Except for his incompetence on the job, I was sure Teri hadn't mentioned seeing him either night. "Milt?"

"Yes, he was making his rounds," she replied as if it was a piece of information I'd forgotten she'd mentioned. I knew I was exhausted, but I was sure she hadn't said anything about it. "I always found that odd," she continued, "because everyone knows that Kevin makes rounds right before he leaves for the evening, but Milt had gotten into the habit of walking the property himself shortly after. I guess it kept him awake."

I thought about the guard in the shack, his chin heavy on his chest with sleep, and couldn't imagine him moving much farther than the TV.

NINETEEN

AFTER I WALKED TERI and Lucy back to their home, I headed back to my mother's. There I found Buzz and Willie standing at her kitchen counter. Each held a fork and were feasting on something from a plastic container. Upon closer inspection, I spied Mom's turkey and veggie meatloaf with mushroom gravy.

"We found this in the fridge," Willie said with his mouth half full. "I hope Grace doesn't mind, but we were both hungry."

I shrugged, knowing she wouldn't. "Mom makes a great turkey meatloaf, but it's better heated up."

"I nuked it for a minute or two," Buzz said. He turned and opened a kitchen drawer, pulled out a fork, and held it out to me.

"You could get some plates, you know." I took the fork.

"More fun this way," Buzz said with a smile. The kid with the missing middle finger was growing on me. Enrique had been mostly silent as he stuck close to Willie as his bodyguard, but Buzz was showing a lot of personality. "Using plates when raiding the fridge is sacrilegious."

"Yeah," Willie agreed, his mouth half full. "Sybil would never let me do this at home."

A tired laugh escaped my lips. Willie, a wealthy fugitive who carried a gun and knew his way around the criminal underground, and who had masterminded a major financial scam, wasn't allowed to eat meatloaf from a plastic container at home. My laugh dissolved into a private smile when I thought about all the times Greg and I had done things like this together. Many a night we clinked forks over Tupperware while seated on the sofa watching a late-night movie. But I did draw the line when it came to drinking directly from milk cartons or juice containers.

Taking my fork, I dug into the lump of meat covered in thick, savory gravy with large chunks of mushrooms and broke off a piece. I shoved it into my mouth. It was warm but not hot. "Mmmmm," I moaned, "that is so good." I took another bite, realizing I was pretty hungry too. The three of us decimated Mom's leftovers while I brought them up to speed on what I had learned from Teri Thomson.

"Well, that hit the spot," Willie said after putting down his fork and wiping his mouth with the back of his hand.

I tore off a few sheets of paper towels from a dispenser fastened under a cabinet and handed them around. There had to be some civility in the world. "See," I pointed out, "if I hadn't been with you, you wouldn't have learned all that. Terri never would have talked to either of you."

"So," Buzz said after wiping his mouth with his paper towel, "Mona could have a motive for killing the Fox woman, and her uncle could be covering for her."

I nodded. "And Fox was beaten, a very personal type of attack." I unwrapped some banana bread that had been sitting near the sink, surprised the guys had missed it in their foraging. "Have some dessert." I placed it on the counter in front of them and they pounced on it like the meatloaf had never happened.

"True," Willie said, "but Teri said she never saw Mona that night." He looked at me with sadness. "It's not looking good for your friend Art. Teri saw him packing up to leave in the middle of the night and he's not been in touch with anyone since. Either he's one cool cucumber and killed Fox, taking off a day later once he realized Grace and Lorraine might discover the crime, or he saw something that scared him to death and took off before he wound up like Fox."

I pinched off a bite of banana bread and popped it into my mouth. It was part of the batch without nuts—the one Mom had made for Art. "I can't see Art killing anyone," I said after I swallowed, "let alone sitting on my mother's patio sipping iced tea less than twelve hours later if he did do it. It's more likely your second theory."

I pulled a pitcher of iced tea out of Mom's fridge and held it up to the men. They both nodded that they wanted some. I got three glasses out of the cupboard and was in the middle of pouring when we heard a car pull up. We all froze. Soon someone was at the front door. Buzz and Willie made a dash for the hall, out of sight. I wanted to go with them but knew I should stand my ground. Maybe it was Mona letting herself in with a passkey. If so, we needed to have a showdown about a few things. If it was Art letting himself in with his key, then I needed to sit him down and find out what was going on.

It was neither.

When the front door opened, I sucked in my breath and held it. A few seconds later my mother sauntered in from the entry hall, her switchblade at the ready, Lorraine behind her.

"What in the world are you two doing here?" I asked as my breath gushed out of me in relief.

"I live here," Mom snapped, making no effort to put away the knife. "What are *you* doing here?"

Willie and Buzz came out from the back. I glanced at them, then said, "We were following up on Art. I left you and Lorraine a note saying that I would be out for little bit."

"Yeah," Mom said, coming close to where I stood. "I got up to pee and saw the note, then couldn't get back to sleep, so I decided to do a little investigating of my own. Lorraine woke up and insisted on coming with me." She looked at Buzz. "Who's this kid?"

"This is Buzz, a colleague of mine, Grace," Willie explained. Willie turned to Buzz. "This is Grace Littlejohn, Odelia's mother. And that's Lorraine Littlejohn, Clark's daughter."

"I'm sure you've heard a lot about my mother, too," I said to Buzz.

In response, he nodded and a wide grin split his face ear-to-ear as he looked at the two of them. "Yes." He turned a 100-watt smile on Lorraine. "But very little about you." Lorraine blushed and looked down at the floor.

Mom stepped in front of Lorraine. "Maybe that's because she has a fiancé in Chicago."

Lorraine's head snapped up. "Not anymore, Grandma," she announced with crisp finality before returning Buzz's smile.

Mom and Buzz took each other's measure, Buzz especially eyeing the knife. "That's quite a knife you've got there, *abuela*," he said to her.

"Thanks," Mom said. She closed the knife and slipped it back into her bag like a squirrel hiding nuts from a competitor. "But I'm not your grandmother, kid."

Buzz smiled again while Willie watched with amusement. Buzz wasn't as classically good looking as his cousin Enrique, but his smile revealed a mischievous charm, one that probably worked on women of all ages, even a hard nut like my mother. "I only meant it as a term of respect, Mrs. Littlejohn." He gave Mom a slight bow, and I saw her icy edges begin to thaw. Lorraine was already a puddle of romantic goo.

"How did you get here, Mom?" I asked.

Mom put her purse down on the counter. "Seems someone took my car keys." Her eyes shifted between all three of us, washing us equally with charges of the crime. "So I took an Uber."

I looked over at Willie and Buzz, giving them my own wide grin, one of satisfaction.

"But we have your house keys too," Willie noted.

"Not all of them," Mom snapped. "Old people tend to believe in spares. Lots of spares."

I thought about Milt at the front gate and his connection with Mona. "Did Milt see you come in," I asked, "or was he asleep at the wheel?"

"He wasn't there," Mom reported. "At least not that I could see when I punched in my code. He might have been in the bathroom. Probably sleeping there." Her voice held traces of disgust.

Teri had said that she'd seen Milt making rounds, which didn't jive with Kevin's report. Maybe he did take walks to stay awake. Maybe he wasn't as lazy as people thought. Then I wondered if he'd been on the prowl while I was talking to Teri and spotted us. If he did, he would no doubt squeal to Mona. But for now, I shoved that out of my mind.

Mom came into the kitchen and eyed the empty meatloaf dish and unwrapped banana bread. "I hope you don't mind, Grace," Willie said, "but we got hungry. The meatloaf was delicious."

Mom waved a hand in the air, dismissing the thought of any intrusion. "Not one of my best efforts, but I'm glad you enjoyed it."

She went into the living area and took a seat in her favorite chair, an upholstered rocker aimed at the flat panel TV affixed to one wall. Neither her chair nor her TV were anywhere near the size of Art's, but they served the same purpose, although the way Mom sat you'd think it was a throne and she was giving a middle-of-the-night audience. Lorraine seemed unsure of where to stand, so I motioned her over to me and the two of us poured iced tea and handed the glasses around. Only Mom waved off the offer. When Lorraine handed a glass to Buzz, I saw their eyes lock and the exchange of shy smiles. A love connection in the works, and if Clark objected, he had only himself and Greg to blame. They'd sent Willie and Buzz to look after us.

"So," Mom began, "have you fools gotten anywhere or have you been standing around eating dry meatloaf for the past few hours?"

We quickly caught Mom and Lorraine up on what had happened at Simon Tuttle's and on my conversation with Teri Thomson.

"Mom, did you know that Mona had a crush on Boaz Shankleman?" I asked, taking my tea and moving to the sofa. Lorraine followed me. The two men pulled chairs from the kitchen table into the living room and sat.

"I heard rumors," Mom answered, "though I don't think it was mutual. Boaz often told Art and me how ridiculous he thought Mona was." She shrugged. "Then again, Boaz was used to women throwing themselves at him. Maybe once in a while he took what Mona was offering. Wouldn't be the first time a man did that."

"What about the Fox woman?" Willie asked. "Teri thought she might be having a fling with Shankleman."

"Very likely," Mom answered. "Obviously Teri doesn't miss a thing, which is why Lorraine and I went to the back of Boaz's place. If Teri Thomson says Fox was visiting Boaz at night, then she was, although Teri's memory has been slipping lately. All the information is in there, you just have to be patient in prying it out." I nodded, remembering how Teri had remembered things like pieces of a puzzle dropped to the floor.

"Grandma," Lorraine said, "you know how you said you saw a light in Boaz's house the night before I arrived?"

Mom nodded. "Yes, we know now that was probably the night of the murder."

"Right," Lorraine continued. "Even though Teri didn't see Mona, maybe she was here and she saw the light on in Boaz's house and thought he might be home so went over there to check on him. After all, she knew people were concerned about him."

"But why would Mona D'Angelo be here that late?" I asked. "She doesn't live on the property, does she?"

"As a matter of fact," Mom answered, "she does. Management has always had someone on-site 24/7. There's a large unit up by the management office just for that purpose. The old manager used to live there, but when she retired last year, she moved to Florida. Mona was promoted from assistant manager to manager and moved on-site."

I remembered the old manager well. She had been in charge when Mom moved to Seaside. Her name was Avery, and she had been a very efficient but friendly woman. I hadn't realized she had lived here as part of her job, but even then we had mostly dealt with Mona. "Does Milton stay there too?" I asked. "Teri told me he was her uncle."

"I don't think so," Mom answered. "He drives a sedan—blue, I think. I've seen him arrive for work at night. If he lived here, he'd walk."

"I see where Lorraine is going with this," chimed in Buzz. "Maybe Mona saw the light, same as Grace did. She went over there, found Fox instead of Shankleman, and attacked her in a fit of jealousy. Because one neighbor's gone and the other's deaf, no one would have heard anything unless it was really loud."

"Do you know yet what the murder weapon was?" asked Willie. "You just said the woman was bludgeoned."

Out of the corner of my eye I saw Lorraine shudder at the memory. "No, the police didn't say anything about a weapon."

"A baseball bat," Mom said, her eyes fixed on the floor as she tried to make a connection. She looked up at us. "Remember, Odelia, you said to me earlier—what if, when Lorraine went through the window, Boaz was home and thought she was a burglar? You said he might have had a gun and shot her or used something else to defend himself and his home." Again I saw Lorraine shudder. "You said," Mom continued, "that you and Greg keep a baseball bat for defense."

"Do you remember Shankleman having a baseball bat?" I asked her.

"A bat could do some serious damage to someone," noted Buzz.

Mom shook her head, "No. Not a baseball bat, but I just remembered that Boaz kept a golf club at hand, and I think that's why. I remember once he had me and Art over for dinner, and Art noticed the club by the front door. He asked Boaz if he played golf, and Boaz said no and made some remark about the club being part of his security system." Mom scratched her head. "Yes, I remember. Boaz laughed and said Ringo was the alarm and the golf club, the muscle."

"Did the police ask you about the club when they questioned you?" I asked.

She shook her head. "No, not a word. Maybe they already had it in their possession." She turned to Lorraine. "Did they ask you about a golf club?"

Lorraine shook her head. "No, they said nothing about a weapon."

Willie got up and started pacing. "If they had the weapon, I'm sure they would have asked about it." He walked back and forth in front of the kitchen counter. "The murderer probably took it with him, whether it was the golf club or not."

"Or her," added Lorraine.

"Or her," Willie said, correcting himself.

"Didn't Teri say that Art was putting something into his car last night?" The question had come from Buzz. Immediately, we three women gave him the stink eye, none of us willing to even consider that Art Franklin would have anything to do with a murder. He caught the glares and quickly added, "As hard as it is to believe, we must consider all the possibilities."

A silence came over the group that Mom finally broke. "Romeo's right. As much as it kills me, we cannot scratch Art off the suspect list, although I can't imagine a motive, especially an emotional one that might have triggered that beating."

"I'm with Mom about this," I said. "Mona had a possible motive: jealousy. The gang Titan was mixed up with also had a motive: revenge on whatever Titan did, but Cydney Fox got in the way. The brutal beating could have been a warning to Shankleman and the other band members."

I turned to Willie, "Are you sure it was the Armenian gang that took Titan out?"

He nodded. "Pretty sure. I'm not clear on the details, but word is he double-crossed them."

"But *he* double-crossed them, the band didn't," I pointed out. "Are they going after Titan's other clients too?"

"Good observation, Odelia," Willie noted. "Do you have a list of the other bands he represented?"

"They would be listed on Titan's website," I said. "If they aren't in danger, then why is Acid Storm?"

Willie pulled out his cell phone and left the room. He headed into the back and we heard a bedroom door shut. The rest of us sat there quietly, waiting, thinking, sleeping with our eyes open. At least I thought I was until the sound of snoring startled me. I straightened up on the sofa and looked around, trying to get my bearings through the fog in my head. The others were laughing softly.

"You nodded off, Odelia," Mom said, with a shake of her head. "And you snore like a freight train."

"Only when I'm overly tired," I said in my defense. "I think I've only had two or three hours' sleep in the past two days."

"Lorraine and I have only had a little bit more than that," Mom pointed out.

"I actually feel quite awake," Lorraine said with a perkiness that made me want to drown her.

"That's adrenaline," Buzz said to her.

We heard the bedroom door open, then the bathroom door close. After a few minutes there was a flush, and Willie rejoined us. "My people are going to check to see if that gang is making any claims or threats regarding others connected to Titan West," he told us. "It could take some time for them to get back to me. It depends on how reliable and connected their sources are."

"So now what?" asked Mom.

"We're kind of in a holding pattern right now, Grace," Willie told her. "But I'd like to take a look around the outside of both Shankleman's and Art's homes."

I got up to go with him, but he waved me back down. "Buzz and I will do that," he said. "We'll be back before you know it." When I tried to protest, he said with firmness, "This is non-negotiable, Odelia. You understand? Besides, you look about to drop."

"He's right, Odelia," Mom said, looking me over. "The zombies on TV look more alive than you right now." I shot her a glare, but it was pretty weak in my current state of exhaustion.

"You ladies try to get in a catnap while Buzz and I are out," Willie said as they headed for the door. "We won't be gone long."

TWENTY

I DIDN'T KNOW HOW long I'd been asleep, but light was peeking through the closed blinds in my mother's guest room when I opened my eyes. I was sprawled facedown on top of the bed. After blinking several times, I rolled over onto my back, swung my legs over the side, and slowly got into a sitting position. I must have dropped onto the bed like dead weight because I had one shoe on and one shoe off. After slipping into my one stray shoe, I stood up and shook my head a few times. My mouth felt dry and prickly. Tilting my head back and my nose upward, I caught the odor of bacon mingled with brewed coffee, and it filled me with resolve to stay upright. Of their own accord, my feet started moving toward the door.

After stumbling my way to the bathroom, where I washed my face and rinsed my mouth out with some mouthwash, I felt some-what ready to face the world—or at least what was waiting for me in my mother's kitchen.

"Well, look who's up?" Mom announced from the kitchen table, where she and Lorraine were nursing coffee mugs. Empty plates were in front of them.

"What time is it?" I asked. I'd left my phone in my bag and the bag in the living room when I'd gone to the guest bedroom. After Willie and Buzz had left, it was decided I'd take the guest room and Lorraine would take the sofa. The guys were barely out the door when we each gave in to our bone-weariness and headed to bed as soon as they left.

"Just after nine," Lorraine said as she got up and shuttled the dirty dishes to the sink.

"Nine?" I asked with surprise. I glanced out the open blinds to Mom's patio, where it was sunny. I shook off my stupor. "Why didn't you wake me when the guys returned?"

"They didn't wake any of us," Lorraine said, sounding a bit miffed. "Just crept in and out and left this note, along with your car keys." She picked up a piece of paper from the table. Next to it were my car keys, which I distinctly remember as being in my bag. "We must have all been comatose from exhaustion," Lorraine added, "because they had to come in to get the keys, then again to leave the note. Kind of like cat burglars."

I picked up the note. The penmanship was awful.

We brought O's car here so you wouldn't need to take Uber home. Go there. Don't stay here!!! Will be in touch soon.—W.

PS: We fed the cat and dog.

Note in hand, I went to the patio sliders and looked out. Sure enough, my car was now parked in the visitor parking cattycorner from my mother's.

"Unbelievable," I said out loud but to myself. I turned and walked back to the table. "Well, let's get going back to my place like Willie ordered. Besides, I have to get ready for work. You two should be safe enough there today, providing you don't go crazy and run off to play cops and robbers on your own."

"Relax," Mom said, "and take a load off. Besides, it's Thursday, and you don't work on Thursdays."

I did a mental walk-back of the week. Mom was right; it was Thursday. Would this week ever end?

Lorraine brought me a cup of coffee. "Grandma and I have only been up about an hour."

I took a sip of coffee. On a plate on the table was some cooked bacon. Several strips rested on a paper towel, shiny and wrinkled like retirees basted in sun block and laid out on a beach. I knew it would be turkey bacon, just as the meatloaf had been made with ground turkey. I grabbed a piece and shoved it into my mouth. The salty crunch was so satisfying, I nearly moaned.

"Would you like me to whip up some eggs for you, Odelia?" my niece asked as a second sliced disappeared into my mouth.

"No, thanks," I told her. "I'd rather get home, and I want to talk to Greg." I licked my fingers. "I should call him now."

"Don't worry about that," Mom told me. "Your phone was going nuts in your bag this morning. It was Greg. I answered and assured him we were all fine. It sounded like he'd already gotten a report from Willie. Then I called Steele and told him you wouldn't be in until Monday."

I had been about to grab the last piece of bacon, but my hand skidded to a halt just short of the plate. "You *what*?" I turned to Mom.

"After talking to Greg," she explained, "I hit Steele's speed dial on your phone and told him you wouldn't be in until Monday." She shrugged and took a sip of her own coffee. "I don't think he was surprised. He asked if we were keeping out of trouble, and I told him yes."

"So you lied to my boss?" I turned fully in my chair and zeroed knit brows at her. "You didn't tell him about us witnessing Titan's murder?"

"No; why should I?" Slowly Mom got up from the table and picked up the bacon plate. At the last minute I rescued the remaining piece and bit it in half with misplaced frustration.

With Lorraine's help, Mom started washing up the few breakfast dishes. Although she had a dishwasher, Mom insisted that hand-washing dishes was more effective. "Steele doesn't need to know everything we do," she said as she added dish soap to the sink. "Besides, it's not like we were dragged in by the police like the other night."

I gulped my coffee down and handed the mug off to Lorraine so it could be washed. I was actually glad Mom had called Steele about my taking the rest of the week off. It had crossed my mind a few times, but it's always tricky with Steele. It was better to have Mom act as my agent in such matters.

When the dishes were washed and dried, the three of us headed out the front door to my car. We'd almost reached the visitor parking when Mona D'Angelo whizzed up in a golf cart like the Wicked

Witch of the West, providing the witch dressed in a pantsuit and rode a broom with four tires.

"So it's true," Mona said with smug satisfaction, "you *did* ignore the order from Seaside's management that she was not to be any-where on the grounds at any time." With a long manicured nail, Mona clarified the "she" by pointing directly at Lorraine.

"It's rude to point, Mona," my mother pointed out.

Mona ignored her. "The guard told me this morning that she came to the property last night."

"The guard?" I asked. "You mean your Uncle Milty?" Mona seemed surprised that we knew but quickly collected herself.

"As a matter of fact, he is my uncle," she said, turning her attention now directly on me. "He told me this morning that your niece came onto the property last night with Grace, and he never saw her leave." She narrowed her eyes at Mom. "I trust you did get the notice I had hand-delivered to you?"

"Yeah, yeah, yeah," Mom said, dismissing the question with a wave of her hand. "I got it."

"And you willfully disobeyed it." Mona's voice was getting shrill, and she was getting excitable. I began to see how she just might get worked up enough to have killed Cydney Fox, a woman she thought might be a rival.

The face-off in the parking area was attracting a small group of onlookers. At first they hung back, but gradually they started coming forward a foot at a time, murmuring amongst themselves. I spotted Teri Thomson and Lucy among them. One roly-poly man in Bermuda shorts, with white socks and sandals and wearing a golf cap, gestured at Mona. "Leave Grace and her family alone, Mona.

They've done nothing to you." The others seemed to be in agreement.

"Yes," a woman with a crackling voice called from the back. "They were just looking after Boaz. They were doing *your* job." Again the mob rallied on Mom's behalf.

Mona turned to the group of residents. "You don't understand. Grace and her granddaughter broke the rules, which are there for your protection."

"Our protection?" called out another man. "What a laugh. That poor woman was murdered right under your nose—and your incompetent uncle's nose."

"He's a disgrace," said Teri. "It's a wonder we're not all attacked with him on the job." Her words brought about a chorus of agreement.

From Mona's reaction, I'd guess she hadn't realized the residents knew Milton was her uncle or that he was widely disliked.

"We heard that you're trying to get Grace to move out," said a chubby woman with curly red hair who was supported by a cane. She shook a finger at Mona. "You can't do that, Mona. We won't stand for it."

"Grace is our friend. We want her to stay," called out another woman. "And her granddaughter too. If you can throw them out, what's to stop you from going after the rest of us over some little thing?"

"Little thing?" Mona protested, but before she could say more, the group moved forward in a small semicircle of geriatric angry villagers.

From somewhere in the back I thought I heard, "Hell no, Grace won't go!" Soon the chant was picked up, and everyone was saying it in unison, over and over. I looked at my mother. She held a hand to her mouth as tears dripped down her face. If she ran for HOA president, she'd win in a landslide.

Seeing her defeat, Mona hissed at me, "This isn't over. Not by a long shot." Her face was beet red with humiliation and anger, and again I could see her easily wielding a golf club at someone. With one last look at the crowd, Mona climbed into her golf cart and beat a hasty retreat while the Seaside residents cheered.

"Well, that was something," I said once we were in my car and headed to my house.

"It rocked, Grandma," Lorraine said from the back seat. "I thought you said you weren't liked."

Next to me, Mom held a hankie to her mouth. Before leaving, she'd choked out a heartfelt word of thanks to her neighbors. The tears had stopped, but she was still overcome with emotion, something that didn't happen often. "I had no idea," she squeaked out.

TWENTY-ONE

BUZZ AND WILLIE SHOWED up at my house shortly after we got there. "The old people at Seaside almost staged a coup," Lorraine told them with animation once they were inside. "You should have seen it! They're really angry that Mona wants Grandma to leave." I caught Buzz beaming at her while she told them what had happened.

"Good for you, Grace," Willie said as he patted my mother's arm. "Seems like more than just Boaz and Art have your back."

Mom gave him a weak smile. "Yes, but we still need to find them. They're my main posse over there."

While I gave Wainwright and Muffin extra pets and scratches, I said to the guys, "Thanks for taking care of the critters this morning. Did you stay here last night?"

"No," Willie said with a smile, "but when we came to get your car in the wee hours, the look on Wainwright's face told me he was expecting breakfast, even if it was still dark out." He motioned toward the living room. "Let's go sit down and talk."

Once we were seated, Willie pulled something out of his pocket. It was a cell phone with World's Best Grandpa emblazoned on the case. The face of the phone was shattered. "That's Art's phone," Mom said with great concern from her seat on the recliner. "Where did you find it?"

"In the bushes near his front door," Willie said. "It was dead, but we took it to a friend of ours. He was able to recharge it and bypass the passcode."

Mom chuckled. "Some tough passcode. It's 1-2-3-4 because Art can't remember anything more complicated."

"Did you learn anything from the phone?" I asked.

"A lot," Willie said with a smile aimed at Mom. "I think it's safe to say, Grace, that your posse is somewhere together."

Mom sank deeper into the recliner with relief at hearing the news. "You mean Boaz and Art are together?" Lorraine sat on the arm of the recliner and put an arm across her grandmother's shoulders.

"Quite possibly," Buzz said, "but we're not sure."

"The last few calls made to this phone were from a burner phone," Willie explained, "but there's voicemail from a man asking Art to help him."

"Did Art call him back?" I asked.

"Yes," Willie confirmed. "We don't know what they talked about, but the calls were made around eleven the night Grace and Lorraine found that body."

"Wasn't that the time that woman with the dog said she saw Art packing his car?" Buzz asked.

I nodded. "Yes, and it was shortly before Mom and Lorraine went through the window."

Willie took a seat on the sofa next to the recliner. He leaned toward Mom, the phone held out. A recording of a man's voice filled the room. The voicemail was urgent, and the caller identified himself to Art as Boaz. He told Art to call him back as soon as possible, that he and Ringo needed Art's help. After imploring Art to not tell anyone he'd called, the call ended.

"Was that the voice of Boaz Shankleman?" Willie asked Mom.

She nodded. "It certainly was. I'd recognize it anywhere, even if he hadn't said who he was."

"But what does this mean?" I asked. "Obviously Shankleman asked Art for help and Art dashed off to give it, but why haven't they called? Especially Art, who would know that people would be worried sick about him."

"And who smashed Art's phone?" Lorraine asked.

"There's something else," Willie said. We all turned our eyes on him, worried that it was bad news. "One of my associates heard back from his contact with the Armenian gang. They did take out Titan, but there's no indication or buzz at all about them killing the Fox woman. The contact said their only target was Titan and his files." Still holding the phone, Willie leaned back against the sofa. "But here's where it gets interesting: the informant said that the reason Titan was targeted for execution was because the head of the gang got word that something was going to go down that would have the police crawling all over Titan West and Acid Storm."

"With Titan West up to his neck in doing favors for the gang," added Buzz, "that meant great exposure to the Armenians and their business. That's why they took his records when they killed him."

"And why he was so paranoid when we got there," I said, piecing everything together. "He was behind locked doors gathering everything up, especially his laptop, so he could go on the run with insurance against the bad guys."

"So somehow he must have known the gang was coming for him," Mom said. "And he must have warned Boaz and the others to get out of Dodge too."

"Exactly," confirmed Willie. "Something was going to rain down on Acid Storm, which in turn would expose Titan's shady business dealings."

"Um…," began Lorraine. We all turned to her to find her white as school paste. "If we had been in Titan's office when they came for him, we probably would have been killed too. Right?"

"It's called collateral damage, honey," Mom said without any sugarcoating.

"Mom!" I snapped, but it was too late.

Lorraine's eyes rolled back in her head as she started to slide off the arm of the recliner, but Buzz, who had been leaning against the wall by Wainwright's bed, hopped forward and caught her in his strong arms before she hit the hardwood floor with a thud. He laid her gently on the floor and started patting her cheeks. I ran to the kitchen to fetch some water and a wet dishtowel while Mom and Willie hovered above her. Even Wainwright joined in by giving Lorraine some slobbery kisses.

Once she came to, Lorraine leaned against the side of the recliner and sipped her water. Buzz sat next to her, holding the damp towel against her neck and making sure she remained stable. After a few minutes, Willie said, "Maybe we should talk about this later."

"No," said Lorraine. "I'll be fine, and I want to hear this." Her color was returning slowly. I wondered if Willie had mentioned any of this to Greg and Clark. My guess was no because if he had, both my cell phone and Lorraine's would be lit up like Christmas trees.

"Okay, to recap," Willie began, "someone, who knows who, alerted the Armenians that something was about to go down involving Titan West and Acid Storm that would cause the police to look into everything having to do with them." Willie had retaken his seat on the sofa but now was back on his feet again, nervous energy almost sparking off of him. "Someone also alerted Titan that the Armenians were about to come after him."

"Maybe it was the same person?" suggested Mom.

"True, but why?" asked Willie as he paced. "In alerting the gang about a possible police investigation, the person who did it had to know that such an action would put a target on Titan's back. Gangs don't leave loose ends for cops to find and follow. Whoever notified the Armenians wanted Titan out of the way and possibly the band members too. In essence, he bought a hit on Titan that he didn't have to pay for."

"It could be that Titan alerted the band members about the gang," Mom suggested.

"Yes," Willie agreed. "If Titan found out, he might have put them on alert, which is why they got out of town. After all, he had a lot of history with these guys and had no reason to see them killed."

"That we know of," Buzz noted from his spot on the floor next to Lorraine.

"Except that Shankleman fired Titan. After the Fourth of July, he was no longer booking gigs for them," I said. "Shankleman gave the job to Cydney Fox."

"The Fox woman is the monkey wrench in this theory," Mom stated. "I could see Boaz taking off once he learned some gang might be after him, but what would Fox have to do with that?" Mom looked at me. "And didn't you say the way she was killed felt personal?"

I nodded, happy that I'd had a few hours of sleep before my brain had to go through these mental calisthenics. "In spite of having the motive of Fox taking away his business with Acid Storm, I don't think Titan killed her. He seemed genuinely surprised by her death." I paused. "And what about the timing?" I asked. "It seems off. Shankleman has been gone a couple of weeks, but it looks like Titan and the other band members just found out about the threats recently. Very recently."

"Good point," Willie said. He stopped pacing and faced us.

"Maybe the gang stuff was a decoy," came a small voice. All eyes turned to Lorraine as she took a sip of water. "We're looking at this as if Cydney Fox was"—she began, then swallowed hard before continuing—"collateral damage. What if her murder was the focus and the gang thing something to blame it on? You know, a cover-up for the real crime. Maybe the murderer wanted it to look like she was just in the wrong place at the wrong time."

"That's a good twist, honey," Mom told her. "Like one of those murder mysteries on TV."

"If that's the case," I said, trying to put all the moving parts together to make a single working engine, "then whoever wanted to kill Cydney Fox had to know about Titan's connection to the Armenians." I put my head in my hands and willed all the pieces to line up nice and orderly, like people waiting for the latest cell phone.

"Maybe the murderer knew them all," Willie suggested, "and this was his way of taking them all out without getting his hands too dirty. He'd do the Fox woman, and the gang would clean up the band and its manager." Willie turned to me. "Didn't you say they pissed off a lot of people back when they were high on the charts?"

"Yes, when the scandal with Kurt Spencer-Hall hit and the band broke up, there were a lot of lawsuits thrown at them from all kinds of places—venues, record companies, music promoters, you name it. The band went bankrupt, I believe. They broke up and lost everything. But wouldn't that be a long time to hold a grudge like that? I mean, the cases would have been settled by now."

"What about the sex scandal part?" Mom said. "Maybe there's some crazy victim or victim's father still ready to swing a golf club at members of the band. Maybe news of the band being back together stirred up old buckets of hate, and someone acted on it."

"Another good possibility," Willie said.

"Except that the sex scandal was all on Kurt Spencer-Hall, not the other band members," I noted. "And why take out Fox, if she wasn't the main target? She'd been seduced by Kurt Spencer-Hall, but she'd been of legal age and had not been drugged by him that I remember or read about. It was when he and Oxman came to blows over Cydney Fox that the truth came out about Spencer-Hall's criminal and skanky behavior with the younger women."

"Someone harboring anger that long could also be linking Fox to the crime, since she was the catalyst for bringing it out in the open," Willie said. "Maybe one of those girls thought Spencer-Hall was going to sweep her away and marry her, but the allegations of rape that came out of the fight between Oxman and Spencer-Hall destroyed her dreams."

"And now that the group is together playing again, it would have given this crazy girl a way to find them," Mom tossed out.

"So we don't think Mona killed Fox anymore?" asked Lorraine.

Buzz got up off the floor and took Lorraine's empty glass from her. He went into the kitchen and returned with it refilled. They exchanged smiles as he handed it to her. Instead of sitting back down next to her, he held out a hand and got her to her feet, resettling her on the sofa next to me. "Would anyone else like anything?" he asked the group. When we all shook our heads, he pulled up a kitchen chair and straddled it. I was really liking this kid, or at least his manners.

"Mona could still be the killer," Willie said. "Is it possible she was one of the women Spencer-Hall drugged back in the day?"

"She could have been," I said, "but Mona's about my age. I was in college when the scandal hit. Except for his dalliance with Fox, he was more into barely legal types and almost-legal types. We might have been too old for him."

"But it's possible?" asked Buzz.

I nodded in his direction. "Anything is possible." I fiddled with the end of my hair, something I did when nervous or thinking. "We need to find Art and Boaz. Boaz should be able to tell us a lot, even if he doesn't know who the killer or killers are." I looked at Mom. "Are you sure you have no idea where Art might have gone or taken Boaz? No favorite spots or hotels he liked to stay at while on his trips?"

"If I did," she snapped, "I would have told you by now so we could check them out." Mom looked troubled, her face overcast with a chance of rain.

"Are you okay, Mom?" I asked.

"I'm just thinking," she answered. "There has to be a way to find Art without talking to the police or worrying Shelita more. If he's helping Boaz, then Boaz must have a good reason for not going to the police."

"Maybe," Lorraine said, "it's time we *do* call the police."

"No!" went up from Willie, Mom, and me almost at the same time. Lorraine shrank back as if slapped, but I caught Buzz sending her a reassuring wink.

"Not yet, Lorraine," Buzz said gently. "They'll only muck everything up and might cause Boaz and Art more trouble, especially if they think Boaz is the killer. You've seen on TV how the cops often overreact."

I patted my niece on the knee. "I'm sorry we shouted at you, but Buzz is right. We need to keep this away from the police until we're sure." I glanced around the room. "For everyone's sake."

We all sat in silence, each of us thinking about how best to move forward. Mom got up and headed down the hall to the guest bathroom. When she came back, she said, "What about credit cards? Has anyone checked those for activity?"

"That information is very difficult to get unless you're the police," Willie said. "Even my people have a tough time getting that. It's easier to get someone's blood type or fingerprints."

"And I'm sure they've checked all of Shankleman's by now," I said.

"But what about Art's?" Mom asked.

"The police would have had no reason to check that, Mom," I told her. "Would Shelita have access to it?"

Mom shrugged. "I don't know, but *I* do, at least if his phone is functional."

Willie still held Art's phone. He looked at it, then at Mom. "It is. Only the screen had been broken."

"Give it here," Mom said as she sat back down. "Art isn't that tech savvy, but earlier this year I set up a banking app on his phone for him. He likes having that info at his fingertips, at least when he remembers to charge his phone. He has a computer but doesn't like working on it very often."

Willie gave her the phone and Mom started looking for the bank app. We all gathered around her to watch. When she found the right app, she tapped on the screen. The username was already filled in and just needed the password. Mom tapped something in, and Art's banking information popped up.

"You have Art's banking password?" I asked with surprise. "You don't even have mine."

"Oh, please," Mom said. "Art's bank password is 1-2-3-4 with a dollar sign before and after. I set it up for him, although I did suggest a more complicated one at the time."

"We really need to educate this guy on passwords," Buzz said.

"Good luck with that," Mom said as she scrolled through the information. "It looks like Art made a $300 cash withdrawal this morning."

"This morning?" I asked.

"Yep, about an hour ago. From a branch ATM in Beaumont."

"Beaumont?" I asked.

Mom looked at me through her thick glasses. "You having hearing difficulties?" She went back to tapping at the screen.

I refrained from snapping back at her. Bigger issues were afoot. Beaumont was a small town about a hundred miles northeast from us. It was a rural town located in Riverside County. The only time I'd been to Beaumont was to pass through it on the 10 Freeway on my way to Palms Springs or Arizona.

"I checked his credit card. There are a few charges, also in Beaumont," Mom said. "Restaurants and a motel charge." Mom got up. "Sounds like we're going on a road trip."

"We don't know if they're still there, Mom," I said. "If Art took out cash today, they might be heading someplace else." I paused. "Tell you what," I said. "Call the burner phone—see if Boaz or Art answers."

"We probably should have done that earlier, don't you think?" Lorraine said. No longer woozy, she was gaining an attitude—the family attitude.

"I did call it. I called this morning as soon as we got Art's phone up and running," Willie said, looking amused. "No one answered."

"Did you leave a voicemail?" I asked.

"Yes," Willie answered. "I told them I was a friend of your family and that Art needed to call Grace ASAP. Who knows, the call might have spooked them into leaving Beaumont."

"Might as well try it again," Mom said as she hit redial. She put the phone on speaker. When she got voicemail, she left a message telling Art to call her, that it was very important and that she knew he was with Boaz. She also said he should call Shelita because she was very worried about him. When she ended the call, Mom looked up. "Maybe if he hears my voice, he'll call."

While we waited I made some coffee for Mom and Willie. Lorraine and Buzz retreated to the patio with sodas. I could see them chatting and laughing while seated at the picnic table. I didn't know what had happened in Chicago between Lorraine and Elliot, but she seemed to be recovering nicely under Buzz's attention. I took the coffee into the living room, along with a tall glass of iced tea for myself. Then I got a legal pad and together the three of us went over the different scenarios again while I jotted down notes and drew diagrams.

It was clear to all of us that there was a good chance that whoever killed Cydney Fox probably knew her, the band, and Titan. More and more it didn't look like her murder and Titan's were unrelated. The slim possibility was still there, but it was slim and too much of a coincidence. Mona could have been around then and had suffered at the hands of either the band's breakup or Spencer-Hall's indiscretions, but then I remembered Shelita Thomas saying that she had gone to college with Mona. And I also remembered that Shelita had told me once that she'd attended USC. Although not out of the realm of possibility, it seemed unlikely to me that a busy USC student would have had the time to be a band groupie. We were all in college about the same time, and I know I hadn't had time to devote to such endeavors. I mentioned this to Mom and Willie, and they both agreed.

"It doesn't mean she didn't kill Fox out of jealousy," Willie noted, returning to an earlier theory. "But it does put our idea about her being one of Spencer-Hall's victims on the back burner."

Almost twenty minutes after Mom had made the call to the burner phone, Art's phone rang. The display showed that it was Shelita calling her dad.

"That's his daughter," Mom said to Willie. "Should I answer it?"

Willie shook his head. "No. If you do, it will only get her more concerned or raise more questions."

"I agree," I told her.

We all listened while the phone rang six times before kicking into voicemail. I know it was six because I counted them while I held my breath. Mine goes to voicemail after four rings. When the ringing stopped, we went back to waiting.

"I almost wished we'd just hit the road for Beaumont," Mom said. "This waiting is killing me."

"Me too, Mom," I told her. "But we could be halfway to Beaumont while Art's halfway to Santa Barbara. We need to find out where they are."

Another grueling ten minutes passed. Muffin had hopped up on the sofa and was making a nest in Willie's lap. He stroked her and told her what a pretty girl she was, which elicited loud purrs from the tiny animal and reminded me of Teri and Lucy.

We'd been waiting over thirty-five minutes when Art's phone rang again. This time the display showed the burner phone's number. After getting a nod from Willie, Mom answered it and put it on speaker. We held our breath.

"Grace, is that you?" came a familiar voice from the phone. Collectively the three of us relaxed.

"Yes, Art, it's me," Mom said. "I'm here with Odelia and a friend of ours. Where are you? Everyone is worried sick, especially Shelita."

"I'm with Boaz and Ringo," he told us. "They needed my help. How did you get my phone?"

"Our friend found it in the bushes by your place," Mom explained.

"Boaz told me to do that," Art said, "so we couldn't be tracked. We're sure glad it was you who found it."

"The police are looking for Boaz, Art," I said into the phone. "For questioning. A woman was found dead in his home."

"Boaz knows that, Odelia. He came back and saw the body, and that's when he asked me to help him. People are after him—bad people."

"The Armenian gang?" asked Mom.

"Yes," came a different voice from the phone. I recognized it from the earlier voicemail. It was Boaz Shankleman—Bo Shank himself.

"This is Willie, a friend of Odelia and Grace's," Willie said toward the phone in Mom's hand. "I have it on good authority that the Armenian gang is not looking for you, but they did kill Titan."

"I know. I saw that on the news," Shankleman said, "but Titan said they would come after us."

"When did you speak to Titan about this?" I asked.

"A day or two ago," Shankleman said. "He called Dave and Simon and told them to get the hell out of town. He left me a voice-mail about it. Dave called me all spooked out, wondering if we should believe Titan since we knew him to be a lying little weasel in the past. I told him we should believe Titan about this. I knew that Titan was in deep to that gang years ago, but he swore that was over when we signed up with him again. Then several months ago I learned he was laundering money for those criminals. The other guys knew nothing about it, unless Titan told them when he told them to leave."

"That's why you fired Titan and hired Cydney Fox, isn't it?" I asked.

"Yeah," Shankleman said. "I didn't want the band involved with that mess in any way. Cyd and I had kept in touch over the years. She was smart, and when she returned to California she needed a job. I knew I could teach her how to handle the bookings, and I had

242

all of the same contacts Titan had. In fact, a lot of the promoters told me they didn't want to deal with Titan anymore. He was always squeezing them for more money, money outside of our contracts. That really made up my mind to leave him for good. He's lucky we didn't sue his ass."

"Was Titan skimming the money he managed to get out of those promoters?" asked Willie.

"Yeah, he was. Just as we found out he was skimming from us all those years ago. It all came out when the band went belly-side up. I told Dave and Simon the skimming was the reason for making the change. I didn't mention the money laundering." We could hear a deep breath being taken on the other side. "I shouldn't have given him a second chance, and I've kicked myself at least once a week for doing it."

TWENTY-TWO

CRESTLINE IS A VERY small town in Southern California located in the San Bernardino Mountains. I'd never been there, but Willie said he had a friend who could provide a safe house for Shankleman and Art and get them off the grid until things cooled down. I drove in my car with Mom and Lorraine. After giving me the address, Willie said he'd meet us there, then he and Buzz took off in their SUV. The last thing Willie told us was to call Greg and Clark and let them know we were okay, but to be careful what we said in case anyone was listening, and then to leave our phones home so we couldn't be tracked. He went out to his vehicle and returned with a burner phone for our use. It reminded me of Mother the hit woman and how she communicated with me. The manufacturers of burner phones must be making a killing off of the criminal community.

We couldn't convince Boaz to come to us. He was afraid he'd be spotted and taken into custody for Fox's murder. His plan was to wait it all out until her killer was caught, and it seemed that Art was totally dedicated to helping him. Willie did manage to convince Shankleman that the Armenians weren't after him, but he was still concerned about someone wanting him dead. Couldn't say I blamed him.

Just as Willie had suspected, his earlier call to the burner phone had caused them to bolt, and the bank withdrawal was so they could travel without credit cards. They had left the hotel in Beaumont and were on the move when Mom called. Now they were heading to Crestline. Willie's friend would meet them and take them to the safe house.

To get to Crestline from Seal Beach, I had to take the 605 Freeway north to the 210 Freeway east, then turn north on Highway 18, which was also known as the Rim of the World Highway. Highway 18 got pretty twisty and hugged the hills, with steep dropoffs on the other side.

"Isn't this pretty," Mom said. "Look how lovely it is, Odelia."

"Mom, I need to be driving, not rubbernecking."

Mom turned to look at Lorraine in the back. "You think it's pretty, don't you, honey?" From the back came a groan.

Mom turned to me. "At the first turnout you see, Odelia, pull off."

"Why?"

"Just do it. Lorraine's green. I think she's carsick."

Another half mile ahead, I saw a wide shoulder and eased into it, my tires leaving the smooth blacktop and crunching over gravel. Before the car came to a stop, Lorraine dashed out and bent over. I could hear retching loud and clear and was glad it wasn't happening in my car.

"Yep," Mom said as she got out to help Lorraine, "there's this morning's eggs and bacon."

I got out and retrieved a couple bottles of water from the trunk. After twisting the top off of one, I handed it to Lorraine. She took a big swig, swished it in her mouth, and spat it out on the scraggly roadside weeds. She did that a few times before cautiously sipping and swallowing some of the water. Fifteen minutes later we were back on the road, with Lorraine stretched out on the back seat, one arm thrown over her face.

"The poor kid has had a rough few days," I said. Checking the GPS, I could see we still had several miles before the turnoff to the address Willie had provided.

"You don't think she's pregnant, do you?" Mom said in a whisper.

"I'm not pregnant, Grandma!" came a surprisingly loud but shaky voice from the back.

Mom twisted around in her seat. "No need to get touchy, little lady. It's just that you have tossed your cookies a few times since you've been here. I thought maybe that's why you and what's-his-name had a fight."

In the rearview mirror I could see Lorraine sit up, think better of it, and fall back down. "His name is Elliot, Grandma," she said, "and you know that. Why do you keep calling Elliot what's-his-name?"

"Because I don't like him," Mom answered honestly. "Never have. But I've never called him that to his face, have I?"

"So if we had married, you were going to keep calling him that forever?"

"Not forever," Mom snapped. "Just for the first ten or so years."

I kept my eyes on the road but my ears on the conversation, happy to be simply a bystander.

"So," Mom said, unable to stop poking the green snake in the back seat, "why did you leave what's-his-name?"

There was a heavy silence, then Lorraine said, "*He* left *me*. You happy now, Grandma? You got the truth out of me. Now leave me alone." In the rearview mirror I saw Lorraine turn her face toward the back. My heart was breaking for her, and had we not been in a moving car, I would have stopped to give her a hug.

Mom, on the other hand, wasn't through poking the snake. "Why would he leave you, Lorraine? You're a gem. Him, not so much."

"Mom," I warned in a low voice.

"Well, it's true," Mom said in my direction. "He's a dullard and not good enough for Lorraine. I've always thought so. I don't know when I've met a more boring individual."

A muffled snicker came from the back seat. "That's rich. He told me *I* was boring." Lorraine shifted back toward the front. "Elliot said I was unfocused and unexciting. He said he wanted someone with more ambition and a sense of adventure." She sniffed back tears. "He left me for a podiatrist."

Mom and I exchanged surprised looks before I shifted my eyes back to the road. "A podiatrist is exciting?" I asked.

"Compared to me," Lorraine said, "one is."

I thought about the last few days and how Lorraine had shifted between kick-ass and a wilting flower almost from moment to moment. "Lorraine, did you climb into Shankleman's house to prove you were adventurous?"

Not a peep came from the back seat.

"I encouraged her," Mom said.

"No, Mom," I clarified, "you gave her the idea and you could have stopped her, but it was her decision. Same as tackling Titan West in his office like a linebacker."

Mom snapped her head around to the back. "You did that and I missed it?" Lorraine didn't answer but went back to sulking.

The GPS said we were almost on top of the road for the turnoff. The side of the road was heavy with trees, and I didn't want to miss it. Fortunately, there was no one behind me.

"Up ahead looks like an opening," Mom said, pointing to the right. In the back, Lorraine righted herself and looked out the window.

Mom was right. Cut out of the tree line was a narrow packed dirt road. I turned onto it and slowly made my way forward, careful in case there were any potholes waiting to devour my car. The road was so narrow, occasionally tree branches dragged along the roof and side of my car. We'd driven down the road for about a mile when it branched out into a clearing with a cabin made of logs and a couple of small outbuildings that looked like small garages.

From inside the cabin we heard the high-pitched yip of a small dog, then it went silent. A man came out of the house and stood on the rough-planked porch. I didn't know him, but he waved and stepped down off the porch. He was toting a high-powered rifle.

"Oh god," came a moan from the back seat. "We're gonna die."

"Oh, relax," Mom snapped. "If he's Willie's friend, then he's on our side."

I glanced over at the cabin, surprised not to see Willie or Buzz anywhere. But I did see a dark face peeking out from behind a thin curtain. Something was said to the guy with the gun, and he nodded. I nudged my mother and pointed in the direction of the window. Without any hesitation, she climbed out of the car. Seconds later Art Franklin bounded out of the cabin and wrapped his sturdy arms around my mother in a bear hug. I didn't see Boaz Shankleman anywhere as Lorraine and I got out of my car.

"Grace, it's so good to see you," Art said, his voice nearly cracking with delight. "I'm so sorry I couldn't contact you and let you know what was going on, but it all happened so fast."

"That's all fine and good," Mom said, breaking the embrace, "but Shelita is worried sick."

"I did call my daughter, Grace, on the way here."

"And what did you tell her?" I asked, approaching them. He greeted both Lorraine and me warmly.

He rubbed his chin. On it was a couple of day's growth that gave off the sound of fine-grade sandpaper as he ran his fingers over it. "As much as I didn't want to lie to my daughter, I felt the circumstances called for it. I told her I'd driven up to Santa Barbara and was going to stay a couple of days, but had dropped my phone and broke it, which is the truth."

"Folks," said the guy with the gun, "we should get inside."

"You must be Charlie, Willie's friend," I said to the armed man, who looked in his fifties and straight off of a secret military mission behind enemy lines. In response he blinked at me.

"Where's Willie?" Mom asked.

"He'll be here directly, ma'am."

Yep. No doubt in my mind that the guy was ex-military.

The inside of the cabin was sparsely decorated. There was a nice-size living room with a fireplace, a kitchenette, and a wood-burning stove. The floors were of scarred wood, and the furniture was mismatched and well-worn. A long table was pushed against one wall and on it rested various pieces of computer equipment. Off to the other side a door led to a room that looked like it contained a bed. I had no idea where the bathroom was and hoped that, should I need it, it wasn't outside.

In a chair by the unlit stove sat a man holding a little dog—a taco terrier I recognized from the photos. The animal growled a warning, but the man shushed it. "It's okay, Ringo. They're friends." He got up and faced us, and I immediately recognized Bo Shank of Acid Storm. He looked road weary, and his eyes and cheeks were hollow. I didn't know if he always looked that way or if the past few days had taken a toll on him. When he saw Mom, a small smile broke across his weathered countenance.

"Grace," he said in a tired voice, "I can't believe you found us, but I really shouldn't be surprised." He and Mom exchanged embraces, and Mom patted Ringo.

"Boaz, this is my daughter, Odelia, and my granddaughter Lorraine," Mom told him, pointing to each of us in turn. He politely shook hands with us, and I had a private, silent fangirl moment.

I noticed out of the corner of my eye that Charlie was concentrating on looking out the window.

"Lorraine was the one who found that dead body in your house," Mom told Shankleman.

Shankleman studied Lorraine with sad, droopy eyes. "I'm so sorry you had to see that," he told her. "It was an awful sight. Poor Cyd." He dropped back down into the chair and lowered his head, burying his face in the small dog's neck.

I approached him. "I have to ask, Boaz. Did you kill Cydney Fox?" I knew he could open-face lie to me but didn't think he would. Everyone, even Charlie, waited, eyes on him, to hear his reply.

"Odelia," Mom said with shock, "shame on you."

Shankleman lifted his head. "No, Grace, she has every right to ask that question. You all do, since you're involved." He turned and looked at me, his eyes wet. "No, Odelia, I did not kill Cydney Fox. I came home the other night and found her like that. That's when I asked Art to help me. I knew I had to get out of there as fast as possible. Whoever killed Cyd was probably looking for me and might come back, and the police would definitely try to pin it on me if I stayed."

"Where have you been for the past few weeks?" I asked. "Did you know before Oxman and Tuttle that the gang was after Titan and probably you guys?"

He shook his head slowly. "Like I said on the phone earlier, I just found out about that myself. I've been on a road trip trying to line up new gigs. It's been quiet for bookings because of changing from Titan, so I decided to make the rounds of various casinos to shake some hands and grease the way for Cyd. I also met with a few promoters who have worked with us in the past to let them know that Acid Storm is ready to work with them without Titan." He put Ringo down on the floor and stretched out his long legs. The dog made a beeline for us and started sniffing first my legs, then Lorraine's. New people, new scents to learn.

"When I found out about that damn gang," Shankleman continued, "I decided the best place for me was to remain out on the road. The only reason I came back was to grab more clothes and more of Ringo's medicine. He has a small heart problem."

At the news we all turned and looked at the little animal, who was now on his hind legs, begging Mom to pick him up, which she did and moved to a chair to hold him on her lap. Lorraine and I put ourselves down on two other hard, straight-backed chairs. Charlie went back to his vigil at the window.

"If you had your car, why did you call Art and get him involved?" I asked.

"I didn't have it at Seaside," Boaz explained, "because I was worried about the gang spotting me. I left it in a strip mall parking lot about two blocks away. Left Ringo there too. Then I slipped into Seaside and made my way to my place. The plan was to grab some stuff, more of Ringo's medicine, and slip back out, go to my car, and take off."

"But didn't you warn Cydney about the danger?" Lorraine asked.

"Sure I did," Shankleman said. "I left her several voicemails as soon as I found out, but I'm not sure she got them. She might have been…gone…by then."

"Why was she at your place with you not there?" I asked.

"With Titan out of the picture as our manager, we were running Acid Storm out of my second bedroom. Cyd was at my place a lot. Sometimes we'd work late into the night and she'd stay over. We were working hard to rebuild the band's contacts and business."

"Then why didn't she go on the road trip with you?" Mom asked as she cuddled Ringo.

"I asked her to," Shankleman explained, "but she thought we'd be better off splitting our efforts—me on the road doing meet and greets and her working the phones. And she was right. Between us we lined up two gigs, with promises of possibly more down the road, and not just these summer fairs that Titan got us."

"So you weren't seeing the Fox woman romantically?" Mom asked.

Shankleman shook his head and offered up a sad smile. "Cyd and I go way back. She's more like a kid sister to me." He got up and walked the width of the room twice while running a hand through his hair. "Cyd and I only pretended to see each other for Mona's benefit."

"Mona D'Angelo, the manager of Seaside?" I asked.

"Yeah," he answered. "We didn't want Mona finding out we were running the band's bookings out of my home. There are strict rules against home-based businesses at that place, and Mona can be a real bitch when it comes to rules." All of us, except for Charlie, quickly nodded in agreement.

"Also," Shankleman continued, "because Mona was really coming on to me. She had been for a long time, but in the past few months she'd amped it up for some reason, in spite of me not giving any encouragement. We thought holding Cyd out as my girlfriend would put Mona's brakes on a bit. You know, like maybe she'd go bother someone else and wouldn't catch on that we were working out of my home."

Shankleman's shoulders drooped and his face dropped toward the floor. "Cyd was there working when they came for me. It should have been me on that floor, not her." The words came out strangled and tight. Sensing his master's distress, Ringo jumped down from Mom's lap and went over to give comfort. Shankleman picked up the dog and held him close to his chest.

The room grew silent, the only sounds coming from the chattering of birds and a slight breeze in the trees outside. We sat on our hard chairs with Charlie keeping watch at the window and gave Shankleman his space for several minutes.

"Like we said on the phone," I said, breaking the silence, "we don't think it was the Armenian gang that killed Cydney."

Slowly Shankleman turned my way. "I know you said that before, but if not them, then who?"

I shrugged. "We're not sure. One theory is that Fox was the target, not the band, and whoever killed her used Titan's murder to deflect the investigation."

"I saw a light on in your house the night of the murder," Mom said. "Although at the time I didn't know there was a murder happening or going to happen. We wondered if maybe Mona saw it too and went to investigate, knowing you were gone, found Cydney there, and killed her in a jealous rage."

Shankleman's eyes popped wide like he'd been squeezed. "Mona is a really odd duck, but murder? Over me?" He shook his head. "I can't see it."

"I can," Mom said sharply. "And with that goofball uncle of hers manning the front gate, he'd probably cover for her if he knew or suspected anything."

"There's another odd one," Shankleman said. "Something's off about him that I can't quite shake or put my finger on. I guess it runs in the family."

I cut my eyes to Mom, then Lorraine. Mom caught my drift and stuck her tongue out at me, quickly, like a lizard. The reference to oddity running in a family went right over Lorraine's head. Give her time and she'd catch on. I glanced at Art. He hadn't missed it at all and was pressing his lips together to keep from chuckling.

"There's another theory," I said, getting back on track, "that whoever did this is someone from the band's past and is taking you all out, including Cydney, for what happened years ago."

"That's absurd," Shankleman said. He started pacing again, carrying the dog with him. "That was decades ago. People barely remember it, if they remember it at all."

"Some people carry grudges forever, Boaz," Mom pointed out. "Mona wasn't by chance one of your groupies back then, was she? Or maybe one of the young women hurt by your friend Kurt?"

"Girls came and went more often than buses back then," Shankleman said. "Cyd was one of the few that made a real connection with any of us."

"She was with Oxman before Spencer-Hall, right?" I asked.

"She was never really with Kurt," he answered, "except for a short fling. She and Dave were having problems. He was partying a lot and cheating on her, and she got back at him with Kurt. Who knew it would blow up into something that would take us all down."

"How did Oxman feel about Fox coming back into your lives?" I asked, remembering how nonchalant the burnout had seemed.

"He seemed okay with it," Shankleman said. "Not jumping for joy, but okay."

"Do you think *he* might have killed Cydney?" Mom asked.

Shankleman let out a short, sad laugh. "Not Dave. The only thing he expends energy on these days is his music and getting high. In fact, he's a brilliant musician when he's high."

"And Simon? How did he feel about Cydney?" I asked. "He wasn't around back in the day, but he can't have been happy about losing some of those gigs."

"He wasn't," Shankleman admitted, "but he has a lot going on elsewhere and a good head on his shoulders. He was with us for the experience. He told me up front that if we couldn't turn it around without Titan, he'd be gone at the end of the year."

"Did you know that he and Oxman were collaborating together on the side?" I asked, remembering what Oxman had told me.

"Yeah, I did." Shankleman put the dog down. Ringo went immediately to Art, who picked him up and started petting him. The animal was a real cuddle hound. "Dave didn't say anything," Shankleman continued, "but Simon did. He liked being upfront on stuff like that. Like I said, Dave's brilliant and has a great ear. Simon was learning a lot from him."

"My money is still on someone from the old days doing this," Mom said.

I nodded in agreement. "Our friend Willie thinks whoever did this alerted the gang that the police were about to crawl all over the band for some reason, which triggered the hit on Titan. Maybe this person is playing with you guys. He also could have given Titan a heads-up about the gang because he was playing with you—getting his kicks out of watching you all run around scared."

"The murder," came a voice from the corner by the window. We all turned. It was Charlie. "The murder was probably what triggered the police investigation," he said, still keeping his eyes on the outside. "The murder was premeditated."

"The murder looked like a crime of passion," I said to him.

"Maybe, but it was probably still planned," Charlie explained, glancing around at us. "From what Willie told me and from what I'm hearing here, my guess is that the killer planned on killing someone—maybe the woman, maybe Boaz. But he could have intended the murder to put the spotlight on the band and that Titan fellow. That would have triggered a panic on the part of the Armenians, and they would have to take Titan out to protect their business, which would cause the rest of you to panic."

He jerked his chin in my direction. "Whoever did this is cold and calculating, especially if he's the one who alerted both the gang and Titan. The lady's right. He's still around, watching it all, playing you for shits and giggles."

TWENTY-THREE

"Is that why you're keeping watch?" I asked Charlie, sidling up to him. "Because you think the killer might show up here?"

"I always keep watch. We all should, all the time," Charlie answered. "Life's unpredictable. Best be ready for it." He cut his eyes to me. "So you're Clark's crazy sister, and that's his crazy mother?" He jerked his head in Mom's direction. His words were flat, but his eyes danced with amusement.

"You know my brother?" I asked, ignoring the "crazy" comment. Before I got the words out, I knew the answer. If Charlie and Clark both worked for Willie in security, there was a very good chance they knew each other. But it did make me wonder if Clark ever did guard duty like this.

"Clark's a good man," Charlie answered. "I like working with him. He's smart and thorough." His attention returned to the outside.

My mind took another leap to a different question. "You don't happen to know my husband, do you?" When Charlie didn't answer, I added, "Come on, tell me—for shits and giggles."

Without looking at me, Charlie said, "Another good man."

I definitely needed to pump Greg for information about his relationship with Willie away from me when he got home.

Ringo was squirming to get down from Art's arms. He put the dog on the floor and the animal made a beeline for the door and made little whining noises. "He needs to go out," Shankleman said. He picked up a leash that was draped over a chair and fastened it to the dog's collar. The dog did a happy dance similar to Wainwright's when he saw his leash.

"He's not the only one who needs to tinkle," Mom said.

"It's right through there, Grace," Art told her, pointing to the other room.

Before Shankleman could open the front door to go out with Ringo, Charlie stopped him. "Hold up. I'll go with you."

Lorraine and I watched as the two men, one armed, and the dog went down the porch steps. Charlie's head did a slow scan of the thick woods and brush while Ringo pulled Shankleman from bush to bush looking for the right spot to do his business. Just as the little dog was about to lift his leg, his nose went up into the air and he started barking.

I saw the assailant about the same time as Charlie did. He was half hidden within the trees, raising a rifle, aiming it at Shankleman. I slapped the glass on the window and screamed out a warning just as Charlie got off a shot. The gunman fired at the same time. Both shots found their marks. Shankleman went down, and we heard a cry from the gunman.

Lorraine let out a long, blood-curdling scream and sank to the floor, her hands and arms over her head in a classic duck and cover move she'd probably learned in grade school. Art ran to the wall on the side of the other window and peeked out while keeping cover. Mom shuffled out from the other room. Taking in the scene, she went to Lorraine and crouched down, trying to comfort her while staying low herself.

Shankleman lay still. Charlie ran to him. Shankleman clutched his shoulder and started to get up, but Charlie motioned for him to stay down and held his gun at the ready. Ringo was running in circles, unsure of what to do, barking and scared out of his mind. Shankleman said something sharply to the dog, and the animal went back to his master and quieted down.

"What's going on?" I called out to Charlie, but he only waved for me to stay put.

It was then we saw a figure coming down the narrow road, his hands above his head. He was dressed in camouflage fatigues, his face dirty, his head covered with a ski mask, even in this warm weather. He limped, and I could see blood oozing from his thigh. Behind him marched Buzz with a handgun to the man's back. Next to them walked Willie, holding a rifle that was probably the gunman's.

Art and I started to tumble out of the cabin, sick with worry, but Willie waved us back. Charlie still held his gun ready and continued to scan the area for more threats. Mom poked her head up, reluctant to leave Lorraine, who was crying. "Why does all the good stuff happen when I need to pee?" Mom complained.

Willie helped Shankleman to his feet and walked him back to the cabin. The dog followed behind, his leash dragging on the ground. Behind them, at a safe distance, Buzz herded the shooter in the same direction. Bringing up the rear was Charlie, walking backward while he continued watching for more threats.

When everyone was in the cabin, Shankleman dropped into his chair by the stove. Willie dragged one of the hard-backed chairs away from the rest of us and placed it near the other small front window. "Take a seat," Buzz said to the shooter. When the man didn't respond, Buzz prodded him in the back with his gun. He sat down. Buzz posted himself on the shooter's other side.

Mom and Art tended to Shankleman's gunshot wound, stopping the bleeding as best they could with clean towels Mom gathered from the bathroom. Art announced that it looked like the bullet hit Shankleman's shoulder. Nothing life threatening, he reported, but it needed medical attention sooner than later.

"Throw a towel my way," Willie said. Art handed him one of the clean ones and Willie held it out to the gunman. "You'd better apply pressure to that," Willie told him. "We might be here a while." The gunman took the towel and pressed it to the wound in his thigh. Although it was bleeding, it didn't look too bad. Both he and Shankleman had been lucky.

Pressed now against a far wall, holding Ringo to keep him out of the way, Lorraine took it all in with an odd mix of horror and curiosity. I wondered if this was enough excitement for her to forget about Elliot and the podiatrist.

When Willie yanked off the shooter's mask we all gasped. It was Kevin Wong, the second-shift guard from Seaside.

"Holy hell!" Mom said. "Kevin, what are you doing shooting at Boaz?"

Willie and Buzz seemed just as shocked at the shooter's identity. Willie leaned back against the doorjamb of the doorway to the bedroom. "Well, you're a big surprise. Frankly, I was expecting to see Milton."

Kevin glanced at Willie, anger in his eyes, but said nothing.

"Why, Kevin?" Shankleman asked, getting to his feet and moving closer. "What have I ever done to you? I'm even generous to you and the other guards at Christmas." Kevin looked down at the floor but said nothing.

Buzz grabbed a fistful of Kevin's hair. "The man asked you a question. Answer him."

I turned to watch Lorraine. Her eyes were glued to Buzz, watching him turn from a sweet-talking hunk to an enforcer. I knew I'd have to have a talk with her about this and about Willie, or maybe it was a topic I should leave for Clark. After all, I'm just her aunt. Aunts don't have to do the tough parental stuff. Still, I hoped that Buzz didn't have to get too physical in front of her.

Buzz yanked Kevin's head back again. This time the guard said, "It wasn't personal."

Shankleman moved closer. "You freaking *shot* me, you SOB!" he yelled. "That's personal!"

Willie pushed off from the wall and came forward. He put a hand on Shankleman's good shoulder and pulled him away. "Take a seat, Boaz. Don't worry, we'll get to the bottom of this here and now."

As soon as Shankleman returned to his seat, Willie whipped around and backhanded Kevin Wong, snapping his head back. Lorraine let out a small half scream. Ringo, agitated and shaking, let out a couple of yips. Shankleman motioned to Lorraine for her to bring the dog to him. When she did, he held Ringo with his good arm and comforted the animal.

"Who paid you to kill Cydney Fox and take out Boaz?" Willie asked.

"Paid?" Mom asked. "What makes you think Kevin was paid?"

Willie turned and smiled at Mom. "When someone takes a shot at someone, Grace, then says it's not personal, usually money is involved." He turned back to Kevin. "Am I right? All other motives are very personal."

"I didn't kill the Fox woman," Kevin said. "I was paid to follow Boaz and take him out."

"Are you a professional hitman?" I asked. "Is that how you supplement your guard's pay?"

From his post at the window, Charlie laughed. "He's no pro. If he was, he wouldn't have failed."

"Charlie's right," Willie said. "You've got skills, Kevin, no doubt, but not the expert skills of a professional killer. Where did you learn to shoot? I'm guessing the military." Kevin nodded.

"Why did you think it was Milt doing the shooting?" Mom asked. "He can barely get off his butt to walk around the property."

This elicited a muffled laugh from Kevin and caused Willie to eye him with narrowed eyes. Kevin stopped laughing and shrunk into himself.

"I think, Grace, you just hit a nerve," Willie said with a smug smile. He turned to us. "I thought it might be Milt because when we brought Odelia's car to Seaside this morning, he was in the guard shack. When we left a few minutes later, he was not. Buzz got out and doubled back on foot and spotted him putting something under Odelia's car. When Milt returned to the guard shack, Buzz investigated, just to make sure it wasn't some sort of incendiary device."

A small involuntary squeak escaped from between my clenched teeth. "But it was a tracker," Willie said, continuing. "After you ladies started on your drive here, we hung back, hoping to spot Milt following you. And good thing we did, although we didn't get close enough to see who it was."

"But how did you know we'd lead you to Boaz?" Mom asked Kevin.

"We didn't," Kevin said. "At least not this quickly. We knew you and your daughter were looking into Boaz's disappearance. We were gambling that you'd stick with it until you found him. We were right."

"So Milt paid you?" Shankleman asked with great surprise. "Lazy Milt?"

"Don't underestimate Milt," Willie warned. "From what we saw, he's pretty agile and fast when no one's looking. I think that lazy guard thing he's got going on is just a ruse."

"For Milt it was personal," Kevin spat. "Very personal. Something from your past, but I'm not sure what. He said he doesn't have any experience with guns, but he knew I did. As they say, he made me an offer I couldn't refuse."

"Personal?" Shankleman was having a tough time understanding that the Seaside guards were out to get him, personal or not. He shook his head and started to stand again, but Art put hands on his good shoulder to warn him to stay still. Instead, he pulled Ringo closer, like a security blanket.

"Did Milt kill Cydney Fox?" I asked.

Kevin Wong shrugged. "Probably. I just know for sure that he was out to get Boaz. That's the only target he mentioned to me."

"Who else could it be?" I asked.

"My money's on Mona," Mom said. "She's his niece and is pretty nasty."

I moved a few steps closer. "Does Mona D'Angelo know about all this?"

Before Kevin could say anything, Shankleman said, "I still don't understand what's personal between me and Milt. Are you sure you don't know what it is?"

Kevin shrugged again but remained silent.

"Shouldn't we get the police involved?" asked a mouse from the corner who looked strangely like my niece.

"Not quite yet," Willie answered. "Not if we want the truth." He smiled at Lorraine. It was a warm smile, genuine and fatherly. "If we take this creep to the police, he'll just lawyer up and we may never learn what's really behind all this."

Willie stretched out a leg and kicked Kevin's injured one. The vibration sent pain shooting up into the gunshot wound, and the guard yelped in pain and went white. "Answer the man," Willie said to him. "What do you know about Milt's motives?"

"Nothing, I swear, but I do know his name isn't Milt D'Angelo, or at least it wasn't always," Kevin said.

"He told you that?" Buzz asked.

Kevin shook his head. "No, I overhead him and Mona talking one night during the shift change. I'd gone out to walk the property and came back a little earlier than usual. They were talking in the guard shack. Mona called him Uncle Kurt."

Shankleman got to his feet, shaking off all attempts by Art to quiet him down. Instead, he handed Ringo off to Art. The poor little dog was being passed around like a bad cold. "Kurt? She called him Uncle Kurt?"

"Yeah," Kevin confirmed, "that's what I heard, although that's the only time I'd ever heard Milt called that."

"That's impossible," Shankleman said, his face exploding with shock. "Kurt Spencer-Hall's been dead for a very long time, and Milt looks nothing like him."

"Hey," said Kevin, "I don't know about the Spencer-Hall part, but Mona definitely called him Kurt."

"Do you have history with anyone else by the name of Kurt?" I asked.

Shankleman paced the room, a hand on each side of his head as if squeezing a zit. He shook his head. "I honestly can't think of another person in my life named Kurt, past or present."

"How about a niece?" asked Lorraine, coming alive. "Do you remember him mentioning his family when you were in the band before?"

Shankleman stopped pacing at the question, gave it some thought, then laughed at a memory. "Kurt, the Kurt I knew, was very secretive about his family, so I have no idea if he had a niece or not. He wanted everyone to think he was English. He always said English musicians got the best girls, but he wasn't from England. By the time Dave and I joined up with him, he'd added Hall to his last name because he'd once heard that name in an English movie and had affected a British accent. Kurt Spencer was actually from Downey."

"Milt's been living in Downey," Kevin Wong said from his chair. "At least since he's been at Seaside."

Willie stared down at Kevin. "You said Milt made you an offer you couldn't refuse to do the hit on Boaz. How does a guard living in Downey have that kind of money?"

Kevin shrugged. "I wondered that myself, but I didn't want to look a gift horse in the mouth, if you know what I mean. He paid half in cash, with the other half to be paid after it was over. I'm divorced, no kids, no future. I was going to use the money to relocate and start over. I couldn't do that on a miserable guard's pay."

"It still can't be the same Kurt," Shankleman said, unconvinced. "Kurt Spencer-Hall died of an overdose in Mexico. That's where he went when things got too hot for him legally."

I was kicking myself for not bothering to read the Marigold report on Kurt Spencer-Hall. I had stopped reading after confirming his death. Then I remembered what Titan had said about Kurt. "We asked Titan about Kurt's death when we saw him," I said. "He told us he went down to Mexico to identify the body. What if he went down to Mexico to give Kurt a new beginning instead?"

All eyes were on me. "I don't know how gangs work," I continued, "but is it possible that Titan used his Armenian gang connection to make that happen?"

Willie was nodding. "We did say that whoever alerted the gang that something was about to go down triggering a police investigation had to have known about Titan's connection to them. If Titan used his connections to help Kurt get a new start, he would know all that."

"It could also mean that this Spencer-Hall could possibly be working for them himself," noted Buzz, "which might be how he had the funds to pay for the hit. Maybe the Armenian gang has a partnership with one of the Mexican gangs. Maybe the Armenians distribute the goods for the Mexicans up here, and Kurt is working for one or the other."

"You mean," asked Shankleman, standing in the middle of the room, his good hand holding the sliding makeshift bandage on his shoulder in place, "that Kurt and Titan could have been working together all these years?"

"Could explain why Milt speaks Spanish like a native," Kevin said, either trying to be helpful or buy into our good graces. "I've heard him myself."

"You know," Willie finally said, "that does make sense. Kurt escapes his troubles by going down south. Through Titan's connections, he gets a new life, a new look, and a new name, and goes to work for the people who helped him." He looked straight at Kevin. "When did Milt start working at Seaside?"

"I can answer that," I said. I'd been sitting in a chair and now got up to add to the nervous pacing crowd. "Teri Thomson told me Milt started just a few months ago. Mona's story is that her uncle had been traveling out of the country and had just returned and needed a job. The other night guard had left, which gave Milt the perfect cover as the new guard."

Mom nodded in confirmation. "That's the story we were all told about Milt."

"A few months ago?" repeated Shankleman. "That's just after Cyd and I started working together and she started coming around Seaside."

"So," I said, thinking and walking, "what if Mona tells her uncle that Cydney Fox, the woman who brought down Acid Storm and brought his other indiscretions to light, has suddenly shown up at Seaside? Maybe he returned to take revenge on her."

Shankleman shook his head and closed his eyes. "Mona did ask me her name when Cyd started showing up regularly, and I told her. She said it was for security reasons."

"So the Fox woman was the target all along?" asked Mom.

"That's what I'm thinking," I said, "or at least the one target Spencer-Hall wanted to take out himself."

"But I've lived there for several years," Shankleman said, his voice heavy with confusion, like a kid who didn't get the math problem on the chalkboard. "Why hasn't he tried to come after me before this?"

"Because he's a patient man," Willie said. "He wanted you all, but mostly her, and she didn't come back to the area until recently, right?"

Shankleman nodded. "But why set up Titan to be killed if they were working together?"

"Because he was a loose end," Buzz answered. "Titan was the only person who knew that Milt was really Kurt Spencer-Hall."

"I'm still confused," said Lorraine. "I understand why this Kurt guy turned on Titan, but why would he call Titan and give him a heads-up about the gang, giving Titan and the band a chance to get out of town?"

"Maybe it wasn't Milt who sounded the alert," Mom said. "Maybe it was someone else?"

We all turned to stare at Kevin, who held up the hand not clutching the towel to his leg. "It wasn't me. I knew nothing about that hit, I swear."

Willie studied him, then said, "I believe Kevin on this. My money is on Mona. She might have been the one to call Titan after she found out about Cydney being murdered. Maybe she thought her uncle was just going to have it out with them, not kill them all. Titan was probably given a heads-up the day you saw him packing. Wasn't that the day after Lorraine found Fox's body? Maybe Mona overheard her uncle discussing his plans with someone or was privy to them."

"Yes, it was the day after, but I can't believe Mona chose to do the right thing," Mom said with a scowl. "I can't see her doing that."

"You don't have to be a nice person to do the right thing, Grace," Art told her.

"Especially if you're worried about being charged as an accessory to a murder," added Willie with a wink. "Maybe she didn't want any more blood on her hands."

"Well," Mom said, raising a fist into the air, "if I get my hands on Mona, her blood is going to be on my hands for putting all of us in danger like this."

Buzz laughed. "You go, *abuela*!"

TWENTY-FOUR

WILLIE KICKED KEVIN'S INJURED leg again. "So what's the setup? Once you killed Boaz, what were you supposed to do?"

Kevin Wong yelped with pain. Sweat beaded on his forehead, even though the cabin was kept comfortably cool in the shade of the tall pines. "I was to call him when it was done. He'd give me a place to meet him and pay me the rest of the money."

"Aren't you on duty today?" Mom asked. "I hate to tell you, but you're already late."

Kevin gave her a half smile. "I called in sick today, with no plans of going back there."

"So Milt pays you off and you hit the road?" I asked.

"Something like that," Kevin said.

"Don't count on it," Willie said with a grin. He glanced at Charlie. "You okay with holding this piece of crap until the police get here?"

"Sure," Charlie told him as he patted his rifle.

Willie turned and faced the rest of us. "Odelia, call the police and tell them you have Kevin here and he tried to kill Boaz, and everything else he told us. For obvious reasons, I can't stick around." He paused. "Wait fifteen to twenty minutes before making that call, and call your friend Fehring—let her have the first crack at this even though she's not the lead on the case. She's your friend in high places; keep her happy. And you might want to give Mike Steele a call just for a heads-up so he can help you maneuver the legalities when the police question you. And tell Fehring to send someone to pick up Mona and Milt if they can find them."

"Who is this guy?" Shankleman asked Mom, indicating Willie.

"Think of him as Batman," Mom whispered. "We do."

While Willie talked, Buzz found some rope and tied Kevin's hands in front of him, giving him enough play to continue holding the towel tight on his leg. "Make sure to tell the cops to send an ambulance," Buzz said in my direction.

Just as Buzz finished securing the rope, a shot shattered the window behind Kevin. Kevin Wong slumped forward, landing on top of Buzz.

"Everyone down!" shouted Willie.

Charlie smashed out the window by him and aimed his rifle out it while keeping back behind the side wall. Buzz untangled himself from Kevin, who fell forward to the floor. His eyes were open, and there was a bullet hole in the back of his head. Lorraine and Mom screamed like a singing duo. With his good arm, Boaz yanked Mom to the floor. I did the same with Lorraine. Art was already flat on the floor, covering Ringo like a precious baby.

Willie, armed with Kevin's rifle, and Buzz, with his own gun, smashed out the remaining glass in the other window and took up positions. Willie turned to me. "Get everyone into the bedroom," he ordered. "There are no windows there."

"You heard him," I told my charges. "Stay down on the floor and crawl into the bedroom. Quickly!"

Boaz and Mom went first, Mom mumbling something about her arthritic knees. I was just happy she was wearing capris and soft-soled shoes today. As she belly crawled along the floor, Mom's big purse, still hooked over her arm, dragged along with them like a dead carcass.

Just before Mom disappeared through the door, Buzz called out to her, "Now would be a good time to bring out that nasty knife, *abuela*."

Next went Art and Ringo. Art was crouched on his hands and knees. He'd let go of Ringo's leash so that the dog could freely follow his master.

I gave Lorraine a shove toward the bedroom. "Now you. Stay low and don't dawdle—and don't puke." She was about to protest when another shot came whizzing into the cabin, striking the chair two feet from her. The guys returned fire. Lorraine took off for the bedroom like one of those speedy little brown lizards that are so common in Southern California. I followed them, the caboose bringing up the rear.

"Odelia," Willie called to me, "make that 911 call—now!"

"But you're not gone yet," I protested.

"Don't worry about us," he said. "Call them and then Fehring to pick up the others."

As soon as I got into the bedroom, I pulled out my cell phone and let out a string of expletives.

"What, Odelia?" Mom asked, this time not chastising me for my language.

"No service." I looked around our little group. They were on their feet now, ready to bolt through the solid planks of the walls, if necessary. The men were standing with the women slightly behind them. Shankleman held Ringo, his injured shoulder forgotten. Mom was holding her switchblade. "Any of you have service?" I asked.

Mom and Lorraine looked at their cell phones and shook their heads. Shankleman glanced at his burner and did the same. We were stuck. It sounded like most of the gunfire was from the good guys, and it made me hope that there was only one gunman outside.

"Who's shooting at us?" Lorraine asked. "Gang members?"

"I don't think so," I said. "There aren't many shots coming from outside. If it was the gang, I think we'd be under siege by a small army with automatics."

"I think Odelia's right," Shankleman said. "If there's only one, our guys might be able to hold off the shooter until he runs out of ammo."

"There's a window in the bathroom," Mom said. "Do you think we might be able to squeeze out and get to safety?"

"Stay here," I told them and went into the bathroom to check it out. The bathroom was very small, with only a small stall shower, a toilet, and tiny sink. The window was small but not tiny; it also wasn't too high. Located over the toilet, a man of average height could easily look outside while peeing. I slid it open and pushed on the screen. It popped out with just a little pressure. I held my breath, waiting for an assailant to pop up, but none came. I poked my head out and realized the window faced the backside of the cabin and the shots were only coming from the front.

I stepped out into the bedroom and beckoned my charges in, one at a time. "Art, you go first so you can help the others as they go out. You okay with that?"

Without hesitating, Art Franklin put down the lid of the commode and stepped onto it. Slowly he hoisted one leg out the window and straddled it. Holding on to the window edges, he lowered himself out, sliding until he freed his other leg, then dropped down, hitting the ground with a soft grunt and gritted teeth. He was going to feel that tomorrow. We all were, except probably for Lorraine. Art waved for the next person.

"Mom," I said, "you're next."

"Just like old times," Mom said as she handed me the knife and her purse and climbed onto the toilet. She was right. It wasn't the first time she'd had to escape danger by squeezing out a bathroom window. But this time the window was larger and lower, she was wearing pants instead of a dress, and I wasn't on the outside trying to yank her through. Art directed her with hand signals like an airport worker guiding a plane to its gate. Once she was on the ground, I reached through and handed her the knife and purse.

"Okay, Lorraine," I said to my niece, "you're next." The gunshots weren't sounding as often but were still occurring, popping like the final kernels in a bag of microwave popcorn.

"I want to stay with you," she said.

"No, you go next," I told her, "or I'll have Boaz shove you out headfirst." She eyed me, making a quick decision on whether or not I meant it. I did.

"Go along now, girl," Boaz told her, "and hurry."

Quick as a bunny, the youngest of us slipped out the window and dropped to the ground. I poked my head out. It still seemed all clear.

"Okay, Boaz," I said to Shankleman. "Give me Ringo, and I'll hand him off to you once you're clear."

"No, Odelia, ladies first."

"But you're hurt," I protested.

"I can toss you out headfirst, one-armed or not," he said with a charming smile, and behind the tired and grizzled face I saw the man I'd once mooned over as a young co-ed. I stepped onto the toilet lid.

Shankleman was the tallest of our little band, but I was the roundest. It was a tight fit, but I managed to manipulate myself through the window and down to the ground with Art's support on the downside. Once on the ground, Shankleman handed Ringo off to me. The poor little animal was shaking like a leaf. Shankleman hit the ground with a muffled grunt and grabbed his bad shoulder. The dog flailed its thin legs toward its master like a tiny child reaching for its mother. As soon as Shankleman was on his feet and stable, I handed Ringo back, and the animal calmed right down.

All together again, we flattened against the back wall of the cabin and looked around. Art pointed to an opening in the trees that looked like a path. It went up a small incline, then disappeared into the dense woods. I nodded and indicated for everyone to head that way. At least it was heading away from the gunfire.

While Art blazed the way, Lorraine helped her grandmother up the incline. Shankleman hung back, but I hissed, "This time you go first." But he shook his head. Before the others had left, he'd given Ringo into Art's care again. That should have been my first clue that

Shankleman was not going to listen to me. He held his injured arm close to his side, but the bleeding looked like it had finally stopped.

"I'm not going to leave them," Shankleman told me, jerking his jaw toward the cabin. "You go."

I shook my head. "I'm not leaving them either. And I need to make that call." He nodded but made no move to leave.

I pulled out my cell phone. Outside the cabin I had service, but it was weak. I called 911. It rang, then the call dropped before being answered. He tried his burner phone with the same results. We walked around the back and side of the cabin, looking for stronger service but found none.

"Shh," I said in a barely audible voice, finger to my lips. "The shooting's stopped." We listened together. Shankleman started for the front of the cabin, but I stopped him. "Not until we get an all clear."

We waited, worried about the silence. Did the guys nail the shooter or had the shooter nailed them? It was three against one—hopefully only one. The math was in our favor. I signaled to Shankleman for us to move back behind the cabin. If we had to, we could beat a hasty retreat into the woods from there.

We had just cleared the corner to the back of the cabin when we heard "Hold it right there." Shankleman and I froze. Out of the woods off to the side, thankfully not from the incline area, came Milt the guard. He was dressed in jeans and a black tee shirt. He looked a lot more fit and robust than he did while on duty at Seaside, but the face, hair, and beard were the same. In his hands and aimed at us was a high-powered rifle. He may have given Kevin Wong the idea that he didn't know how to handle a gun, but that had been as much of a ruse as the whole guard persona. If Kurt

Spencer-Hall had been working with gangs in Mexico, dollars to donuts he'd picked up some good shooting skills.

"That you, Kurt?" Shankleman asked.

"What, you don't recognize me, Bo?" Milt laughed. "It's been a long time, and I've been through a lot of changes."

"Just go, Kurt," Shankleman said, moving slightly forward to shield me. "Cydney's dead. Titan's dead. Even Kevin Wong is dead. There doesn't need to be any more killing."

"But I'm not done, Bo. Dave's with the cops right now, but he'll be released someday, and I'll be waiting."

Inwardly I was relieved. Mom's stunt with Oxman's tires hadn't cost the man his life.

"The Tuttle kid is safe. I have no beef with him," Milt said and raised the gun, taking aim at Shankleman's head.

"Let them go," said a voice from the corner. It was Willie and Buzz, guns trained on Milt. "Like the man said, there's been enough killing."

"Tell you what," Milt said, not lowering his rifle. "Let me kill old Bo Shank here, and I'll let the lady go." He adjusted his rifle lower, to me. "But stop me, and she'll die first. What's it to be?"

Only the subtle sounds of the great outdoors could be heard— a breeze in the treetops, birds chirping and calling, a woodpecker knocking on a tree trunk, and the subtle crackling of needles and leaves as tiny, unseen critters crawled through them. Overhead the sky was bright blue and cloudless. I knew in my heart this was a no-win situation. Milt/Kurt wasn't about to kill Shankleman and let me go. He'd fight until we were all dead or at least until he was. I looked up. If I couldn't die looking one last time at my beloved Greg, then

I wanted my last vision on earth to be of something pretty. And I prayed my mother wasn't watching.

A gunshot fired close. My ears exploded, and I fell to the ground on my knees, my hands cupped over my ears like earmuffs. When I opened my eyes, Shankleman was next to me, eyes open. He was shaking his head back and forth like a dog's and looked disoriented.

Willie ran up to us, yelling, "Are you okay?" I couldn't hear what he was saying, but I could lip read the few words. I nodded, then shouted, "Yes, but I can't hear."

My eyes moved to the side, where Milt had been. He was on the ground, crumpled like a rag doll. Crouched over him was Buzz. Buzz looked at Willie and shook his head. I saw Willie glance up, so I did too. Above me, in the open bathroom window, was Charlie, his rifle resting on the lower ledge of the window. It had been his shot that had bludgeoned my eardrums. While Willie and Buzz were trying to talk Milt out of killing Shankleman and me, he'd crept into the bathroom, lined up his shot, and taken it like a trained sniper.

TWENTY-FIVE

EVEN THOUGH CLARK'S HOUSE was pretty big, even larger than ours, we were a bit cramped, but it was a happy squeeze. Lorraine and Mom bunked together in one guest bedroom. Greg and I had the other. There was no way I could convince Greg to continue his trip until he saw for himself that I was okay. So after the police were done with us, Mom, Lorraine, and I piled into my car and headed for Arizona. Wainwright came with us while Muffin was shuttled off to Art's place.

Poor Art; when the truth of what had happened came out, Shelita went on a rampage to get her father to move, but Art dug in his heels, saying all his friends were at Seaside and now that Mona and Milt were gone, it was a very safe place. Since Mona had been a longtime friend of Shelita's, Shelita could hardly throw stones at my mother any longer for being a bad influence. She could try, but it wouldn't hold water considering what Mona, her inside snitch, and Mona's uncle had done. Seaside also promised better vetting of their guards and management people in the future, and better communications with their residents. I'm sure somewhere in stuffy corporate offices their legal counsel was circling the wagons, ready for an onslaught of lawsuit filings.

Even after he saw me and touched me and kissed me, Greg wasn't satisfied. He insisted that I go to Colorado with him and meet his friends. I argued that Steele would never stand for me taking another week off, but a quick call from my mother and Steele was A-OK, even thrilled to get us all out of his hair. I made a mental note to use Mom as my negotiator with Steele in the future. We sent Boomer on ahead to Colorado. Greg and I would drive there in my car with Wainwright while Mom and Lorraine stayed to visit with Clark and look after him. I intended to use the time alone in the car with my husband to pump him on his relationship with Willie outside of my knowledge.

Buzz and Willie took off from the cabin before we called the police. With the cabin being so remote, no one had heard the gunfire and called ahead of us. With the danger out of the way, they took a few minutes to pick up the casings from Buzz's gun but left those for the rifle Willie had used, while we gathered everyone back from the woods. Willie wiped Kevin's gun clean and added prints from Kevin's cold hands on the butt and shaft. Then Shankleman mauled it with his handprints. The story we all agreed upon in fast order was that it was Boaz Shankleman who had fended off Milt with Charlie and had used Kevin Wong's rifle to do it. Kevin had been shot in the leg by Charlie but killed by Milt, and Shankleman had been shot by Kevin, which was all true. While Charlie, who did turn out to be a trained military sniper, held off Milt by himself,

Shankleman and I had herded everyone out the back window and into the woods, but Milt found us and was about to shoot us when Charlie shot him from the bathroom window. It was all true except for Willie and Buzz's presence and who was handling Kevin's rifle.

I don't think Fehring believed the entire story. Nor did Detectives Gonzales and Mack or the local authorities on the scene, but we all stuck to it; even when they questioned us separately, we couldn't be cracked, not even jellylike Lorraine or my crazy mother. Lorraine told us later that Willie Proctor's name even came up in her questioning, and she claimed she had no idea who he was. They'd asked each of us about him. Shankleman and Art also claimed they had no idea who he was, and Mom only said she thought he was a friend of mine and Greg's. That much the police did know.

Willie and Buzz were in the wind—gone like a puff of smoke. No one had been able to prove that they were ever at the cabin or at my house or even, thanks to the broken security camera, at Seaside.

While Shankleman called the authorities, I called Fehring and gave her a heads-up on Mona D'Angelo, who was rounded up about the same time as police descended on the cabin. Mona claimed she knew nothing about any of it. It's believed that Milt did kill Cydney Fox. Shankleman's golf club was found in the trunk of Milt's car, with his prints and Fox's blood and brain matter on it. The police removed the tracking device from my car and also found one on the undercarriage of Kevin's car, which was parked down the wooded lane. They believe that while Kevin was following me Milt was following him and planned to kill him, and probably all of us, as soon as he killed Shankleman.

That night, after all the questioning, Mom, Lorraine, and I snuggled into beds at my house and slept like a trio of Rip Van Winkles. When we finally crawled out of bed the next morning, we hit the road for Arizona, unanimous in our decision to head out of town.

Clark, in spite of his broken ankle, grinned from ear to ear with happiness to have us all under his roof and waiting on him hand and foot. He sat in his recliner like a pontiff, the cast on his injured ankle festooned with colorful comments from friends and family. Lorraine fussed over him and played cards with him. Mom cooked and baked for him.

I was sitting on Clark's large front deck enjoying the evening with Greg beside me in his wheelchair, holding my hand, when Clark hobbled out on his crutches and joined us. At our feet, Wainwright snored and farted happily. Although it was August, the area was experiencing a brief break in its usual relentless summer heat.

"Lorraine's decided to stay on here for a while," Clark announced. "She needs time to sort out things concerning Elliot and Chicago. She's not even sure she wants to go back except to pack up her stuff. She said she's calling her employer on Monday and quitting."

"Is Mom staying here too?" I asked.

Clark shook his head. "She said she wants to go home as soon as you two return from Colorado. She said she has things to do." He chuckled. "She probably wants to soak in the glamor of being involved in the shootout. So once you get home, call me and I'll stick her skinny ass on a plane."

While we sat quietly, a motorcycle pulled into Clark's driveway. The driver lifted one long leg over and slid off while taking off his helmet. Much to my surprise, but not Clark's, it was Buzz.

"Hi, folks," the young man said as he bounded up to us. "Lorraine ready?" He didn't say a word about what had happened in Southern California just a couple of days ago. Instead, he crouched down to stroke Wainwright, who lifted his head and wagged his tail at the attention.

"Here I am," Lorraine said as she came out of the house.

Buzz beamed at her. "You look amazing."

And she did. It was the first time since arriving from Chicago that Lorraine looked truly happy.

With a kiss to her dad's forehead and a wave to us, Lorraine put on the extra helmet Buzz handed her. Then they climbed on his motorcycle and took off.

"Is he the reason Lorraine wants to stay?" Greg asked.

Clark shrugged. "She could do worse, and has." He shifted his cast with a grunt. "I never liked Elliot. He's a pompous ass. I just never told Lorraine how I felt. I say good riddance. Buzz is a hardworking and educated young man from a nice family, and he's going places. Like his cousin Enrique, Willie is grooming him for the organization's management team."

Greg and I both continued to stare at Clark. "And?" I asked, not feeling the need to say more.

Clark took a deep breath. "And I had a long talk with Lorraine last night about Buzz and Willie and who Willie is and why I work for him."

"And?" asked Greg, taking his turn.

"And she said she understands and is okay with it after spending time with both of them and seeing them in action." He laughed again. "She said Mom called Willie Batman, and that's how she's going to think of him."

"And I suppose that Buzz is Robin?" I asked with amusement.

"No," Clark answered with a smile. "Buzz is Alejandro. That's his real name."

THE END

ACKNOWLEDGMENTS

Once again, I take my hat off to the usual suspects and partners in crime: my incredible agent, Whitney Lee; my editors at Midnight Ink, Terri Bischoff and Rebecca Zins; and everyone else at Midnight Ink/Llewellyn Worldwide who had a hand in making this book, and all those before it, a reality.

WWW.MIDNIGHTINKBOOKS.COM

From the gritty streets of New York City to sacred tombs in the Middle East, it's always midnight somewhere. Join us online at any hour for fresh new voices in mystery fiction.

At midnightinkbooks.com you'll also find our author blog, new and upcoming books, events, book club questions, excerpts, mystery resources, and more.

MIDNIGHT INK ORDERING INFORMATION

 Order Online:
- Visit our website www.midnightinkbooks.com, select your books, and order them on our secure server.

 Order by Phone:
- Call toll-free within the U.S. and Canada at 1-888-NITE-INK (1-888-648-3465)
- We accept VISA, MasterCard, American Express and Discover

 Order by Mail:
Send the full price of your order (MN residents add 6.875% sales tax) in U.S. funds, plus postage & handling to:

Midnight Ink
2143 Wooddale Drive
Woodbury, MN 55125-2989

Postage & Handling:

Standard (U.S. & Canada). If your order is:
$30.00 and under, add $4.00
$30.01 and over, FREE STANDARD SHIPPING

International Orders:
$16.00 for one book plus $3.00 for each additional book

Orders are processed within 12 business days. Please allow for normal shipping time.
Postage and handling rates subject to change.

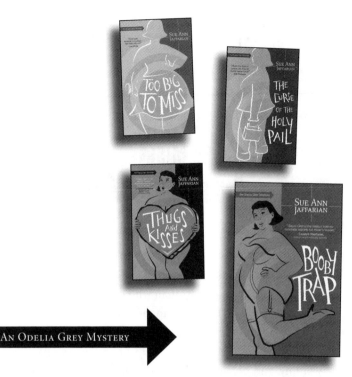

An Odelia Grey Mystery

The hugely popular mystery series that features unforgettable amateur sleuth Odelia Grey

You'll love Odelia Grey, a middle-aged, plus-sized paralegal with a crazy boss, insatiable nosiness, and a knack for being in close proximity to dead people. This snappy, humorous series is the first from award-winning, critically acclaimed mystery author Sue Ann Jaffarian.

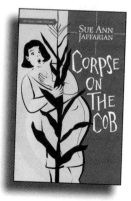

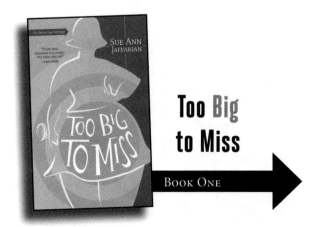

Too Big to Miss

Book One

Too big to miss—that's Odelia Grey. A never-married, middle-aged, plus-sized woman who makes no excuses for her weight, she's not Superwoman—she's just a mere mortal standing on the precipice of menopause, trying to cruise in an ill-fitting bra. She struggles with her relationships, her crazy family, and her crazier boss. And then there's her knack for being in close proximity to dead people…

When her close friend Sophie London commits suicide in front of an online web-cam by putting a gun in her mouth and pulling the trigger, Odelia's life is changed forever. Sophie, a plus-sized activist and inspiration to imperfect women, is the last person anyone would ever have expected to end her own life. Suspecting foul play, Odelia is determined to get to the bottom of her friend's death. Odelia's search for the truth takes her from Southern California strip malls to the world of live web-cam porn to the ritzy enclave of Corona del Mar.

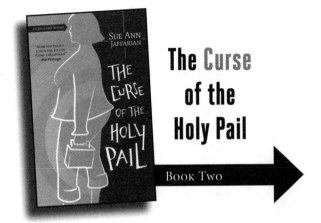

The Curse of the Holy Pail

BOOK TWO

I s the "Holy Pail" cursed? Every owner of the vintage Chappy Wheeler lunchbox—a prototype based on a 1940s TV Western—has died. And now Sterling Price, a business tycoon and client of Odelia Grey's law firm, has been fatally poisoned. Is it a coincidence that Price's one-of-a-kind lunch pail—worth over thirty grand—has disappeared at the same time?

Treading cautiously since her recent run-in with a bullet, Odelia takes small bites of this juicy, calorie-free mystery—and is soon ravenous for more! Her research reveals a sixty-year-old unsolved murder and Price's gold-digging ex-fiancée with two married men wrapped around her breasts—uh, finger. Mix in a surprise marriage proposal that sends an uncertain Odelia into chocolate sedation and you've got an unruly recipe for delicious disaster.

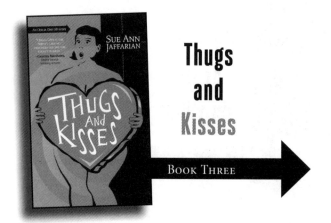

Thugs
and
Kisses

BOOK THREE

With the class bully murdered at her thirtieth high-school reunion and her boss, the annoying Michael Steele, missing, Odelia doesn't know which hole to poke her big nose into first. This decision is made for her as she's again swept into the action involving contract killers, tangled relationships, and fatal buyer's remorse. Throughout this adventure, Odelia deals with her on-again, off-again relationship with Greg and her attraction to detective Dev Frye.

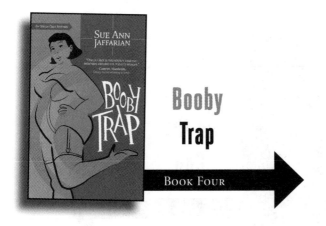

Booby Trap

BOOK FOUR →

Could the Blond Bomber serial killer possibly be Dr. Brian Eddy, plastic surgeon to the rich and famous? Odelia never would have suspected the prominent doctor of killing the bevy of buxom blonds if she hadn't heard it directly from her friend Lillian—Dr. Eddy's own mother!—over lunch one day. This mystery gets even messier than Odelia's chicken parmigiana sandwich as Odelia discovers just how difficult—and dangerous—it will be to bust this killer.

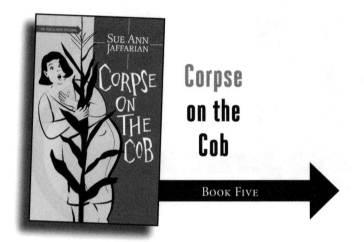

Corpse on the Cob

Book Five

What do you have to lose when you go searching for the mother who walked out of your life thirty-four years ago—besides your pride, your nerves, and your sanity?

Odelia finds herself up to her ears in trouble when she reunites with her mom in a corn maze at the Autumn Fair in Holmsbury, Massachusetts. For starters, there's finding the dead body in the cornfield—and seeing her long-lost mom crouched beside the corpse, with blood on her hands…

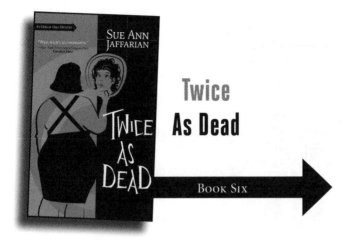

Twice As Dead

Book Six

Corpse magnet Odelia Grey is at it again—stumbling across a dead body at a wedding reception while "Achy Breaky Heart" plays in the background. Bodies are turning up so fast that Odelia enlists the help of her family and friends—Greg, Seth, Zee, Detective Frye, her half brother Clark, even her pompous boss Michael Steele. But solving a mystery is twice as hard when the victims have more secrets than the killer.

Hide
and Snoop

BOOK SEVEN

A merger at Odelia Grey's law firm has put her job in jeopardy, and her new icy-cold boss, Erica Mayfield, has it in for her. The humiliation doubles when Erica dumps her three-year-old niece with Odelia and disappears for the weekend. The nerve! Primed for a confrontation, Odelia impulsively goes to her boss's house in the middle of the night—and finds Erica's sister murdered. Before she knows it, Odelia's madcap misadventure to prove her own innocence ends up in a cuddly cradle of crime.

Second-hand Stiff

Book Eight

Thanksgiving with her fault-finding mother has Odelia Grey stewing in her own juices. But her husband's cousin Ina—who shows up to dinner alone with ugly bruises—clearly has it worse. Things quickly go downhill after Odelia's mother decides to extend her visit a few extra days to attend a storage auction with Ina, who owns a consignment shop. The day of the auction, the thrill of bargain hunting gives way to tragedy when Ina's husband is found inside a storage locker—dead.

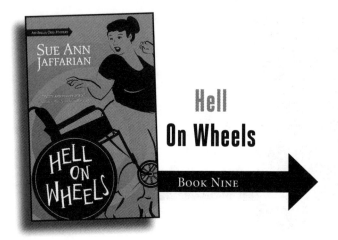

Hell On Wheels

BOOK NINE

When Odelia Grey and her husband, Greg, attend a rugby match to cheer for their quadriplegic friends, the last thing they expect is to witness a murder on the playing court. Complicating matters is their friendship with the killer—and with the second person who turns up dead. It doesn't help that Odelia's pompous boss, Mike Steele, is embroiled in a mystery of his own—one that leaves more than his super-sized ego bruised and battered.

Odelia enlists the help of family and friends, and gets some surprising assistance coming out of left field. But with a murderer calling the shots, Odelia wonders if she can tackle this dangerous case or if she's out of her league.

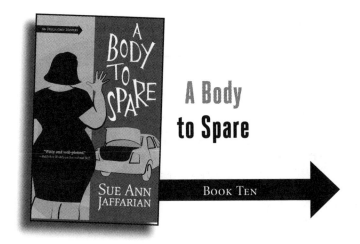

A Body to Spare

BOOK TEN

Odelia Grey's relaxing day of errands is ruined when she finds a body folded like an origami crane in the trunk of her car. And it's not just any dead body—it's the corpse of Zach Finch, a young man who had been kidnapped eight years earlier. But why was he put in Odelia's car? Where has Zach been all these years?

With her name at the top of the suspect list, Odelia and her husband, Greg, are determined to find answers. They'll do whatever it takes to uncover the truth, even if they have to give the slip to an arrogant FBI agent and delve into the dangerous world of contract killers.